A CHRISTMAS PROPOSAL

Unable to stop himself, Connor took Sarah's hand and lifted it to his lips. "Sarah, I know you will think this sudden, but I am drawn to you. My heart is becoming seriously engaged."

Sarah pulled her hand from his. "Lucy, bring your boat," she called to her daughter. "We must go home."

She stood up and Connor stood up with her. "Forgive me. I have been too blunt," he said. "I am not experienced in courting. But my devotion is real."

"Connor, I can see that you are a decent man with the highest of principles. I find that appealing. But I think your emotions are colored by our shared adversities in the workhouse."

Connor grasped her shoulders and looked down into her face. "Certainly, I have warm memories of that young girl, but, believe me, my dear, it is the grown Sarah, not little Sissy, who has captured my heart. My intentions are honorable. Let me prove it to you. . . .

—from "A Promise Kept" by Alice Holden

<u>BOOK YOUR PLACE ON OUR WEBSITE AND MAKE THE READING CONNECTION!</u>

We've created a customized website just for our very special readers, where you can get the inside scoop on everything that's going on with Zebra, Pinnacle and Kensington books.

When you come online, you'll have the exciting opportunity to:

- View covers of upcoming books
- Read sample chapters
- Learn about our future publishing schedule (listed by publication month *and author*)
- Find out when your favorite authors will be visiting a city near you
- Search for and order backlist books from our online catalog
- Check out author bios and background information
- Send e-mail to your favorite authors
- Meet the Kensington staff online
- Join us in weekly chats with authors, readers and other guests
- Get writing guidelines
- AND MUCH MORE!

**Visit our website at
http://www.kensingtonbooks.com**

A KISS FOR CHRISTMAS

Alice Holden

Lisa Noeli

Melynda Beth Skinner

ZEBRA BOOKS
Kensington Publishing Corp.
http://www.kensingtonbooks.com

CONTENTS

A Promise Kept

Alice Holden

One

Sarah sat in a straight-backed chair beside the glass door to the terrace, opened to catch a breeze. She was keeping an eye on her four-year-old daughter, Lucy, who played with a black-and-white kitten on the flagstones. The day was sunny and unseasonably mild for November.

Knitting needles and a ball of yarn lay in Sarah's lap. Her black bombazine gown was a relic from her days of prescribed mourning for the death of her young husband in a riding accident three years before. She—like the other two occupants of the parlor, her sister-in-law, Cynthia, and her spinster aunt by marriage, Augusta Lawton—was waiting to get a look at the important visitor, one Lord Lyle, who was talking business with her father-in-law, Silas Lawton, in the library.

Little Lucy whispered into the flattened ear of the small ball of fur as though the two of them shared a secret, bringing a smile of affection to Sarah's lips. Only Lucy made her life bearable. Were it not for her fear for her daughter's welfare, Sarah would have left this house with its frigid atmosphere long ago.

She picked up the knitting needles and pulled a strand from the blue woolen ball in her lap. She had just started to cast on stitches for a winter scarf she was knitting for herself when her hands stilled. She looked toward the parlor door, drawn by the sound of male voices coming from the hall.

On the ornate rococo sofa across the room from Sarah, Cynthia smoothed the flounces and frills on the skirt of her pink silk gown that was more suitable for a female younger than her twenty-two years. Beside her, Aunt Augusta laid her hand over her niece's in a sign of solidarity and encouragement and said, "You look lovely, dear."

While Silas Lawton's aim was to convince the wealthy Lord Lyle to make a much needed infusion of cash into his faltering textile mill, the ladies had marriage on their minds. Lord Lyle was an eligible bachelor, and Cynthia was in the market for a husband.

Silas ushered the visitor into the parlor, talking animatedly to him. The stranger's answering voice was rich and deep.

Sarah drew in her breath. Lord Lyle was not handsome in the classical sense, but his looks were striking, in contrast to her portly father-in-law with his shiny bald head and bushy brows. Silas was of average height; Lord Lyle several inches taller. His hair was full and black; his eyes looked dark.

"Let me make you known to my sister and daughter," Silas said to Lord Lyle, who sketched a bow to the ladies on the sofa and brought his lips very properly to just above each of their proffered fingertips. He said all the right things in the manly baritone of a cultured gentleman.

The butler placed the tea things that Aunt Augusta had ordered earlier onto the sofa table in front of the spinster while -across the room Sarah went back to her knitting.

She was seldom introduced to visitors, and, so, was not surprised to be ignored on this occasion. She was sometimes mistaken for Lucy's governess since Aunt Augusta saw no reason to incur the expense of hiring a nursemaid when Sarah could make herself useful and look after her own child.

Aunt Augusta would not have been pleased to know that

this "chore" suited Sarah perfectly. Lucy was her all. It sometimes seemed to Sarah that Augusta's purpose in life was to make her niece-by-marriage's life as miserable as possible. It was on this thought that Sarah glanced up from her knitting to meet Lord Lyle's steady stare. Her heart thumped when his handsome mouth burst into a luminous smile.

"Sissy, I can't believe it!" His long stride brought him to Sarah in a flash. "It's really you, Sissy! It is!"

Sarah's heart began to pound heavily. How did he know that name? She had not been called Sissy in ten years!

Lord Lyle seized both her hands and pulled her up from the chair, her knitting tumbling onto the rug.

"Sissy Eaton," he said in wonder, looking deep into her eyes. His tone softened. "Imagine finding you after all these years. Look at you. How beautiful you have grown. You cannot believe how often I wondered what had become of you."

Con? Sarah felt a tentative shock of recognition. *Connor Hamil? It must be Con.* A frisson of fear hit her. She must stop him before he said too much.

"My lord, you have mistaken me for someone else," she dissembled, her voice shaky. "I am Mr. Lawton's daughter-in-law. His son Ellis's widow. My given name is Sarah, not Sissy. I was Sarah Farrell before my marriage, not this Sissy Eaton."

Lord Lyle looked unsure, bewildered, skeptical, but he let go of her hands. "I beg your pardon, madam. I was certain that you were a childhood friend, but it has been ten years. Please forgive me if I have caused you distress."

Sarah's breath came fast. "Of course," she murmured.

Leaving her knitting on the rug where it had fallen, she hurried through the opening in the glass door onto the terrace and scooped up the tiny kitten. "We must take Bitsy back to the stables now, Lucy," she said and snatched her daughter's small hand and started down the steps into the garden, silently commanding her knees to stop trembling.

Lucy stared up at her. "Your hand is shaking, Mama," the child said.

Sarah gave Lucy a feeble smile. "I forgot to put on my shawl, sweetness. The air is more chill than I thought."

Sarah longed to run, but set a pace to accommodate Lucy, who skipped along beside her with the kitten pressed against her chest. Her mind was in a turmoil. *Lord Lyle must be Connor Hamil from the workhouse. Con, grown into a man. But how did he become a lord?* She could see little of the boy she remembered in the man, except his dark good looks. Connor had had the same beautiful black eyes. He had been tall at fourteen, but direly thin. Who would have expected him to become this imposing, powerful gentleman. *Gentleman! Connor Hamil?* The cheeky boy she had known had been raised on the streets of London until his aunt and uncle died in the influenza epidemic. He had been placed in the workhouse as an indigent youth. How had he come to be a titled wealthy mill owner?

Inside the stables, Lucy took the kitten from Sarah's hands.

"Here's Bitsy, Agnes," the child said and scratched the mother cat between the ears. Agnes licked the restored kitten with a small pink tongue.

The horses neighed their greetings from their stalls. Feeling more calm, Sarah waved to a stable boy who was repairing tack at the other end of the long corridor. Her heart had finally reverted to its normal beat, and she left the stables.

As she walked back to the house, she promised her pretty brown-haired daughter, "I shall send for milk and cake when we get back to the nursery."

Lucy chattered in detail about the strawberry tarts Cook

had baked that morning. But Sarah's mind was still on Lord Lyle. She had probably made things awkward for him, but she had to think of Lucy. She could not let the Lawtons learn that she had never been Sarah Farrell. She would have to find a way to speak with Connor privately and explain her situation, to ask him to keep her secret. He, of all people, would understand.

As she navigated with Lucy toward the back stairs to avoid the parlor and Lord Lyle, she shook her head in wonder. Who would have thought that the two destitute orphans from the workhouse would land on their feet— Con splendidly, it seemed, while she not quite so? But she had no right to complain. She had gotten out alive. She felt ashamed to decry her present situation whenever she thought of the stupendous death rate of the children who had been left behind in the workhouse. Only as an adult had she learned how truly fortunate she was.

Connor walked back across the Persian carpet to the Lawtons. The butler had left, but the family gazed wide-eyed at him. He smiled a bit sheepishly. "I seem to have made a foolish blunder," he said. "I mistook Mrs. Lawton for a friend from my younger days. I trust I have not discomfited her."

"Think nothing of it, Lord Lyle. Sarah's sensibilities are of no consequence," Augusta Lawton said, dismissing the incident. "Sit there in the wing chair. It is the most comfortable. You take the armchair, Silas, and share the side table between you with his lordship. Cynthia will bring both of you your tea and a plate of cakes."

Connor did not care for the sixtyish gray-haired woman's high-handed manner toward young Mrs. Lawton. For some reason, Ellis Lawton's widow was not held in proper regard in this household. But he was a guest.

Speaking in Sissy's favor might make matters worse for her. And, she was Sissy Eaton. He was sure of it. Her honey-brown hair was the exact shade it had been when he last saw her, the day the former Lord Lyle saved him from the workhouse. Her hazel eyes were the same, more brown than green. A person's eyes did not change color from thirteen to twenty-three.

"I will take you on a tour of the mill tomorrow, Lord Lyle," Silas Lawton said, interrupting Connor's thoughts. "I think you will find it worthy of your investment. We ran into a patch of hard luck with some accidents and the breakdown of equipment recently. It left us short of cash, but the business is basically sound; it just needs a bit more capital."

Connor set the cup of rich brew Cynthia handed him beside a plate of cakes on the table provided.

"Cream or sugar, my lord?" she offered.

"No, thank you," he said, but his mind was on Mr. Lawton's contention.

Rumor had it that the "patch of hard luck" had been going on for some time. Connor suspected that Lawton's textile mill was poorly managed and would need more than "a bit of capital." He hoped to talk the mill owner into giving him a controlling interest, although he would have preferred to buy the mill outright. But most owners were reluctant to sell the family business even when they suffered yearly losses and found themselves periodically under the hatches.

"I look forward to seeing your enterprise, Mr. Lawton," Connor said. "But let's not talk shop. I am sure we will only succeed in boring the ladies whom I would like to get to know better." It was no bad thing and politic to tell white lies now and then.

"Well said, my lord," Lawton agreed with a robust laugh

and took a bite from a slice of sponge cake he lifted from the plate on their shared table.

Cynthia simpered at Connor's words. She did not have Sissy's natural beauty, but neither was she what polite society would unkindly call an antidote. Her hair was a pleasing shade of blond and her blue eyes were clear. Her short stature was rounded in all the right places, yet Con knew that Silas Lawton's daughter was not for him.

"Do you travel to London often, Miss Lawton?" he said, to make conversation.

Before Cynthia could answer him, her aunt intervened. "Dear Lord Lyle, I fear both Cynthia and I are Miss Lawtons. Perhaps to avoid confusion, you could address her by her given name and leave me the sole Miss Lawton."

Connor smiled politely. "Of course, madam."

Mr. Lawton looked eager. "Perhaps you would do me the honor of calling me Silas, my lord." Connor knew it would be better when conducting business to maintain a degree of formality, but he had consented to accept Lawton's hospitality for a few days. It would seem churlish to deny the man's simple request when he seemed to want it so much.

Connor nodded. "Silas," he said by way of consent. "And why don't you drop the lordship and lord and simply call me Lyle as my friends do."

Silas beamed. "Kind of you, sir. Most kind."

"Now, Miss Cynthia," Connor said, turning back to her, "do you make sojourns to the capital?"

Cynthia Lawton looked like she was going to faint from happiness at being singled out by him. "Yes, my lord," she said. "I have gone to London for the Little Season."

"Well, then, my dear, I would be pleased to hear your impressions of the City."

Connor sat back with his cup of tea and prepared to be bored.

Two

Fifty-year-old Gideon Lambert held out the dark blue superfine coat to his charge, whom he had served for the past ten years since the old Lord Lyle had taken a shine to Connor Hamil. The street urchin had beguiled the old gentleman—and Gideon, too, for that matter—with his keen intelligence, curious mind, and mature attitude that had belied his humble beginnings.

For years the former Lord Lyle had fostered lads from the workhouse, educated the orphans, and found them positions in the working world. But the wealthy aristocrat had found something in Connor Hamil that he had not seen in any of his other "charities," and he had taken a fatherly interest in the boy.

"What did you learn below stairs about Mrs. Lawton, Gideon?" Connor asked as he pushed his long arms into one sleeve and then the other of the red silk-lined coat. The tall valet straightened the garment over the broad shoulders of the young man whom he had come to love and respect. He had approved completely when Lord Lyle changed Connor Hamil's status from foster child to adopted son and heir.

"Nothing that ties her to the workhouse," Gideon said, moving to the oak dresser and rooting around in a jewelry box.

An erudite instructor had taught Connor to read and saw

to his formal schooling, but Gideon's reclusive employer had insisted that Connor have a social life. So, it was the valet who had coached the graceless lad in the ways of the upper classes and arranged for invitations to functions to be tendered from the right people. Long before he became Lord Lyle, Connor Hamil could have held his own in the company of the Prince Regent himself.

Connor lifted his chin for Gideon to arrange his neck-cloth and to poke a ruby stickpin into the spotless cravat.

"If Mrs. Lawton is the girl whom you knew as Sissy," the older man said, "the servants are not aware of it. They believe her to be the daughter of a Mrs. Farrell, who is now deceased. Her mother was a seamstress and her father a sailor who drowned when she was a baby."

"Of one thing, I am certain: if Mrs. Lawton is Sissy, Mrs. Farrell was not her birth mother. Sissy was born on the wrong side of the blanket to an aristocrat and his mistress."

"You could be wrong, Connor. It has been ten years." Gideon Lambert's easy familiarity from when he had nurtured Connor as a boy had carried over into his pupil's adulthood.

The brown-haired valet with just a touch of gray at his temples removed an expensive gold signet ring from the jewelry box and handed it to Connor, who placed it on a slender finger of his right hand.

"Perhaps, Gideon, but I swear Mrs. Lawton knew the name Sissy. She appeared nervous and took off like a scared rabbit with a pretty little girl in tow. The child has the look of her. Is she her daughter, do you know?"

"Yes, she is the deceased son's issue. The mite is called Lucy. The staff praised Mrs. Lawton for being a good mother, and she is generally well liked by them."

"Even as a child, Sissy had a generous spirit," Connor said.

The dinner bell rang at that moment, warning him that he had five minutes to get below stairs or appear rude.

Gideon took one last critical look at the result of his valeting. "You'll do, my boy," he said as he always did.

Connor turned at the door. "Leave off making any more inquiries, Gideon. I do not wish to draw the family's attention to the fact that Mrs. Lawton is a matter of interest to me."

But Connor broke his own command within five minutes after sitting down to dinner with Silas Lawton, Cynthia, and the aunt.

"Isn't Mrs. Lawton dining with us?" he asked, unable to quell his curiosity. As a member of the family she should have been there.

Beside him Cynthia made a small sound that could have been surprise or disapproval or a little of both. Across the table from him, Augusta Lawton appeared nonplussed as a seemingly bewildered Silas looked to his sister on his left to supply an answer.

"Sarah is not comfortable in the company of quality folk," Miss Lawton supplied after a clumsy pause. "She is of low birth, you know. Her mother was a widow woman who kept a dressmaking shop in London. Mrs. Farrell had a deplorable accent, and while Sarah has learned to mimic acceptable speech, she still feels the stigma of her inferior background and shies away from her betters."

Connor prudently minded his manners, for he had been taught to treat all women with courtesy, but he was sorely tempted to mention his own mean birth just to squelch Miss Lawton's lofty airs. Had the stars not been lined up right the day Lord Lyle came to the workhouse, Connor might be peddling vegetables from a handbarrow on the streets of London instead of living a privileged life.

Silas took a portion of lamb cutlets with French beans that a servant offered him from an enormous platter and said, "You must understand, Lyle, Sarah Farrell would not have been my choice as a wife for my son. Ellis should have looked much higher, but he became besotted with the girl while in London and married in haste, informing us of the union after the fact."

Augusta Lawton was tall and spare with a long nose. She pulled a sour face. "Not only did he bring Sarah to live here, but also her mother, who sold out her business. You can imagine how embarrassing it was for us to be forced to make such a low person a member of our household."

Connor gave a noncommittal grunt and ate a piece of grilled cabbage.

Cynthia apparently misread the sound as sympathy, for she said, "I think you see, Lord Lyle, how awkward the whole affair was. I found it difficult to face my friends."

"Since none of it was your doing, Miss Cynthia," Connor said, blandly, "I fail to see why you should have felt ashamed."

"Yes, too true, sir. My brother was the one who humiliated the family, not I."

Miss Lawton took a sip of wine before she continued her mild diatribe on her late nephew's faults. "But, unfortunately, we are the ones who are the heirs to Ellis's poor choice."

To Connor's surprise, Silas became visibly annoyed.

"Ellis is dead. We will not malign him. He left us a precious gift in Lucy. Let us not forget it."

"Yes, Lucy is a gem," Miss Lawton said, tempering her tone. "We all love her."

Connor felt that her palliation lacked fervor, although Augusta Lawton seemed to take her brother's admonition to heart, for she changed the subject adroitly to court gossip about the Prince Regent.

Connor decided that the Lawtons, like most people, knew nothing of his past. They took him for a born aristocrat. Among his friends, the former Lord Lyle had made no secret of how Connor had come to him, but the old gentleman was a private person. Connor had heard the often-told tale that he was Lord Lyle's bastard son. Nothing could be further from the truth. He was born of poor but legally married parents, who died when he was three. It was then he went to live with his apathetic aunt and uncle in London.

The rest of the dinner passed in civil, though uninspired, conversation until the ladies were excused at the conclusion of the meal. The two gentlemen remained at the table to enjoy a glass of wine and an imported cigar.

"I pay a good price for my port these days," Silas said as he filled Connor's crystal wine glass.

Connor took a sip. "Excellent bouquet," he said, sincerely.

Although not much of a connoisseur of tobacco, he had to admit that the cigars, too, were a better blend than he was normally offered. Silas liked to live well.

The mill owner blew a cloud of smoke over his bald head. "How deep are you considering investing?"

"Substantially," Connor said, not surprised that the topic would be broached now that the ladies had withdrawn, "but, you understand, I will need to examine your operation and your books before I commit to a figure." He knew Lawton was anxious to hear a number.

"Of course, of course," Silas said. He continued to extol the productivity of the mill, pushing for an estimate, but Lord Lyle had been Connor's instructor in the world of business. Connor never made a financial decision without considering what his adoptive father, the wisest man he had ever known, would have done. While he indulged

Silas's rhetoric, he had no intention of throwing out an amount until he had all the facts.

Connor smoked his fine cigar partway down before he snuffed it out in a glass receptacle provided for the purpose.

"It has been a long, tiring day," he said to his host and begged off from the custom of joining the ladies in the parlor after the port and smokes.

"Please make my excuses to Miss Lawton and Miss Cynthia. I rose before five this morning to get here by three this afternoon. I want to be fresh for our tour of the mill tomorrow."

Silas graciously liberated Connor from the social duty. "You are a better man than I, Lyle," he said with a smile. "The longest I can recall traveling by carriage, even in my youth, was six grueling hours."

Connor had just reached his bedchamber when a door closed at the far end of the hall with a soft click. A wall sconce illuminated Mrs. Lawton coming down the passage, a tray of dishes in her hands. She stopped for a moment when she noticed Connor, but, then, continued to walk toward him.

He did not move. He wondered if he should stop her as she passed him, confront her, get her to admit she was Sissy. But there was no need.

She came up to him and gazed into his eyes. Softness crept into her voice as she said, "Hello, Con."

Three

"I knew it," Connor said. "It is you, Sissy!"

She laughed with him, but put a finger to her lips. "Sh," she whispered, looking toward the stairs. "They mustn't hear us."

Connor opened the door to his bedchamber and, lowering his voice, said, "Come inside. I have so many questions to ask you."

He stood aside as she passed by him. He took the tray of dirty dishes from her and set it on a table beside the door.

Connor looked down at her. "Damn, but you are beautiful, Sissy."

She frowned a little. "Don't call me Sissy, Connor. No one has for ten years now. Mrs. Farrell, who took me from the workhouse two weeks after you left, said it was a silly nickname. I did not know it, but I was registered as Sarah Eaton."

"Is Sarah your birth name?"

"I suppose it must be, but Mama never called me anything but Sissy, nor did Jack. But then neither of them were very forthcoming with information."

Connor knew that Jack had been her mother's lover and Sissy's father.

She looked toward the door. "I cannot stay, Con. Jessie, one of the maids, is with my daughter, Lucy. She will wonder what is keeping me. I am just supposed to be returning our supper tray to the kitchen."

"But I do so want to talk with you. Just a little bit, Sis . . . Sarah." He reached out a hand to her.

Connor wanted to hug her, but did not dare. Their last day at the workhouse when he had decided to go with Lord Lyle, she had flung her arms around his waist and wailed tearfully, "Don't go, Con! Please don't leave me!"

His hands had stayed at his side then, too, for giving comfort or getting it had been alien to him then. He had put her from him clumsily and had given her reasons why he had to leave, but he could not recall them now.

Sarah sat down with him on the blanket chest at the foot of the bed. "How did you come to be a lord?" she asked.

"Lord Lyle adopted me and made me his heir," Connor replied and told her of the circumstances.

She shook her head in wonder when he finished and said, "Imagine that."

"Did you love Ellis Lawton very much?" he asked. She appeared puzzled by the question.

"Love Ellis?" she murmured.

"I understand that you have been a widow for three years, yet you still wear deepest black," he said. Connor wondered if he was jealous of a dead man. He was terribly attracted to Sissy. No doubts. The attraction was there, strong and sharp. And sudden.

Sarah's smile seemed a little bitter as she looked down at her black dress. "Not by choice. Aunt Augusta's allocation of funds for clothes does not stretch as far as my wardrobe. Perhaps when I start patching these widow's weeds, she will loosen her purse. As for Ellis, I was fond of him. Oh, he liked to gamble and drink, but he was not nasty when he was foxed. In fact, he found everything funny when he was in his cups. And, he was faithful."

"Though not a marriage made in heaven?"

"Hardly. I married him because Mrs. Farrell threatened to return me to the workhouse if I refused Ellis's proposal. But he was a nice, gentle man, and I did like him. Mrs. Farrell saw the son of a wealthy mill owner as an answer to her prayers and my marriage as a way to retire from the drudgery of dressmaking. Ellis was mad for me and when she passed me off as her natural daughter from whom she could not bear to be parted, he agreed to let her live with us."

"And she moved in here," Connor added, for he had learned that at the dinner table.

Sarah nodded. "But after less than a year, she came down with some unidentifiable malady and died within a week."

"But why all the secrecy, Sarah?"

She sighed. "I could not wed Ellis without telling him the truth. I made him aware that Mrs. Farrell found me in the workhouse and that I was the product of a union between an aristocrat with a family of his own and his mistress, an opera dancer. Ellis was not put off by it, but he made me promise never to tell his father or his aunt. Being the supposed legitimate daughter of a seamstress and her husband who had been lost at sea was barely acceptable, but Ellis was certain his father would seek an annulment if he learned of my true background."

Sarah got up as if to leave, but Connor pulled her back.

"Please, not yet. Did Mrs. Farrell treat you kindly?"

"Mostly indifferently. I was an investment. She threatened when she sought to get her way, but she did not physically abuse me. I worked hard in the dress shop, and she had no complaints from her customers, which was all she cared about. What of Lord Lyle? Was he kind?"

"Always," Connor said. "He was all that a son could wish in a father. For the first time in my life, I felt as if I had been born under a lucky star. I was heartbroken when he died."

Sarah got up again, but, this time, she shook off Connor's hand. "No, Con. I must go now. You won't tell the Lawtons about me, will you?"

He stood up and looked down into her worried face. "Gad, Sarah, I would never do that. Those months in the workhouse, it was you and me against the world." He let a grin climb his cheek. "Remember how we would hide when we didn't like the looks of the visitors who came to lay claim to one of the inmates?"

Sarah gave him a smile. "Until Lord Lyle showed up."

Connor sighed. "There was something about him, Sarah. I know you felt betrayed, but I was a green boy of fourteen. I was so sure that it was the chance I had waited for. I was not wrong."

"Dear Con, there is no question of betrayal. I am not blaming you," she said. "A child in our position had to count itself fortunate to be given a home where there was no brutality. I cried a bucket of selfish tears, but I was only thirteen and frightened."

Connor walked with Sarah to the door. She picked up the tray from the table. "Will you please look to see if the hall is empty?" she said. "I would be courting trouble if I were to be seen coming from your room."

He reached around her to open the door, but paused with his hand on the doorknob. "I must see you again, Sarah. I am touring Mr. Lawton's mill tomorrow, but perhaps we could get together in the late afternoon?"

"That would not be wise. Cynthia and Aunt Augusta would be in a fret if you paid attention to me."

Sarah did not have to spell out the problem for Connor. Cynthia was setting her cap for him with her aunt's help. He had seen the signs in designing females too often not to recognize them.

"Isn't there somewhere that we could be private?"

Sarah shook her head, but he hurried into speech, for he was not going to give up. He was already enamored of her. He had to test how deep his emotions ran.

"There must be someplace."

Sarah looked thoughtful. "There's a gazebo near a small pond not far from here," she said.

She set the tray down again and walked to the window beside the carved cherrywood headboard of the bed, motioning Connor to follow her.

She pulled aside the heavy brown drapes and pointed. "See those evergreen trees? Hidden behind them are the pond and the gazebo. I will be there at three o'clock, the usual time that Lucy and I walk."

She went back to the table, Connor following, and picked up the tray. He opened the door and looked up and down the empty hall. "Until tomorrow at three," he said.

Sarah slipped past him. He watched her turn toward the stairs to complete her belated errand to the kitchen, then closed the door before someone noticed him.

Four

Connor closed the business ledger and leaned back in the office chair that belonged to Ambrose Sykes, who managed the textile mill for Silas Lawton. Connor had been at the factory for hours, inspecting the machines and facilities and poring over the books.

Sadly, Lawton employed some children barely out of leading strings for ten or twelve hours a day with no breaks except for the noon meal. At Connor's own mill, he hired no children under twelve, an unprecedented practice for a mill owner in England. He knew of only one businessman, Robert Owen, who had instituted any reforms close to Connor's own. But Owen was able to preach his revolutionary ideas far and wide, even to Parliament, while Connor could only work quietly, doing what he could to make life better for the employees of his small enterprise.

Connor folded his hands beneath his chin. If he were to invest in Silas Lawton's business, he would have to demand some changes. For one, Ambrose Sykes, Lawton's longtime manager, would have to go. Con was good at accounting. He could analyze and verify financial transactions flawlessly. He had had an excellent teacher in Lord Lyle.

Con was all but certain that Ambrose Sykes was stealing from Silas. He had detected signs of embezzlement, but was not yet ready to make an accusation. He would want Jerome Jepp, an honest worker from his own mill who supported Connor's reforms and had trained under Con's manager Warren Suggs, to replace Sykes.

Connor lifted his gold watch from his vest pocket. Lud, it was already after two o'clock. He did not intend to miss his rendezvous with Sissy. He had to remember to think of her as Sarah so that he did not make a mistake in front of one of the Lawtons.

Connor smiled to himself. The attraction he had felt for Sarah yesterday had not faded. He had never been in love before, but he was sure that he was in love now. It had come like a bolt out of the blue. Lord Lyle had taught him to be a careful man, a prudent man, not to trust his emotions. But how did one stop such overpowering feelings? Apparently, love struck when one least expected it. And, wise or not, he was not going to deny something as wonderful as this odd little happiness rolling around inside him.

The door opened as Connor was rising from the manager's chair. He came from behind the desk and met Silas Lawton halfway as the mill owner walked into the room from an outer office.

His eyes questioning, he inquired, "Well, Lyle, what is your opinion? Not a bad company is it?"

Connor's reaction was not ebullient. "I need some time to digest my impressions and perceptions before making a firm commitment. There are some sensitive areas where we may have disagreements on a change in employees. But I beg your patience, Silas. Give me one night to sleep on it. I give you my word, I shall enter into serious negotiations with you tomorrow."

Silas's mouth pruned. "I cannot imagine where we would come into conflict. I have good people," he said rather testily.

Connor did not like to be prodded, but he concealed his annoyance beneath a half-apologetic smile.

"I know you are anxious to conclude our transactions, but Lord Lyle demanded that I reflect on every aspect of a financial deal before signing a contract. I have always found it a commonsensical requirement when doing business. Now, I would like to return to the house. I have been cooped up inside for far too many hours on such a fine day. I am looking forward to taking a long solitary walk this afternoon to clear my head."

The mill owner's face revealed that he recognized the futility of pressuring Connor.

"My carriage is parked out front, Lyle," he said, but the strain to make his voice sound cheerful showed.

It was past three o'clock when Connor hurried toward the verdant trees that Sarah had pointed out to him from his bedroom window. He made his way through the grove and came out onto a private park that was surrounded by evergreens of various species, some of which were of the type that flowered in the spring.

Sarah sat on the gazebo's wooden steps of white peeling paint. Dense shrubbery grew against the sides of the peak-roofed summer house that overlooked a pond where the child Lucy was sailing a toy boat tethered by a long string.

The little girl looked over toward Connor and cocked her head, the afternoon sun giving her light brown curls a golden tinge.

"Mama, a man," she called to Sarah.

"I see, darling. Come here and I shall introduce you."

Lucy pulled the boat from the faintly murky water to the white-pebbled shore, dropped the string, and ran to the steps where her mother sat.

Connor approached them, smiling. "I am so glad you

are here," he said to Sarah. "I was afraid you might have changed your mind."

She returned his smile with a faint shake of the head. "How could I, Con? I still find it hard to believe that I am seeing you again after all these years. I have thought of you often and wondered what had become of you." She pointed a gloved hand toward Con. "This is Lord Lyle, Lucy, an old friend of Mama's. Make your obeisance, dear."

Lucy executed an inept curtsy, barely keeping her balance. Her fine pink coat and matching bonnet looked new, at variance with her mother's sad-looking black garments.

Con was charmed by the pretty little girl. He put his hands on his knees and bent down toward her. "Hello, Lucy. What a lovely curtsy. You must have been practicing."

Lucy's small face became serious. "Lots," she said, "but Aunt Augusta says I am not profi . . . profi . . . something." She looked up at her mother for help.

"Proficient," Sarah supplied.

"It means not good enough," Lucy said with a frown.

"How old are you, poppet?" Connor asked.

"Four," she said, holding up the requisite fingers.

"Well, then, I think Aunt Augusta is too fussy," he said. "Your proficiency matches your age quite splendidly."

Lucy looked unsure. "Is that good?"

Con threw his head back and laughed. "Very good indeed."

Lucy beamed at her mother, who was smiling.

Connor could see the mutual love between Sarah and her daughter. He reached in his coat pocket and pulled out two wrapped comfits and handed them to the little girl.

Lucy's blue eyes grew big. "I love candy. Aunt Cynthia sometimes buys me some when we go to the confectioner's in the village."

She tucked one piece of candy into her coat pocket and began to unwrap the other sweet.

Sarah prodded gently. "What do you say to Lord Lyle?"

"Thank you, Lord Lyle," she sang out.

"You are quite welcome, Lucy."

Connor sat down beside Sarah on the steps. He stretched out his long legs and watched Lucy as she walked back toward the pond.

"What a darling little girl," Connor said.

Sarah looked proud. She gazed over at her daughter who was running toward the trees, her blue-and-white vessel abandoned on the pebbled shore.

"Lucy," Sarah cried and the child stopped in her tracks and stared back at her mother.

"A bunny, Mama," she called.

"Stay where I can see you, dear. Don't go into the trees. The rabbit has already gone into its hole."

Lucy made a face, but returned to her boat.

Sarah's daughter was so protected, secure, and happy, Connor thought. "I still think about the babies and little children that died in the workhouse the months we were there," he said. "It had a profound affect on me."

"You shielded me so successfully," Sarah replied, "that at the time I blocked a lot of the ugliness from my mind. I was so spoiled. I did not let myself believe that some of the children there were dying."

Connor reacted to her remorse. He put his hand over hers. "We were children ourselves, Sis . . . Sarah," he said to ease her self-reproach. "We arrived there the same day and sat together in a corner on the dirty floor and never separated again. You were so afraid, your face stained by tears. I never cared about anyone before. Yet I kept you close, and we stayed together without any conscious design."

Connor thought how strange it was that a single decision

had changed his entire life. At fourteen he could have run away when the rent collector came to his house to evict him and turn him over to the parish, but winter was near. He had reasoned that if he was a ward of the parish and went to the workhouse, he would at least have shelter and two stingy meals a day. Completely on his own, he might have died of starvation or frozen to death. The choice had brought Sissy into his life and, later, Lord Lyle.

"The workhouse was so chaotic with all sorts of people thrown together, young and old, male and female, all poor, many in rags, undernourished, so many sick," Sarah said, her voice somber.

"Yet it was that disorder that made it possible for us to be lost in the crowd," Con said. "Too many children were orphaned by influenza for the keepers to single us out. I suddenly found it useful to have been raised by Aunt Maude and Uncle Bert after my parents died. They were indifferent to my comings and goings. I was not much bigger than Lucy when I first pilfered an apple from a stall."

Sarah gave him a dismal smile. "Your experiences on the street made you savvy and nimble-witted. You managed to open the padlocks on the storerooms where the food for the overseers was kept. At times we got to forgo the thin gruel and watered-down soup given to the inmates and dined instead on bread and cold meats."

Inwardly, Con shuddered, remembering the folly of it. Stupid boy. Both of them would have been flogged if he had been caught, the sort of severe beating which would have left them maimed for life.

Con gazed at Sarah's profile. She was so beautiful that he could not stop staring at her.

In the distance Lucy babbled to an imaginary playmate.

"I thank the Lord every day that my daughter will never go to a horrible place like that," Sarah said with feeling.

"No child should," Connor replied. "It is why I bought

a cotton mill after I came into a fortune when Lord Lyle died."

Sarah gave him an incredulous stare. "But factories are notorious for working young children for long, long hours."

Connor nodded. "I know. But I have set up schools for the children who work for me, and I do not hire the very young. I know what education can do for the mind and the soul. Their families need the money so I have to give the youngsters duties to earn their wages, but I have cut the hours and made the daily lessons part of the workday. It's not a lot, but it is something that makes a difference."

Sarah's mouth stood open. "Con, that is wonderful," she said.

"But a long way from Utopia," he replied. "I would like to buy Mr. Lawton's mill, but he only desires investment. Yet I will be able to institute a number of reforms for the children through the manager I plan to bring in if Silas and I can strike a deal."

Sarah touched his shoulder. "You have made a start at improving the lives of children. I wish I could do something for the orphaned workhouse waifs. Not many end up as fortunate as you, or I."

"No," Connor said, but he knew what oddities he and Sarah truly were. Most children died in the workhouses. Those who were taken out were more likely to be worked to death by uncaring masters than to live to adulthood. It would take government intervention to stop the abuses, but there was little sentiment among the powerful for meaningful reforms. Most owners cared only about profits and nothing for the betterment of their workers.

These concerns had been almost a constant in Con's daily musings for years. The former Lord Lyle had not been involved in politics. His name was not known in official circles, as Robert Owen's was, and, lamentably,

Connor's new title carried little weight. But he put these cares aside. His feelings for Sarah were new, and for the first time in his life, his mind was filled with thoughts of a woman.

Unable to stop himself, Connor took Sarah's hand and lifted it to his lips. "Sarah, I know you will think this sudden, but I am drawn to you. My heart is becoming seriously engaged."

Sarah pulled her hand from his. "Lucy, bring your boat," she called. "We must go home."

She stood up and Connor stood up with her. "Forgive me. I have been too blunt," he said. "I am not experienced in courting. But my devotion is real."

"Connor, I can see that you are a decent man with the highest of principles. I find that appealing. But I think your emotions are colored by our shared adversities in the workhouse."

Connor grasped her shoulders and looked down into her face. "Certainly I have warm memories of that young girl, but, believe me, my dear, it is the grown Sarah, not little Sissy, who has captured my heart. My intentions are honorable. Let me prove it to you."

"I don't doubt you, Con," she said, giving him hope. "But I would rather that we not make the family aware of your interest."

Connor did not like the evasion, but he did not want to make things difficult for Sarah with Cynthia and Augusta Lawton. He suspected that the two women were jealous of her.

"I can carry that off," he promised, although he did not know how he would squelch the warmth in his eyes.

"Can we meet again tomorrow?" he asked. Given time, he was confident that he could get Sarah to agree to marry him. She was not immune to the man he had become. Her open facial expressions did not hide a certain admiration for him.

His faith was rewarded when she said, "Cynthia and Aunt Augusta are taking Lucy visiting with them and will be gone from the house between one and three, but Silas will be there, most likely working in the library."

"All right, then, I will meet you here at one o'clock. I have business with Silas in the morning, but we will have concluded our affairs before noon."

Sarah watched Connor until he disappeared into the trees. He was making a positive impact on the lives of poor children. She would have liked to do the same. But high-minded principles were a luxury she could not afford without money of her own. At thirteen, she had come to the workhouse from a pampered childhood, unprepared for the harshness. Con's protection had saved her sanity; Mrs. Farrell had saved her life by taking her from that awful place. She never wanted to end up on the parish dole again.

Sarah held her daughter's free hand; the child's other hand clutched her boat.

Lucy looked up at her mother. "Lord Lyle is a very nice man, Mama," she said.

Sarah squeezed her daughter's hand. "Yes, he is, dear, very nice."

Her passions were running surprisingly parallel to Connor's. Just talking to him made her feel alive again. It was the suddenness that made her wary. But his words seemed to come straight from the heart. Her own heart and mind were attuned to his. It had been an eternity since someone had made her feel special. In all honesty, as odd as it was, she felt that she was already in love with Connor Hamil.

Five

Silas sat at Ambrose Syke's desk looking lost, a business ledger open before him. Connor leaned over the desktop and ran a long finger over the numbers on the page.

"See there and there," he said. "The amounts don't make sense. Exactly where did this expense come from?"

Silas frowned. "I don't precisely see what you mean," he said. Connor suspected that the mill owner did not have an aptitude for numbers.

Within minutes, his suspicions had been confirmed. Silas Lawton knew nothing about keeping accounts. It became clear that as long as Sykes had turned over an adequate sum that he claimed represented the quarterly profits, Silas had been satisfied. He accepted excuses of machinery breakdowns and decreasing business, taking Sykes's word as gospel without an independent audit.

Ambrose Sykes had gotten away with embezzlement for years while the business prospered, but the Lawton Mills had hit a bump in the road, as it were, over the past year. Sykes had become accustomed to siphoning money from the company, but with the downturn of business he could no longer satisfy both his greed and Silas Lawton's expectations.

Patiently, Connor explained the issue in layman's terms to Silas and watched the mill owner's face turn red with rage as he finally grasped the truth.

He leapt from the office chair and rushed to the door, flinging it open. "Mr. Cobb," he called to the clerk who sat in the outer office on a high stool, "did you say earlier that Mr. Sykes was off the premises on business today? Isn't that highly irregular?"

The thin bespectacled employee shrank visibly into his black coat as if he were being accused of a dereliction of duty. "Not exactly, but, yes, not usual for him, I suppose."

"Send a boy around to his house to enquire of his whereabouts and leave a message that I wish to see him."

The clerk jumped from the stool. "Immediately, sir."

Connor had been watching from the doorway of the manager's office. "I think Sykes realized the jig was up when he saw me examining the books yesterday," he interjected. "I would bet a farthing the boy you send around will find Sykes's house shut up tight and his servants gone."

Eyes downcast, Silas pushed past Connor and sat back down at the desk. He propped his elbows on top and dropped his head into his hands.

Connor closed the door and lowered himself into a chair that faced the distraught mill owner. His arms folded over his chest, he waited for the enormity of Sykes's treachery to sink in. Their embezzler was probably far away by now, perhaps even already aboard a boat sailing for the Continent.

Silas did not say anything for a very long time. At last, he sat up, stiffening his spine and lifting his chin. "I suppose, Lyle, you are about to tell me that I am ruined and that you are not going to throw good money after bad."

Connor kept his face impassive. "No, nothing quite so drastic, Silas. Actually, Mr. Sykes could have done greater financial damage than he did. The sales were quite brisk up until ten months ago. Only when they dropped did he run into trouble and he could not live beyond his normal salary as he had been doing *and* give you the money to which you were accustomed."

Silas still looked concerned, but his eyes also revealed a measure of optimism at Connor's words.

Connor reached into his inside pocket and pulled out a folded sheet of paper.

"Everything I have learned from my investigation leads me to believe that your paramount interest in the mill is as a source of income so that you can live well. Tell me if I am wrong."

"You are correct. I do like my comforts. Except for a piece of London real estate, I have no other significant means of livelihood, and I have three women and a child to support."

Connor was satisfied with the honest answer. "Then, let us get down to business," he said and leaned over and handed the paper across the desk to Silas. "I have made a breakdown of the capital I am prepared to invest and the allocation of the funds as I see them."

Silas unfolded the informal document and stared at the numbers. He looked over at Connor, his eyes growing large. "You will infuse this amount into the business?" He was clearly stunned. But Connor was not surprised by his reaction. He had come up with a sum designed to get him the concessions he wanted from Silas. The mill owner had taken the bait.

But Connor felt obligated to say, "You had better listen to my conditions before you make a snap judgment."

"All right, give them to me." But Silas was all but rubbing his hands together in delight.

"I must bring in my own manager, Jerome Jepp, who will run the mill without interference. He has been trained at my cotton mill. Some of my changes may not sit well with you since I do not treat my workers in the accepted manner employed by most factory owners."

Silas held up his hand. "Say no more, Lyle. You may be as hard as you wish on the employees as long as you guarantee me my dividends as stated here." He tapped the paper with his index finger.

Connor made no effort to correct Lawton's pompous misconception. Matters had turned out better than he had originally thought they would. Although he would not own the mill outright, the contract would give him autonomy over every phase of the business. Sykes's perfidy had worked to Con's advantage. Had he been an honest employee, Connor would have had to initiate reforms slowly. But with Sykes gone, Jerome Jepp could step right in and make drastic changes.

"When can we sign a contract?" Silas asked eagerly.

Connor motioned with his head toward the outer office. "In speaking with your Mr. Cobb, I found that he is a notary and can put my notes into a legal form."

"Yes, Cobb is astute in the language of business and, as you say, he is certified to handle such matters. I will see that he has the contract ready to sign by morning."

"I agree, then," Connor said and the two men shook hands.

Long after Lord Lyle left, Silas stared at the number that represented the money earmarked for his household expenses. He would not have to cut back on his standard of living. He had expected to dismiss a number of his servants and put his sister on a tight budget, but, miracle of miracles, young Lyle was saving his hide intact. He almost felt giddy at his good fortune.

Sarah pulled the dark woolen cloak around her against the chill wind. Dark clouds blotted out the sun. She felt a flutter of happiness when she caught sight of Connor stepping from the grove of evergreens, which needed only a sprinkling of snow to look like a Christmas forest. The Lawtons did not celebrate the holiday, and she missed the merriment from her childhood.

Jack had spent Christmas mornings with his legitimate family, but late in the day he came to their house bearing gifts. The cook served up a feast with roast goose and plum pudding. A small yule log burned in the fireplace and Jack dipped spicy wassail from a crystal bowl into cups and made a gay toast for their little family's continued happiness.

Sarah's thoughts turned from her lost family to Connor, who was walking with long strides around the pond and coming toward where she waited on the top step of the gazebo. The skinny boy who had protected her in that terrible workhouse had grown into an exceedingly handsome man. He was intelligent and kind and decent. She admired those qualities in a gentleman.

Sarah walked down the steps to greet him. "I can see by your face that your business with Mr. Lawton went well."

Connor took her hands in his and smiled down into her eyes.

"Auspiciously so," he said. "As long as Silas makes money, he does not care how the mill is run. Within a few weeks, I will have all the reforms in place that I have made in my own factory. But, just now, my dear, I was thinking that you are the most beautiful woman I have ever laid eyes upon."

Sarah laughed. "Flatterer," she said, but was pleased.

"I love you, Sarah," he said softly. She backed away a little. The rising wind whipped her cloak around her ankles. Her heart sang, but she felt the need to protest.

"Oh, Con, other than those few months we were together while we were children, we have only known each other for these three days."

Raindrops began to fall from the dark clouds above them, but neither of them paid attention.

He put a hand on her shoulder. "I could let myself be ruled by my head instead of my heart and wait three weeks or three months or three years to say I love you, but it would not change a thing."

Just then a wild wind came from nowhere, and the sky burst open in a torrent of rain. Connor put an arm around Sarah's shoulders and hastened her up the steps into the shelter of the gazebo. Some of the wooden slats were split, and runaway ivy twined around the struts, but the floor was solid.

The blinding rain came straight down in sheets. The gazebo was made secure by the impenetrable foliage. Only the stairs were exposed to the elements.

Connor untied the bow of Sarah's bonnet, removed the black hat with the purple silk lining from her head, and placed it beside his own tall beaver on the built-in bench. His arms around her waist, he brought her gently against the solid length of his body, lowered his head, and moved to claim her lips.

With a little sob, Sarah's arms went around his neck. She savored the series of slow, sensual kisses that sent desire sweeping through her. Her mouth opened under his as the kisses increased in heat and intensity, sending her emotions into a spin and her head reeling.

Both of them were breathing hard when Con lifted his mouth from hers and curled his fingers into the front of her cloak.

"Now, convince me, my sweet, that we are not head over heels in love in three days."

"I cannot," she said softly.

Connor held his hand along the length of Sarah's face.

"I want to marry you, Sarah. Will you have me?"

"Yes, oh, yes," she said, leaning her cheek into his palm.

"I will inform Silas when we get back to the house," Connor said, smiling happily.

Nervous tension spiked Sarah's chest. She shook her head. "No, Con, don't, not until after your business with Mr. Lawton is concluded."

Connor's smile faded, and he dropped his hand from her face.

"Why?"

Sarah sighed. How to make him understand? She moved apart from him and looked toward the steps. The rain still came down hard.

"Aunt Augusta is not going to like our engagement by half. She had visions of you courting Cynthia."

"But, my dear girl, that was never going to happen whether I fell in love with you or not," Connor said, sitting down on the bench.

"Be that as it may, Cynthia fancies you. I know what that can mean." Sarah sat down beside him, folded her hands in her lap, and looked down at her black boots.

"Once before, Lord Collins, an eligible young man, was invited to a house party, specifically for the purpose of getting him to propose to Cynthia. But he would not come up to scratch. Worse yet, he began to woo me. I did everything I could to discourage his attentions, for in truth, I did not welcome them. But he became obsessive in his pursuit of me until, finally, I could take no more. I ripped up at him and told him rather bluntly that he was no gentleman. He took offense at my plain speaking and left in a huff within hours of our quarrel. I was accused of ruining Cynthia's chances by throwing myself at the man and giving him a disgust of me, driving him off."

Connor put his hands over hers. "I see. So, you expect

some sort of unpleasantness when we announce our intentions."

Sarah nodded. He looked off into the distance.

"Tell me," he said. "Why are you excluded from taking meals with the family?"

"That only occurs when there are guests. Given my so-called lowly lineage, Aunt Augusta claims that I will be more comfortable taking my dinner with Lucy than in polite company."

"What nonsense!" Connor's expression became fierce, his voice vibrant. "You will dine with us tonight, Sarah, or I shall raise a rumpus."

Sarah laughed. "A rumpus? I would like to see that," and he laughed with her.

Connor stood up and his voice sobered. "I mean it, darling. I will insist that you be included at dinner. I will not tolerate them showing you any disrepect."

"Perhaps I am overreacting, Con," she said. But she knew she was not. Connor had no idea how vicious Aunt Augusta and Cynthia could be. Sarah had been called a slut and a trollop after the contretemps over Lord Collins, even though she had been innocent of any wrongdoing, unless one counted losing her temper.

She stood up, too, and touched his arm. "Indulge me in this, Con," she said. She had no reason to believe that once Connor announced their betrothal that the two women would gracefully accept the engagement. She might be a coward, but she intended to put off the inevitable until the last possible moment.

Fearing his silence, she pressed. "Promise me you won't say anything about our plans to wed without my permission?" She needed a verbal assurance.

He waited so long to answer that Sarah expected him to argue with her. Finally, he shrugged. "I don't like it, but all right," he said. "I agree."

Satisfied, she gazed toward the opening by the steps. "Look, the rain has stopped," she said.

The downpour had ceased as suddenly as it had started. The sky had lightened as a fresh wind began to blow away the storm clouds. Faint patches of blue were visible in the distance.

"I must go, Connor. Aunt Augusta and Cynthia will be returning from their visitation soon."

"They take Lucy with them, but not you?"

"Yes, she is invited to go along when they make calls to homes where there are children. The aunts are kind to Lucy, and she enjoys playing with her little friends. I cannot fault them on that score. I don't mind not being included," she lied. She would have liked to have a friend or two.

The look on Connor's face told her that he was rankled by the things she had told him.

He picked up her bonnet from the bench and placed it on her head. Bending his knees to her lesser height, he tied the black ribbons under her chin and set a sweet kiss on the tip of her nose.

There was such tenderness in his dark eyes and sincerity in his voice when he said, "I shall soon take you and Lucy away from here; I promise to be the best of fathers to her and the most devoted of husbands to you," that Sarah was overwhelmed with love for him.

He picked up his own hat and offered her his arm. "Let me walk you back to the house."

Sarah acquiesced. If anyone asked, she could always say that she and Lord Lyle had met by accident.

Six

The mahogany dining room table was set with the Lawtons' best china and crystal while a tall candelabra at the unoccupied end added light to what was provided by the brass wall sconces.

Silas Lawton sat at the head of the table which could have accommodated twelve guests, but was set for five.

A footman waited nearby for a signal from his master to bring in the fish course.

"Where the devil is Sarah?" Silas said. "I do not like it when food meant to be hot is served cold."

On her brother's right, Augusta Lawton's lips pursed in rebuke as she looked across the table at Connor.

"Silas has said that you asked that Sarah be included in our company this evening, Lord Lyle, but I fear that she might not fully appreciate the honor you have bestowed upon her. She lacks the niceties that one who is raised in a proper family would possess. Her mother was in trade and her father was a lowly seaman, you know."

Connor sat across from her beside Cynthia. The spinster's words raised his hackles, but he kept his voice even. "So you have said before, Miss Lawton." He once again reminded himself that he was supposed to treat women as ladies even if they did not deserve it.

But it was for Sarah's sake that Connor held his tongue. She had not overstated her in-laws' animosity toward her.

He wanted very much to set them straight, but he had promised Sarah to behave and he would.

Cynthia sniffed as she turned toward the door. "Here is the miscreant now," she said.

Connor left his chair and intercepted Sarah as she came hurrying into the room. She took Connor's proffered arm, but said to her father-in-law a little breathlessly, "Please excuse me, Mr. Lawton, but Jessie was late in arriving to look after Lucy. I came as soon as I could."

Silas waved off Sarah's apology as Connor seated her.

Once Connor returned to his own place at the table, Silas signaled the footman to serve the first course.

Connor was aware that Miss Lawton's mean eyes narrowed in disapproval. But he would not take his own eyes from his love to appease Augusta Lawton. Let the spinster stew. Sarah's golden-brown hair was arranged into a chignon, which, in its simplicity, cast Cynthia's corkscrew curls into the shade. She smiled at him and his pulse accelerated.

While the fish course was being served by the liveried footman, Augusta Lawton opened the dinner conversation by directing her remarks to Connor.

"I had a letter just today from Lady Winfield, Lord Lyle," she said, before taking a bite of the turbot with lobster sauce.

Connor drew a blank, for he knew little of the cream of London society, and cared even less.

"I have never met Lady Winfield, ma'am," he said.

Augusta frowned. "Lady Winfield travels in the Prince Regent's circle and knows all of the latest gossip about everybody who really matters," she said as though such shallowness were admirable.

"Lady Winfield informed me of the birth of Lord Bemington's by-blow with Mrs. Colby," Miss Lawton said.

"Their liaison, of course, is hardly a secret. She says Mrs. Colby will not keep the child, but will foster it out."

Connor did not find the gossip appropriate for table talk in a mixed group, but once again he held his tongue.

"What do you mean by 'fostered out,' Auntie?" Cynthia asked.

Sarah answered her. "Unwanted children of the aristocracy are farmed out to families in the country who will board them for a fee, rather than abandoning them to a parish workhouse." Her disgust was apparent, her tone heavy with sarcasm. "The money soothes their consciences, and the paid caretakers have an incentive to keep the waifs alive, but not to treat them humanely."

"You are being impertinent, Sarah, to make judgments about your betters," Augusta said. "No person of sensibilities wants to keep a flesh-and-blood reminder of a social misstep."

Connor was infuriated by the woman's callousness and her set-down of Sarah and spoke his mind at last.

"We are speaking of infants, madam. Their own children. Mrs. Lawton has the right of it."

Until now Silas had seemed more interested in the food and wine than his sister's talebearing, but he must have sensed the anger in Connor's voice, for he said, "Turn to something other than coarse London gossip, Augusta. Does not this correspondent of yours have some inoffensive amusing stories?"

Augusta's laugh was false. "To be sure," she said and launched into some mildly humorous *on dits*. Cynthia provided a counterpoint that kept Miss Lawton from noticing that Con's own responses were curt and his few smiles decidedly weak.

Sarah picked at her fish, finding Aunt Augusta's juicy tidbits boring. But the topic of illegitimate children revived thoughts of a happier time. She blocked out Augusta's voice for her own memories. Her mother and father had loved one another, and her. Jack had already had a family of his own when he fell in love with her mother, Jeanne. But even if he had been free, marriage between an aristocrat and an opera dancer would have been impossible. Jeanne always would have remained his mistress.

Yet, Jack had never rejected them. He kept Sarah and Jeanne in comfort in a snug cottage in a good neighborhood near the outskirts of London town, visiting often. He remained in their lives, and Sarah had known she was loved by both her parents.

But when the influenza epidemic swept through the city, Jeanne had died and no one had come to claim Sarah. She could not search for Jack because she did not know much about him. The servants addressed him only as "milord." Yet she knew in her heart that he, too, had succumbed to the disease, for never would her father have abandoned her.

Sarah came out of her reverie with a start when Silas said, "What's wrong with your quail, Sarah?"

"Nothing," she said, surprised that her fish course had been replaced by the game bird, new potatoes, and asparagus. She had eaten most of the vegetables without being aware that she had.

"Well, then, finish up," Silas said. "The rest of us have cleared our plates and are ready for the pudding."

Pushing her plate aside, Sarah said, "I've had enough."

Silas called for the dishes to be removed and the pudding brought in. He made some lighthearted remarks apropos of nothing.

The table was cleared and clean plates laid for dessert while a second footman filled the coffee cups.

Augusta Lawton's voice became warm as she addressed Connor. "I would like to arrange a party for you to meet the neighbors, my lord. Nothing elaborate, of course, on such short notice, a buffet and dancing, I think. I know everyone who is anyone will want to meet Silas's new partner in the mill."

Silas perked up. "Splendid suggestion, Augusta," he said.

She waited for a footman to pour cream onto her bread pudding before she said, "Cynthia would be happy to act as your partner for the evening and introduce you to our neighbors and the worthies from town, Lord Lyle." She gazed over at her niece. "Wouldn't you, my dear?"

"Oh, most assuredly, Auntie," Cynthia said with a simper. "To do so would give me the greatest pleasure."

Connor brought his long fingers, tip to tip, under his chin, and made no response.

Silas went on as if Con had agreed and asked his sister, "How long will it take for you to get the invitations delivered and the arrangements made for the food and a musical quartet, Augusta? Mind, I don't want it to be a shabby affair."

"As if I would plan anything that would shame you," Augusta said indignantly. "Three days should do it."

Silas said, "Can you spare us a few days now, Lyle, or would you rather we held something a little more elaborate later next month, perhaps during Yuletide?"

"I fear I must decline either," Connor said. "I expect to be announcing my forthcoming marriage tomorrow." He looked over at Sarah. "It is better to be honest about these things."

Sarah's nod of capitulation was faint, but unequivocal.

The Lawtons were stunned into a heavy silence.

"I have asked Sarah to marry me," he said, "and she has accepted."

There was a rush of indrawn breaths. Cynthia's hatred leapt into her eyes as she stared across the table at Sarah. *You viper!* Only her lips moved; her voice was mute.

But Augusta fumed. "He is your lover!" she accused, her voice shrill. "You have been carrying on an affair with him behind our backs."

Sarah did not have a tempestuous nature, but her composure snapped. "When would I have been able to do that, Aunt Augusta? I have been imprisoned in this house since Ellis died. I sleep here every night with Lucy in the next room."

Silas, surprisingly calm, put a restraining hand on his sister's arm. "There is no need for that kind of talk, Augusta. I am sure that Lord Lyle and Sarah have done nothing inappropriate."

Connor glanced at Sarah, seeming to say, *See, everything is going to be fine,* before he turned to Silas, obviously encouraged by the older man's support.

"I recognized Sarah that first day, but it took her a little longer to make the connection that we had known each other as children." He smiled at Sarah, affectionately. "When we saw each other again, we had one of those moments that sometimes happens between a man and a woman that is commonly called 'love at first glimpse.'"

Augusta's unladylike snort communicated her opinion of his romanticism.

"I see no reason Sarah and I should not be married as soon as I procure a special license," Connor said. "I want her and Lucy to accompany me when I leave for home, tomorrow."

Silas lifted his shaggy salt-and-pepper eyebrows. "Tomorrow, eh?" He turned to his sister. "Augusta, excuse us," he said with limp courtesy. "I wish to speak to Lord Lyle and Sarah alone in the library." He pushed back his chair.

Sarah felt the chill of the women's icy glares, but she fixed her eyes on Con, who slipped her a wink as he stood up and reached out a hand to her.

* * *

Inside the library, Silas said, "You had better sit down. Both of you."

He remained standing, resting his backside against his stout desk as Sarah took a wing chair and Connor sat catty-corner to her in a gentleman's old leather lounger.

"You two may wed and Sarah may leave, but Lucy stays here," Silas said.

"No!" Sarah cried, leaning forward. "Impossible!"

Connor looked more perplexed than incensed. "Sarah is Lucy's mother. You have no right to demand that the child remain with you."

"Oh, but I do, Lyle. You see, Ellis gave me guardianship over Lucy until she is twenty-one or she marries, whichever comes first."

Sarah's heart sank. "Ellis would not do that," she said, but she was sure that he had. Silas was not given to bluffing.

Silas waved a hand nonchalantly at her and spoke to Connor. "My son was weak. He was an amiable idler who loved his frivolous amusements. The only productive thing he ever did was to give me a grandchild. Although I loved him, I did not trust that he would do right by Lucy." He paused. "Ellis was always short of money. I threatened to cut off his allowance unless he signed over the care of his daughter to me. You see, Lyle, my son could not stand the thought of making his own way in the world. And I think he knew I would be the better guardian for the child."

"That will not stand up in court," Connor said.

Silas smiled. "Of course it will. You forget, sir, a father holds all the rights over his children, the mother none. Ellis legally passed all those rights to me."

Sarah felt as if she would faint.

"What about me?" she said, her voice trembling.

Her father-in-law looked relaxed and confident. "You can go with Con, as you call him," he said.

"My given name is Connor Hamil," Con explained. "It is what I was called when Sarah knew me before."

Silas smirked. "Oh, yes, about that. I guessed that there was something havey-cavey about your relationship since that first day when you called her Sissy."

"It was her nickname," Connor said.

"It won't wash, Lyle. She denied ever having been called it. But it doesn't matter now. Whoever she is, or was, she married Ellis and that can't be changed."

Sarah felt the tears coming into her eyes. Her throat became tight. "Surely, you are not going to keep Lucy from me, Mr. Lawton?"

Silas lifted his shoulders in a light shrug. "Ellis refused to sign anything until I added a codicil to our agreement that said that you will have a home with me as long as you want, although it was quite unnecessary. I would never have thrown you out. Your presence, Sarah dear, does not bother me as it does my sister and daughter. You have a choice. Stay here and take care of Lucy as you always have, or marry Lord Lyle and go live with him."

Seven

Sarah's face was pinched and ashen. Connor reached out a hand toward her in comfort. "Sarah," he said. He ached for her.

She got up slowly, refusing to meet his eyes. Like a sleepwalker she went to the door, opened it, and was gone.

Connor got to his feet and approached Silas, holding on to his temper. "Can't we come to an accommodation, Lawton? I would bring Lucy to visit you frequently. I am sure Sarah would agree to let her daughter spend some holidays with you. You could even visit us whenever you wished."

"I am Lucy's guardian. Sarah is the one who is free to visit my granddaughter whenever she wants. Why should I oblige you or her?"

"Why? The milk of human kindness springs to mind," Connor remonstrated with some acerbity. "Threatening to separate a mother from her child is cruel."

Con's appeal to Silas's better nature failed miserably. The older man held on to his stubborn position.

"Lucy is my charge, and she stays under my roof. Sarah is free to do as she wishes. And if this cancels our mill contract, so be it. I shall have to find the funds somewhere else to put me back on my feet."

Connor gave up trying to pierce Silas's conscience. "I have never resorted to blackmail in order to close a business deal," he said, "and I don't intend to start now. I will sign our agreement and honor our terms."

But it was the children who worked in Lawton's mill that Connor had on his mind. Ambrose Sykes's safety record was abysmal. The children's fate was in Connor's hands, and his own conscience would not allow him to let them down.

"I will see you in the morning, Lawton," he said, abruptly. Further talk was bootless. "For now I shall seek my bed."

Without a backward glance, Connor left the library, went up the stairs, and turned toward Sarah's bedroom, which connected with the nursery. He stopped short of her door. He could not ask Sarah to give up Lucy and come with him. For one thing, she would never do it. And, if she were the kind of woman who could leave her child for a lover, Connor would be the one who would not want her.

Con set his mouth in a line as stubborn as Silas's had been. Nothing had been settled as far as he was concerned. Sarah would be his wife, no matter how long it took. He loved her and always would. Determined to find a way out of their dilemma, he turned and went back to his own room to spend a sleepless night in contemplation.

Sarah had loosened the top two buttons on the bodice of her black dress when she heard someone coming down the hall. The footsteps stopped before reaching her door. She immediately sensed that it was Connor. Her heart beat faster as she held her breath waiting for him to come closer and knock.

She would not answer, not let him in. If she did, he would surely take her in his arms to attempt to soothe her with well-meaning words. But her pain was too great to be assuaged even by Con's tender touch.

To her relief, she soon heard him walking away down the hall. Her shaking hands went back to her buttons. She took off her clothes, hating Ellis and Silas for what they had done. She had never suspected that her husband had made his father Lucy's guardian. All this time she had had no real say in Lucy's life and had never even known it.

Sarah pulled the white cotton nightgown she had laid out earlier over her head, tied the blue ribbons at the neckline, and climbed into her brass bed. Angry tears of indignation filled her eyes. How dared Ellis and Silas do this to her? On a heartbreaking sob she turned her face into her pillow. Sarah had allowed herself to dream of being happy. She had found a true love in Con, a worthy man. She and Connor and Lucy were going to be a family. But Ellis and Silas had killed that dream.

She cried for a long time until there were no more tears left. Finally, she sat up and blew her nose in the handkerchief she kept in the drawer of the bedside table.

Her love for Con was real, the sort of love that would last a lifetime. But she could not marry him, not if it meant giving up Lucy. She could never desert her daughter to be raised by someone else. Never!

Yet, Silas had not interfered in Lucy's upbringing before. He had left his granddaughter's welfare in Sarah's hands. It was the reason that she had never questioned Lucy's guardianship. And, he had said that she could bring up Lucy as she always had. The knowledge did not make her like her father-in-law any better, but it gave her hope.

Connor was lost to her. She had to put him behind her, no matter how much it hurt. Her future lay in devoting her life to making her precious child happy. "I will raise Lucy with the same depth of love that Jeanne and Jack showed me," she said aloud. It would be enough; it would *have* to be enough.

* * *

In another wing of the house, Augusta and Cynthia sipped tea in a nightly ritual. Aunt and niece sat on green velvet boudoir chairs in the sitting room between their bedrooms.

Cynthia adjusted a peach silk and Alsace lace robe around her knees. "Do you think Sarah will marry Lord Lyle now that Father has revealed that he will not let Lucy go with them?" she wondered aloud.

The two women had eavesdropped at the door to the library and had heard everything. When Sarah left, they had melted into the shadows, and she had been too distraught to notice them.

Augusta, wrapped in a blue flannel robe, a frilled nightcap over her gray hair, let out a derogatory sound.

"Hardly," she said. "More's the pity, but she hasn't the gumption to leave her child for a sterling suitor, and Silas is too mule-headed to allow Lucy to be taken away by Sarah and Lord Lyle. Alas, I fear that Sarah is going to be with us for a very long time."

A servant had set a butler's table at Cynthia's elbow to hold her refreshments. She set her teacup down onto it.

Her lips formed into a sulky scowl. "Father should have sent Sarah away after Ellis died," she grumbled. "You have seen how she throws herself at a man. Even hints to that foolish Lord Collins of her low birth did not keep him from being taken-in by her. And now Sarah has stolen Lord Lyle from me. It is the outside of enough."

A current copy of *La Belle Assemblé* rested on Cynthia's lap. She picked up the lady's periodical and paged fiercely through the magazine.

Augusta did not blame her niece for being agitated. Sarah had been a thorn in their sides ever since Ellis had brought her to this house, but more so since he had died.

When her nephew had been alive, he drank and played cards nearly every night in the village tavern. Rarely did he join the family for dinner when outsiders were present. Sarah, too, invented reasons to stay away from the table then, for she had found it awkward to make excuses for her absent husband.

Since Ellis's death, Sarah could not be kept from sight when guests came for a prolonged visit. Somehow she always showed up where she would be noticed, as she had the day Lord Lyle arrived. Despite her low birth, she could hobnob with gentlemen of quality and not seem out of place. The brazen female was skilled in pulling the wool over a man's eyes. Cynthia was no match for such an experienced wanton, Augusta thought bitterly, and came to a decision.

"I have a solution to our quandary, my dear," she announced.

Cynthia looked up from the magazine. "You have a plan to rid us of Sarah?"

"Something better," Augusta said. "I was thinking, Silas owns that town house in London that he leases out. I believe it is standing empty now. You and I will remove to the City and take up a permanent residence there."

"But Father has said he needs to rent the London house for the income. We had to cut our visit short when we stayed there last year."

"True, my dear, but, you see, that was because Silas would not pay for other lodgings as well as our social expenses. It costs a small fortune to make a splash in the *beau monde*. But I have money I inherited from my grandmother that I never used since your father provided for all my needs. The investments have grown over the years. It is time I dipped into the profits for your benefit. At my demise, you would have received the entitlements through my will. But why wait?"

Cynthia perked up, a gleam in her eyes. "You mean you will lease a house for us?"

"In truth, I like Silas's town house. It is a grand place that can impress even a pink of the ton. But I think I can talk your father into letting us have the residence in exchange for my taking up the expenses that will keep you in the kick of fashion and ensure that you will be invited to all of the best affairs."

Augusta smiled smugly. "Given my wherewithal, there is no reason you cannot look as high, as say, an earl." She had pulled a title out of the air that she knew would please and impress her niece.

"An earl? Truly, Auntie?"

"Why not? Although you are past the first blush, you are not yet considered on the shelf."

"How delicious!" Cynthia cried, clapping her hands in delight like a small child at her aunt's optimistic forecast.

The next morning from his bedroom window, Connor saw Sarah and Lucy walking across the fields toward the park. He grabbed his greatcoat, shrugged into the warm garment, went downstairs and outside through the front door.

Gideon Lambert had already packed Connor's bags. Bob, his driver, had been informed by the valet that Lord Lyle's coach, which had been housed in the mews during his stay, was to be driven to the mill at eleven o'clock with Gideon aboard to pick up their master.

Connor was determined to speak to Sarah before he left. He loved her with every fiber of his being. He must convince her to remain strong and continue to believe as he did that someday they would be man and wife.

He walked toward the pond, a steeliness in his stride that spoke of purpose.

* * *

Sarah sat on the gazebo's steps, working hard to persuade herself that it would be best if she did not see Connor before he departed. It would only make her feel bad. She had left the house by the seldom-used back stairs to keep from running into him. But when he stepped from the trees, her heart betrayed her good intentions. Suddenly, her doubts disappeared, and she felt glad that he had come to say good-bye.

Nearby, Lucy rolled a large red ball down a grassy incline in the wintry sunshine. Connor stopped beside her. He said something to her that made her giggle.

Sarah sighed. Connor would have made a wonderful father for Lucy but it was not to be. The thought left her extremely sad.

When Connor reached the gazebo, he put one brown half boot on a lower step and leaned an arm across his thigh, bringing him in line with her face and making her look into his eyes.

"I am to leave for the mill with Silas in his carriage in a half hour to sign the contract," he said after a perfunctory greeting. "I will be going home afterwards. Bob, my coachman, and Mr. Lambert are meeting me at the plant. But I had to see you, Sarah. I want you to know that this is not the end. I love you with all of my heart and soul, and I will find a way for us to be together."

Sarah shook her head from side to side.

"You must forget me, Con."

"Never!" he said, his dark eyes flashing. "What nonsense. I will be coming back here frequently on business concerning the mill. What do you want me to do? Pretend I don't love you?" He stood up. "We will see each other then. If Silas bars me from the house, we will meet here or in the village until our problems are solved."

Sarah shook her head again. "Seeing you will only make things harder."

Connor snorted. "Don't let me hear you say something asinine like staying apart will make it easier for us to forget one another. Call me selfish, but I don't want you to forget me, Sarah." He let out a long breath, and his voice grew softer, kinder.

"I know the world seems bleak right now for us, darling, but we are made for each other. I promise you I will find a way for us to be married."

Sarah absorbed his words, wanting so much to believe him. "I will love you forever, too, Con," she admitted, but her throat was constricted by unshed tears.

Connor leaned over and tenderly ran the pad of his thumb down her cheek. "I must go now, but I will soon return to you, my love. Don't ever doubt it." He kissed her brow, then walked away toward the house. He spoke once more to Lucy and waved to Sarah before he vanished into the trees. Only then did Sarah let the tears flow freely.

Eight

Silas was content to trade the rent on the London house for shedding his financial responsibilities for his daughter and sister. But after being besieged by servants for three days with unwelcome questions about their chores, he relegated Augusta's former household duties to Sarah. The staff respected her and cheerfully obeyed her instructions, for she was much more diplomatic than Augusta or Cynthia had ever been.

Then, after four days, Silas became weary of his own company at the dinner table and insisted that Sarah join him for the evening meal. Initially, their conversations were forced and woodenly polite. But without the overbearing presence of Augusta and Cynthia, both Sarah and Silas unbent and became comfortable with each other.

One evening over their dessert of apricot cake, Silas asked her, "How long since you bought new garments?" He had noticed that her clothes were rather dull and worn.

Sarah's faint smile was bleak. "Not since I went into mourning for Ellis."

"Lud, girl, whyever not?" But the reason was apparent when he recalled that Augusta handled the household money. He had not realized that his sister had disliked Sarah quite so much as to deny her decent clothes.

He put down his fork, pushed back his dining chair, and clasped his hands over his ample stomach.

"Never mind," he said. "I can guess. But, you obviously need to replace every garment hanging in your armoire. Go see Mrs. Bartles. She has a shop in the village and is a rather skilled seamstress, I believe. Pick out a complete wardrobe."

He could see Sarah's surprise. "Mr. Lawton, the expenditure . . ." Her jaw dropped.

He held up a hand. "I won't hear of anything less."

He had an account at Breck's Emporium and directed her to buy shoes and bonnets and other necessary apparel there.

"And, don't let Mrs. Bartles or Mr. Breck sell you inferior stuff. I don't buy things on the cheap," he said.

Sarah managed a sincere thank you before she left to tuck in Lucy.

After she was gone, Silas remained at the table drinking his port and smoking a cigar, chiding himself. A gentleman did not neglect a woman given into his care. He should not have left Sarah's welfare totally to his sister's discretion. But Silas was not one to wallow in guilt. One could not undo the past, he thought philosophically. He was doing right by her now. In the long run, it was all that mattered.

The next day Sarah drove herself to the village for her shopping expedition in the same one-horse chaise in which Augusta and Cynthia had run errands and made calls on their neighbors.

She was still stunned by Mr. Lawton's generosity, or change of heart, or whatever it was. The small carriage was solely hers to use now. Even more than the new clothes, she valued this privilege, for it meant that she would be able to leave the premises without permission whenever she wished.

Yet, as she pulled up to the curb in front of Mrs. Bartles's dress shop, she was thinking that she did not want to get her spirits up too high, for Mr. Lawton might revert to his old self if Cynthia and Aunt Augusta came back.

Sarah's state of uncertainty vanished while she happily selected styles from Mrs. Bartles's pattern book and fabrics from the many bolts of cloth on the shelves.

Going on to Breck's Emporium, she bought intimate apparel, two pairs of shoes, some stockings, and two bonnets. A cheerful clerk carried the many boxes to the chaise and piled them into the boot.

Back at the house Sarah left an accounting with Silas's valet of the debts she had accumulated and went to unpack her purchases in her bedroom. Twenty minutes later she was interrupted in her task by a footman who informed her that Mr. Lawton wished to see her in the library. Made a little nervous by the peremptory summons, she worried that she might have spent too much.

The large leather chairs and oversized furniture gave the library a masculine aura that Sarah found attractive. A fire roared in the hearth. She had been inside the room only once before. But she had not noticed the congenial ambiance on the night she and Connor had learned that her father-in-law was Lucy's guardian. The memory was still painful. She was resigned to the legality, but by no means had she completely forgiven Silas.

He sat behind his desk, a ledger open in front of him.

"Are you any good at keeping accounts?" he asked.

"Fair to middling," she said, honestly. "I used to do them for Mrs. Harrell's dress business. But it has been a long time."

Silas put down the quilled pen. "You are bound to be better at it than I. Numbers confound me. I shall leave the household ledger here. If you don't mind, I would like you to see what you can make of the accounts."

"All right," Sarah said, surprised that he would trust her with such a personal matter.

"Good," he replied and reached into his interior breast pocket and pulled out the paper on which she had itemized her purchases.

"You can practice by entering your charges in the proper columns," he said, tossing the list down onto the desk and leaving his chair. He walked deliberately past Sarah and crossed the room to a long table filled with scale models of houses and churches.

Sarah followed him, curious about the small buildings of all sizes and shapes that she had not seen before. She had often wondered what he did in the library for hours and hours. Now she knew.

"You made these," she said. His amazing talent astounded her.

His smile was wider than she had ever seen it. "Every single one is authentic," he said proudly. "Years ago, I traveled all over the country drawing sketches and making detailed notes."

He picked up one of his creations that was nearly as tall as it was wide. "For instance, box-framed houses with bases of sandstone like this are found in Shropshire."

He showed her some others from Cornwall and the Cotswold Hills.

His collection of England's architectural diversity was fascinating. Silas had constructed a perfect example of a 15th-century timbered house, reproduced the raised plaster work called pargeting on an Elizabethan home, and copied the distinctive pattern of English thatching he found on the roof of a house in Norfolk.

"And this is Salisbury Cathedral," Sarah said, recognizing the majestic building.

"You know the church," he said, clearly pleased that she could identify it from his reproduction.

"Yes, I once visited it." She almost said with my father. Jack had taken her mother and her to Old Sarum on a week's holiday when she was ten.

Drawing pads and notebooks were piled in open bookcases. And a raised worktable where her father-in-law apparently did his fabricating stood near to an undraped window through which natural light spilled into the room. Cluttered around the table were dozens of bins with all sorts of stones and darkened wood and dry plaster.

"I strive to make all of the buildings true-to-life," Silas said as Sarah peered into the boxes.

She was truly impressed. "Your models are marvelous," she said. He gave a little modest wave that turned out to be a sign of dismissal. He then sat down on a high stool in front of the raised worktable and took up a small hammer and began to chip away at a piece of marble.

Leaving Silas to his task, Sarah said, "I will have a look at the books now before Jessie brings Lucy back from their walk."

Silas's hammer remained poised in midair. "Sarah, the library is forbidden territory to Lucy."

There was no heat in his words.

"Yes, I understand," she said. "Lucy would see the houses as toys and they are not."

"Hmm? There is that." His words were so soft as to be almost inaudible. Sarah saw him glance at some mysterious object too large to be one of his model houses covered by a white sheet, but he said nothing more and turned back to his work. She shrugged mentally and went to examine the books.

Sarah often marveled at the changes in her life since Augusta and Cynthia had left. Now that she no longer felt like a prisoner, she began to see the house differently. It was really quite a wonderful old country manor.

She began to plan ways in which she could spruce up the rooms and add a touch of her own personality. Besides an allowance for herself, Silas had budgeted funds for household expenditures that she could use to implement her many ideas.

Her life was more interesting and free, but was clouded by moments of longing to be with Connor. Reliving his kisses never failed to do funny things to her heart and make her yearn so much to be in his arms again.

Sarah entered the dining room one evening and asked the footman who was serving dinner, "Where is Mr. Lawton, Banks?"

Silas was usually there before her, partaking of a before-dinner drink.

Sarah, herself, was a little late, for she had just returned from calling on Lady Jenna Keats, a neighbor, who had introduced herself to Sarah at Breck's and invited her and Lucy to tea.

The pleasant woman told Sarah that the Misses Lawton had brought Lucy with them when they came to visit and that her own son and daughter missed their little playmate.

"Mr. Lawton is indisposed, ma'am," the footman said, in answer to her question. "The doctor was called."

Sarah had been feeling lighthearted, for she had made a friend in Jenna Keats that afternoon, but now her appetite was suddenly diminished. She picked at her food.

If a doctor had been summoned, Silas's illness could not be minor. She skipped her dessert, for she was anxious to speak to Mr. Walsh, his valet, who was taking care of him, and to learn the extent of Mr. Lawton's ailment.

When she knocked softly, Walsh opened the bedroom door and stepped into the hall. "Mr. Lawton is asleep,

ma'am. Mr. Trask, the physician, dosed him with lau-
danum."

The valet was a hale and hardy sixty-year-old longtime
retainer with intelligent eyes and a very correct but ap-
proachable manner.

"What happened, Mr. Walsh?" Sarah asked, her hand to
her throat.

"The master collapsed this afternoon after coming back
from a horseback ride. The doctor suspects his heart and
recommends a week's confinement to his bed."

Sarah volunteered to take a turn sitting up with Silas.

Mr. Walsh thanked her and smiled kindly but said, "No
need, ma'am. I have pressed the factotum Finney into service as a nurse. We shall take turns sleeping on a cot in the
dressing room at night until the master is well again."

Sarah had to be content with the arrangement. She could
not see to Mr. Lawton's needs as well as the two men
could.

The next morning she stuck her head in the sickroom
door to ask about his condition and found Silas awake.

He motioned her inside. "Stupid thing to do, crumpling
like that," he said when she asked him what had happened. "But I suppose I had best heed old Trask and get
some rest."

Her father-in-law looked very pale, his voice was rather
weak, and his hands trembled. He lay back with his head
slightly elevated on two pillows.

"How did your visit with Lady Keats go?" he asked,
for he knew that Sarah had been invited to tea.

"We became instant friends," she said. "Lucy and Lady
Keats's children, Dougie and Mary, are quite compatible,
for the most part." She laughed. "There were very few ar-
guments, and Lucy only stuck her tongue out at Dougie
once."

Silas's answering smile was wan.

Sarah did most of the talking, relating more about the visit. She kept to herself the fact that Lady Keats had been sympathetic to Sarah's plans to open a nursery for the infants and toddlers of the women who worked at the mill, and that she wanted to help. Mr. Jepp had agreed to let Sarah use a large storeroom for her project. Mrs. Jepp, too, had offered her services.

But Sarah saw that Silas was tiring. "I will come back later," she said. His eyes closed even as she got up to go.

During the week, as Silas gained back his strength, Sarah read to him and played chess and cards with him. He surprised her one day when he said, "Tell me who you really are, and how you came to know Lord Lyle. I would like to know the truth."

Sarah looked at him for a moment. A month ago she would have wondered if he wanted to trick her into admitting something that he could use against her. But she trusted him now. She took a deep breath and began her story.

He listened without any visible emotion, only nodding now and then. She explained about her mother and father and the influenza epidemic that had taken Jeanne and Jack. With no relatives to claim her, she had been sent to the workhouse where she met Connor Hamil.

"Damme," he said. "I thought he was the old Lord Lyle's bastard son."

Since Sarah knew that Connor made no secret of how he came to be a peer and would reveal the truth to anyone who asked, she told Silas everything she knew about him.

"Con was only fourteen, but he was a street boy and wise in the ways of staying alive under harsh conditions. You must know that the mortality rate for children in those horrible places is astronomical. Con took excellent care of me." Sarah thought she saw a flicker of sympathy in Silas's eyes, but she could not be sure, for it was gone in an instant.

"Shortly after Con left to go with Lord Lyle, I was taken out by Mrs. Farrell. She taught me to sew and to perform other duties in her dress shop. Ellis followed me home one day after I had made a delivery and was obviously smitten. When he proposed, Mrs. Farrell saw her chance to leave a life of hard work behind. It was then that she insisted that I call her Ma and passed me off as her daughter."

"Did my son know about your true origins?"

"Yes, I could not bring myself to marry Ellis without telling him, but he begged me not to say anything to you. He was afraid that you would seek an annulment. Would you have?"

"Probably," Silas said truthfully. "It doesn't matter to me now, but I would rather you continued to keep mum about your real mother. Knowledge of your background could easily jeopardize Lucy's future position in society."

"Con . . . Lord Lyle knows."

"I assumed as much. His own beginnings explain why he has turned things upside down at the mill with all those reforms."

Sarah wasn't surprised that he knew about Connor's considerable improvements, although he had not been to the mill since Mr. Jepp arrived and had never mentioned the revolutionary changes before. He must have his sources.

He looked smug. "I also am aware that you have spent the money I have allotted for your personal use on equipping a room at the mill for the babies of the working mothers."

Sarah smiled faintly. He indeed had his sources. "Mrs. Jepp is assisting with the children, and Lady Keats is donating money so we can hire extra help. It seems Lord

Keats favors the reforms and has given his wife his support both emotionally and monetarily."

"Humph, I find you are as big a do-gooder as Lord Lyle. Well, you will be happy to know that he will be here by the end of the week for an inspection tour of the mill. I have invited him to stay at the house."

Sarah could not contain her joy and broke into a bright smile.

"You still miss him," he said, dryly.

Sarah nodded. Connor was the last one she thought about before she fell asleep, and the first one she thought about when she woke in the morning.

"You think I am a mean, old ogre to keep you two apart, don't you?"

Sarah did not know how to answer him, but before she was forced to form a reply, both of them looked toward the door where Lucy was peeking around the doorjamb at them.

"Come in, child," Silas said, beckoning to his granddaughter.

Nine

Lucy took a step into the room, stopped, and glanced at her mother. Sarah gave her daughter a smile and nodded her encouragement.

Lucy walked to where Sarah sat in a bedside chair and looked over at her grandfather. "Does your tummy hurt, Grandpapa?"

"You might say I hurt in my heart, Lucy," Silas said. "But I am feeling more the thing every day now." He pointed to the bath chair in the corner. "Tomorrow Mr. Finney is going to wheel me around the house in that invalid's contraption."

Lucy gazed at the odd-looking chair, but seemed to have something else on her mind. She moved to the bed and leaned her elbows on the high mattress below her grandfather's head and propped her little chin on her hands. "Why doesn't Father Christmas come to our house?" she asked.

Silas and Sarah exchanged a surprised look at the unexpected question. Sarah's baffled expression led Silas to believe that she had never mentioned the symbol of Christmas to Lucy.

"Who told you about Father Christmas, Lucy?" Sarah asked, confirming his supposition.

"Dougie Keats," she answered her mother, but kept her eyes on her grandfather. "Dougie is seven," she said, as if his more advanced age gave added weight to her answer. "He said that it's almost time for Father Christmas to come to their house as he does every year. That's why he has to be 'specially good so he gets lots of presents. Why doesn't Father Christmas come to our house, Grandpapa?" she repeated.

Silas was taken aback. "Maybe he will come this year, Lucy," he said to placate the tiny moppet, adorable in her white pinafore and pink-flowered dress.

"Will he, Mama?" Lucy said, turning to her mother, her blue eyes big and hopeful.

Sarah looked unsure. "You heard your grandpapa," she equivocated. Lucy seemed to take this as an affirmative response and climbed up into her mother's lap and leaned back against her bosom as Sarah's arms came protectively around her daughter.

Silas looked at them and felt a novel emotion, one he had not felt for a very long time. He loved the pretty child and had grown fond of Sarah. She was a fine woman, with a good heart.

What had happened to Christmas in this house? When his lovely Norah was alive, Christmas had always been celebrated with decorations and a feast and small presents. Ellis had been a sweet little boy, and Cynthia, an innocent babe. But afterwards, in his grief, he had given up Christmas while mourning his dead wife.

The holiday had turned into just another day. Augusta and Cynthia went to church; his sister ordered a singular meal. But there were no gifts, no jolly adornments. Even the mill workers did not get the day off. He grunted. Lord Lyle and his man Jepp would, no doubt, change that.

"What say you, Sarah? Shall we keep Christmas this year?" he said in a light tone.

Sarah smiled. "I think that would be splendid, Mr. Lawton."

Silas raised a bushy brow. "I know you would find it awkward to call me Father, but do you think you could manage Silas?" he said, suddenly wanting to put their relationship on a more intimate level.

"Yes, Silas, I would be pleased to," she replied, with a faint smile.

"Well, then," he said, a little gruffly, "make some tentative plans for the holiday, and we will discuss your ideas later when little ears are otherwise engaged."

Sarah was in a state of bliss when the butler came to tell her that Connor had arrived as expected. The December day was blustery and cold. She found him in the drawing room, warming his hands by the fire. His smile was broad as he came and took both of her hands in his and kissed her gently on the lips. She wore one of Mrs. Bartles's creations, a light-wool violet gown trimmed in white lace at the neck and at the cuffs of the long sleeves.

Hands linked, Con looked down into her eyes and said, "I have missed you dreadfully, dearest."

"And I you," she said gazing up into his wonderful face.

"Come." He led her to the sofa.

"You look so young and pretty in that dress. I had forgotten how beautiful you are. You take my breath away."

Sarah smiled. "You put me to the blush with such an excessive compliment. How have you been, Con?"

"Miserable," he said. "I have not tolerated our separation as well as I thought I would. Sarah, I have set an agent to look for a property that might be up for sale in the vicinity. I want to be close enough to visit you whenever I wish."

"What of your mill?" she said.

"I have a manager whom I can trust. He sees eye to eye with me on my reforms and will keep them in place and protect the children. Going back for periodic visits should be sufficient to see that the mill is still being properly run and to take care of my other business interests."

Sarah went quiet. Connor touched her cheek. "Don't you want me near to you?" he said, his voice growing tense.

"Of course, I do. I . . ."

"What?" He removed his hand from her face, looking concerned.

"It is so unfair to you, Con." She meant it.

He grinned. "Is that all?" He gazed toward the door, which stood open to the hall. Lowering his voice, he said, "If I can get a property in this district, I might be able to convince Silas to let Lucy live with us, and we could get married. He might be more amenable if he could see his granddaughter every day."

Sarah put a finger to her chin. She wasn't sure. "Perhaps he would," she said, tentatively. "Silas has changed since he originally issued his cruel edict, and he and I have been rubbing along quite well together."

Her words gave him a lift. When Sarah went on to describe her new status, she was so enthusiastic about her new duties and her improved relationship with Silas that Connor could not doubt that she sounded happy. A dread mixed with jealousy began to rise in Connor's breast.

"It is amazing, Con. All those years I thought I despised this house, but it was really my treatment here that I hated."

Connor felt a little numb. Was Sarah not as determined to marry him now that she had found a place for herself with Silas?

Before he could take the thought further, his eyes were drawn to the door by the sound of footsteps in the hall and the groan of an invalid's chair.

A servant, whom Connor did not know, wheeled Silas into the room. Connor got up from the sofa and shook hands with the mill owner, who was paler and thinner than on Con's last visit.

"You can go, Finney," Silas said to the servant, who straightened the plaid shawl on his patient's lap before he left.

"Been to the mill yet?" Silas looked up at Connor, his manner cool.

Con gazed over at Sarah and winked. "Being this close to Sarah I could not bring myself to detour. I shall go later today, before closing."

"Closing is earlier now, you know," Silas pointed out to him tartly.

"Yes, it's what I ordered," Connor said mildly and sat back down beside Sarah. "It hasn't affected the productivity."

"Humph," Silas muttered and pulled a dour face. "The jury is out on that yet. I suppose you know that Sarah has started a nursery for the children of our female workers. Your man Jepp gave her space in one of my buildings to house the enterprise. He never asked me."

"Our agreement gives me and Mr. Jepp, as my agent, autonomy on that kind of decision," Connor said, trying to ignore Silas's whining tone and his own rising irritation. "I thought it was an excellent idea. In fact, come the spring we can build a separate facility in a more pleasant area down closer to the river and away from the noise of the machines."

Sarah let out a delighted gasp. "Oh, Con, how wonderful! We can have a fenced-in playground so that the children can go outside in clement weather."

"It will eat into the profits. It's no way to run a business," Silas sneered. "Nurseries and Christmas food baskets with five-pound hams for every family. Charity can go just so far. We already pay a higher wage than common."

Connor wondered where Sarah saw a change for the better in the man. He was actually more disagreeable than Connor remembered him to be.

"I am footing the bill for the Christmas hampers and the new building from my personal account," Con told him, even as he wished the mill owner to perdition. He felt his jaw tighten while he waited for Silas's next attack on his liberality, but apparently Sarah's father-in-law was through with that phase of his complaints at least.

"Speaking of Christmas," Silas said, "I have decided to keep the holiday this year for Lucy's sake. Sarah, no doubt, will want you to spend a few days of the Yule with us, Lyle."

Sarah looked so happy that Connor could not bring himself to be overtly rude to Silas despite the backhanded invitation.

"I would like it above all things," he said, squeezing Sarah's hand and addressing himself to her.

Blessedly, with this opening, Sarah turned the conversation to Lucy's fascination with a holiday that had not been fully celebrated in this house in recent years, and Connor relaxed beside her.

After a time she rose to her feet and said, "You must come up to the nursery and say hello to Lucy, Con." He got up with her. "She has been eager to see you again."

"And I her," Con said.

Silas's man Finney had been hovering near the door, waiting for a signal from Sarah. He came in, then, and wheeled out the invalid, much to Con's relief. The man positively set his teeth on edge.

"I notice you call him Silas," Connor said when he and Sarah reached the upstairs hall. "It was Mr. Lawton the last time I was here."

"He asked me to use his given name." Sarah hesitated.

"My life here is greatly improved, Con. For all intents and purposes, I run the household. Silas never interferes with Lucy's upbringing and leaves every decision concerning her to me."

Connor could not begrudge Sarah for having the sort of life she deserved. He just wished he had been the one to put the bloom back into her cheeks and the happiness into her eyes.

Sarah opened the nursery door and Connor started forward, genuinely pleased when the small girl shrieked and rushed to him and flung her small arms around his legs.

As much as Connor wanted to be near to Sarah, he could only stay another day. He had several important business appointments to clear from his December calendar if he was to come for a longer stay at Christmas.

He yearned to hold Sarah in his arms and kiss her thoroughly. But the weather had been bitterly cold, and going to the gazebo was out of the question during the wintery conditions. While inside the house, doors had to be left open in the interest of propriety. Anyone passing by could come in without knocking and interrupt any passionate moment he might dare to initiate. But he tamped down his frustration, glad just to be with her.

During their full day together, Connor sat with Sarah in the conservatory, where the sun came through the floor-to-ceiling glass and warmed the room and grew the plants. He would be leaving for home early the next morning.

"I was thinking about Christmas Day at the workhouse when we were children," he said softly, content to hold her hand.

"I remember that day," she said, her mind retreating into the past in a vivid memory.

After standing in line at the workhouse's women's lavatory and washing her face and hands in the icy water, Sissy Eaton joined Connor Hamil.

"Why are those bells ringing?" she asked him. She could hear the church bells from every direction in the city.

"It's Christmas morning, ninny," Con said.

"Christmas? Oh, no!" A sob escaped Sissy's lips and tears spilled down her cheeks.

Hands in his pockets for warmth, Con slipped down the wall onto one of the chair cushions he had filched from somewhere.

"Aw, Sissy, don't be carryin' on so. Come sit beside me." He nodded at the second cushion that he toted around for her comfort.

Sissy sat down beside him. "I miss my mama and Jack," she sobbed, "and the Christmas goose."

"Christmas goose?"

Con laughed at the inanity.

"You're a fribble, Sissy," he said and pulled his clasped hand from his pocket. "I won't give you your Christmas present if you don't stop your wailing."

"A Christmas gift?" Sissy was so flabbergasted that she stopped crying and dried her tears on the sleeve of her coat. "Let me see," she said, touching his clenched fist.

Connor opened his hand and revealed a shiny penny.

"For me?"

He nodded.

"Where did you get it, Con?" she asked, suspicious.

"Brought it from home," he said, pointing to his sack. Both of them carried around their few possessions all the time to keep their paltry goods from being stolen.

* * *

The adult Connor, in the plant-filled room, smiled at Sarah. "I didn't steal the penny, you know," he said, reading her thoughts. "I really did have it in my bundle when I was taken to the workhouse by the parish beadle."

Neither of them spoke for a long time. Their youthful companionship in the workhouse had been brief. But fate had brought them together as adults and revived the memories and the emotions that had faded, but had been too momentous ever to be forgotten.

"I must have adored you even then, love, to give you the one thing I possessed of any value, however trifling it seems now," Connor said.

Sarah's lips quivered. "Mrs. Farrell took the penny away from me when she went through my things. I cried and cried. I missed you so much."

Connor lifted her hand to his chest and held it against his heart. Somehow the emotions from then and from now became entwined. "But miraculously I found you again. I know somehow it is all going to come right for us."

His promise was not an empty one; he would keep it. He cast aside his insecurities from the previous day. He, of all people, knew that it could take just one moment of good fortune to change everything.

Ten

Sarah came halfway down the staircase and hesitated when she saw a stranger being escorted to the front door by the butler. The gentleman of middle years was of medium height with a slender build, well dressed, although not fashionably, and with a head of thinning fair hair. He put on his hat and stepped outside, a gold-knobbed cane tucked under his arm. The butler closed the door against the sharp cold.

Sarah came downstairs as the butler went back to the servant's wing. Curious about the identity of the visitor, she went to seek out Silas in the library for the answer. Her father-in-law spent almost all day, every day, working on his models now that the doctor had given him permission to leave behind his rolling chair.

Sarah stopped to straighten a red bow that graced the greenery twined around the gilded frame of a hall mirror. She had cut evergreen boughs from the woods around the pond, and had bought yards and yards of red ribbon from the dry goods store in the village to decorate the house for the holidays.

It was three days before Christmas and Connor would be arriving today. She couldn't wait to see him. She loved Con so much. No man had ever had the effect on her that he did. He lived with her in her daily thoughts. But his last visit had left her bereft and unfulfilled. When he raised her hand to his lips and tenderly kissed her finger tips, it was sweet, but it made her yearn for more, much more.

The library door was ajar, and Sarah went in without knocking. Silas sat in a fireside chair, staring into the blazing fire. Strewn in his lap were sheets of writing paper.

"Who was your visitor?" she asked as she sat down across from him in the companion wing chair.

He smiled at her rather mischievously. "My future son-in-law," he said.

Sarah's eyes grew big. "Cynthia has made a match?"

Silas nodded. "A rather good one, I must say. Sir Claude Mendenhall by name, a childless widower. He holds a baronetcy and commands a decent income." He gathered the papers in his lap into a neat bundle. "These are letters from Augusta and Cynthia."

Sarah felt a touch of envy. Her deep love for Connor welled up. How she wished that it was he who was announcing their betrothal.

"Are Aunt Augusta and Cynthia coming for the holidays?"

"No, the baron has invited them to his country estate to meet his parents on Christmas Day. I was asked, but tendered my regrets after I explained to Mendenhall that I am recuperating from a recent illness. But, in truth, I would rather keep Christmas with you and Lucy."

Silas handed the letters to Sarah who took a few moments to read the two messages.

"Aunt Augusta and Cynthia seem very happy with the match," she said, starting to hand the correspondence back to Silas.

But he said, "Put them in the top drawer of the desk for me, will you, please, Sarah."

She did as he bid, but as she turned to come back around the desk to sit down again, she heard a commotion in the hall.

Lucy and Connor came into the room, the child hanging onto his arm. "Look, Mama, Lord Lyle is here. Mr. Lambert has a pile of gifts this high," she said, raising her little arms over her head.

Sarah smiled at Con as he came to her. He had shed his greatcoat, scarf, gloves, and hat, but his face was cold as he touched cheeks with her.

Lucy begged Connor to tell her what was in the gaily wrapped boxes that Mr. Lambert had carried upstairs.

"I am Father Christmas's emissary, and I will not allow anyone to peek inside until Christmas Day," Connor said, affectionately tweaking her tiny nose. "So you might as well stop your cajoling, poppet."

Since Lucy had had no idea what Father Christmas looked like, Sarah had bought a book at the village bookstore with an illustration of the mythical gentleman. Now, obviously remembering the picture of the bearded figure in the long coat with a wreath of ivy on his head, and not understanding the word "emissary," Lucy frowned and said a little crossly, "You don't look anything like Father Christmas, Lord Lyle."

"Lord Lyle means that he is standing in for Father Christmas, dear," Sarah explained, "not that he is the gentleman himself. An emissary is a messenger."

Lucy brightened at this, but Sarah saw that Silas was gazing nervously toward his prized collection of houses, which were in full view.

"Let us remove to the drawing room, Sarah," he said. She intercepted his pleading glance and complied with his silent request.

"Yes, of course, we will be more comfortable there," she said to Connor, taking her daughter's hand and leading her to the door before Lucy spied the models, which would have proved irresistible to her.

Once everyone was seated in the drawing room, Sarah

ordered tea, and Silas delivered the news to Connor of Cynthia's engagement.

"Augusta has gone along to act as chaperon at the baron's country home, so neither she nor Cynthia will be here for Christmas," he said. He did not sound the least regretful.

Only days ago Silas had confided to Sarah that he found the house more peaceful without his sister's constant sniping and his daughter's incessant complaining. "You never have a bad word to say about the servants, whom I notice go about their chores more cheerfully these days," he had told her. Sarah had relished the praise, not a common commodity in the past, from the master of the house.

During tea, the two men spoke about the month's production of textiles. Silas was no longer grumpy when discussing management of the mill. Sarah knew from working on the books that her father-in-law's income had actually increased on Mr. Jepp's watch.

She found herself smiling again and again at Connor, and she saw that he could not keep his eyes from her. She wore a flattering dark-rose gown with pink pearl buttons.

Silas left after a time to go back to the library to work on his Lilliputian architectural achievements. Jessie, who looked after Lucy when Sarah was occupied, came to fetch the little girl who had begun to squirm and look bored with the adult conversation.

Connor pulled Sarah up from her chair. He took her in his arms and kissed her long and deeply, whispering endearments in her ear, heedless of the proprieties.

"Say you love me," he said, breathlessly.

"You know I do," she replied.

"Say it."

"I love you, Con," she said.

After that, Connor led her to a settee for two that faced the windows and not the door.

"My agent hasn't been able to find a house for sale anywhere in the vicinity," he said when they were seated.

His fine lips were turned down at the setback.

"The world seems to be merrily hurtling on while we are no closer to being man and wife than we were weeks ago."

Sarah did not know what to say to quell his gloomy mood, for she felt much the same way.

A muffled rap at the tall window in front of them gained their attention. Lucy had her mittened hands cupped around her face and was peering inside, a bright yellow scarf pulled up to her mouth.

"Let's get some air, too," Connor said. Sarah stood up with him. He guided her by the elbow to the hall to get their warm coats. "Perhaps the cold, wintry air will cool my frustration." He muttered the thought, his voice a mere whisper, as if he meant the words only for himself.

On the afternoon of the twenty-fourth, Connor was poking around in the library. He stopped by the table that was filled with Silas's little houses. He was alone, for Sarah was busy with the preparations for Christmas.

Connor admired the museum quality of Silas's models. Lawton may not have a head for figures, but he had a keen eye for architectural details.

He noticed a series of old drawings of a manor house pinned to the wall beside the window. Beneath a diagram of the exterior were the words *Drawings of Ezra Lawton's Country Home.* Con quickly deduced that the sketches were of this house. But he was puzzled to see rooms that were designated as the "east wing." He had never been in that part of the house. Intrigued and loving a mystery, Con set out to find the missing rooms.

He found the east wing sealed off from the rest of the

house by a locked door, but the key hung on a hook beside it.

Connor put the key in the well-oiled lock, pushed the door open, and stepped into a large empty room. To his left was a flight of stairs to the upper floor. Off the main room were two smaller, unfurnished chambers.

Connor examined all of the fireplaces, as well as the ceilings, the woodwork, and the windows, which were clean and showed no evidence of leaks. Needed repairs had obviously been made in a timely fashion.

Taking the stairs two at a time, he went up to the second floor, where a pair of empty bedchambers were in tip-top condition. He prowled the length of the rooms, an idea beginning to form in his mind.

As Connor descended the stairs, his excitement grew. Over and over, he had promised himself that he and Sarah would eventually be together. He had said the words, yet, lately, he had been having trouble believing them. Now his optimism returned. But it all depended on Silas.

Connor locked the door and returned the key to the hook. Sarah claimed that Silas had mellowed, so it was worth a chance. Still, he tried to tamp down his eagerness as he opened the library door.

"I am composing a belated Christmas letter to Cynthia and Augusta," Silas volunteered from behind his desk.

Despite Con's best efforts, his face must have been animated, for Silas said, "What's put you into such high spirits, Lyle? You look like you won the French lottery."

"I fear, Silas, I have been nosing around," Con said, backing into his agendum.

Silas raised his bushy brows.

"How so?" he asked.

"I looked at the drawings of this house there on the wall." He nodded in the direction of Silas's work area.

"So? The old drawings are hardly secret documents, or I would have them under lock and key."

"Yes, well, I learned of the vacant rooms in the east wing from them and went there," Con said. "I know I should have asked your permission, but the key was too handy to ignore. I went inside."

"My dear Lyle, there is no harm in that. The rooms are completely empty. I have the servants sweep them out occasionally and bring in a man to check for any flaws that may have developed in the walls and ceilings. Cracks and such, you know."

"Why are the rooms not used?" Connor asked.

Silas leaned back in his desk chair and said, "Sit down, Lyle. I'm getting a crick in my neck staring up at you."

Connor turned a plain wooden chair to face Silas and obeyed.

"Ezra Lawton, my grandfather," Silas said after a moment, "had the house built, anticipating a large family. But the Lawtons have not been prolific breeders. My father was the only one of three children who lived into adulthood. Augusta and I were his sole offsprings. As you already know, Ellis died, producing just Lucy. Previous generations were thinned out during England's many wars. I know of no long-lost cousins. To put it succinctly, there never have been enough family members living here to warrant opening the rooms."

Connor leaned forward on the hard chair. "I have an idea for the use of the rooms," he said, and proceeded to reveal his plan.

To Connor's abundant astonishment, the mill owner not only gave his unbridled endorsement, but modified Con's idea with an eminently sensible suggestion of his own.

Sarah was sent for and dropped into a chair rather dazed when she learned what the two men had decided.

"You mean we are to live in the same household apart

and yet together?" she asked. She knew about the rooms, but it had never entered her mind that she and Con could live here with Silas.

"Lyle thought to lease the east wing for you and him and Lucy, but that would be foolish, so we worked out a financial arrangement whereby the house will eventually belong to him. I will make the east wing my private quarters, a bachelor's apartment as it were, while you and Lyle will live in the rest of the house."

Sarah was elated. She gazed at Connor for validation. He nodded and grinned. Her heart burst with happiness. She would have Con at last, and the house already seemed like hers.

"That is, if you have not changed your mind about marrying me," Connor said, but he did not look like a man who feared that he was going to be turned down.

He drew her from the chair into his arms for a soft, lingering kiss. Sarah did not care that Silas was watching, although had she deemed to look, she would have seen that for once, the odious man was not scowling, but had something resembling a smile on his lips.

On Christmas morning the family gathered in the drawing room, decorated with holly, ivy, and red carnations from the gardener's glasshouse. Presents for everyone were plentiful and wonderful.

Lucy's grandest gift was a doll's house, which her grandfather had made for her in the Dutch-gable style found in the fens of Lincolnshire. When he removed the white sheet, the little mite's blue eyes became wide. She raised up on her tiptoes, pulled down Silas's head, and kissed his shiny baldness, causing him to blush.

Lucy's banishment from the library now became clear to Sarah. Silas had not been hiding his models, but rather his secret gift. He said, then, that he had been building the doll's house even before they had decided to keep Christmas, but the occasion had presented a perfect opportunity to give his gift to Lucy.

Silas leaned over and removed the back to give the little girl access to the interior of his creation. One at a time, Lucy took out each piece of tiny furniture, and showed off a chair, a table, a bed, and a dresser to her grandfather, as if he were not the builder of each carefully crafted piece.

With Silas and Lucy thus occupied, Connor took Sarah's hand in his and led her from the drawing room into a small parlor off the hall where callers, customarily, waited while the butler announced them.

Connor shut the door and turned the key in the lock. He reached into his coat pocket and drew out a magnificent ring and slipped the symbol of their betrothal onto Sarah's finger.

"Oh, Con, it is so beautiful," she said, as she held up her hand to admire the diamonds and emeralds that sparkled in the sunlight coming through a window adorned with a holiday wreath. Her heart was filled with him.

Connor drew her closer and leaned his forehead against hers.

"Happy Christmas, Sarah. Did I not promise you that I would find a way for us to marry?" His voice was tender, gentle, loving.

"A promise kept," she whispered. "The most wonderful Christmas gift I could ever receive."

"And the best I will ever have to give you."

Sarah's heart expanded with joy as she melted into Connor's arms and his warm, eager lips met hers in a long, passionate kiss that predicted a lifetime in a loving marriage.

A MERRY
GENTLEMAN

Lisa Noeli

One

The hearth was cold and the kitchen silent. A tall man felt his way along the wall, casting a supernaturally long shadow as a result of the candle he held in his hand. He stopped at the shelves that held clean dishes in tidy rows above the deep stone sink.

Quietly, carefully, he took down a plate and placed it on the deal table in the middle of the room, resuming his mysterious quest.

The pantry door was open, though darkness enveloped the room beyond it. The man entered, holding the candle next to boxes and baskets sealed tight against marauding mice. He opened one box and peered inside. A sticky, sinister lump seemed to squat within. With a muttered exclamation, he quickly closed the lid.

Would his Aunt Venetia never cease making fruitcake?

He reached toward the back of the shelf, toward a covered china dish that held the remnants of his favorite Stilton cheese, and drew it carefully, quietly, toward himself.

A wedge of Stilton, plain wheaten bread, and a small glass of sherry. That would quiet the grumbling in his belly. Perhaps then he might sleep. He set the cheese on the kitchen table and found the loaf, tearing off a piece but dripping candle wax upon his nightshirt in the process.

Annoyed, he stuck the candle in the dish rack and put

the piece of bread on the plate, adding a bit of cheese. But where was the sherry? Not in the kitchen, surely. His Aunt Venetia was certain that the plump, red-cheeked cook and the butler, her supposed comrade in crime, were nipping the spirits and watering the whisky.

Lord Henry thought she might be right about the butler, who had been a ship's bosun and had a taste for rum. But he would trust the cook with his own life.

His aunt kept a close eye on all intoxicating liquors, which she poured liberally upon those unspeakable fruit-cakes, soaking them for months before giving them away to the villagers. Wasn't it enough that she, a stickler for tra-dition at all costs, provided them with these dubious treats *and* a feast in the Great Hall to celebrate Christmas? Did she have to pour good whisky onto cakes that most people did not like but ate anyway?

He hoped and prayed that Venetia had not used the sherry as well. He would look for another bottle in the case that he had hidden in the small cabinet by the walnut side-board, which stood between two suits of armor and below the ancestral portraits in the cavernous dining room.

Not a cozy setting for his midnight repast, but he needed a drink. The coming of Christmas always rattled his nerves, though men were not supposed to have nerves, this being a privilege reserved for ladies, with whom the great house was about to be filled.

Some were his cousins and some were not. He supposed he would have to be nice to the cousins, but he drew the line at the friends of cousins.

There would be a great deal of chattering by the fire-place in the best ballroom, and the blazing Yule log duly admired for its great size and the colored sparks that danced upon it.

There would be carol-singing. His cousins would trill "The Holly and the Ivy" in piercing sopranos, as always, and he would stumble through the obligatory Sir Roger de Coverly dance as he did every year. Some of the servants and most of the villagers would indulge in the old rural customs of wassailing and mummery, to everyone's annoyance. There was nothing like Christmas cheer to give a man the blue-devils—and Lord Henry had 'em.

He picked up the plate that held his small feast, retrieved the candle from the dish rack, and headed the way he had come.

Something brushed his ankles and he stepped upon its tail. The same something let out a caterwaul loud enough to wake the dead, causing him to drop the candle, which miraculously remained lit.

Lord Henry sighed, reaching down to stroke the cook's beloved pet, Sir Puss. "Now you've done it. Mrs. Hannigan will be here in a flash."

A plump figure, wearing a mobcap and a voluminous wrapper tied with obvious haste over her nightgown, bustled in. "What seems to be the trouble, my lord? Has the cat been at the cheese again?"

"Sir Puss is innocent of all wrongdoing. I have been at the cheese, Mrs. Hannigan."

She bent down to put the softly purring cat into its basket. "Oh—and a fine thief you make, if you don't mind my saying so. Bare legs and all."

He looked down. "Do forgive me. I could not find my drawers in the dark."

She chuckled. "I have seen manly legs before. My Wincent had a sturdy pair, he did."

This familiar exchange would have caused Aunt Venetia to purse her lips, as she did not believe in fraternizing with servants. But Lord Henry had known the cook from his childhood and was very fond of her.

Her Wincent had served as steward at one or another of his family's houses for many years, but the good old man had gone to help St. Peter keep the keys of heaven, as Mrs. Hannigan put it, and only a month had passed since his funeral at the village church.

Henry hoped the Christmas season and its memories would not make her sad.

At the moment, she seemed preoccupied with the fire in the cookstove, lifting an iron lid to see if the coals were properly banked.

"Would you like a cup of tea then? I might enjoy one meself, if you don't mind."

He thought about the sherry and decided in favor of the tea. "I would."

She beamed and blew upon the fire to rouse it from ashy slumber, then filled a kettle with water and set it upon the stove.

Lord Henry put his plate upon the table and began to eat.

"Has my aunt finished with the baking?" Not that Venetia actually performed this messy chore—but she supervised it, keeping an eagle eye upon the currants, figs, raisins, spices, flour, and sugar.

"Almost," sighed the cook. "It is going slower than usual, as herself insists upon the finest ingredients—sultana raisins, sugar from the Barbados, and the like."

He nodded thoughtfully. "She always has been a most particular person. But the results do not seem worth the expense."

"You never liked fruitcakes, nor the rest of it."

He shuddered. "No, Mrs. Hannigan, I do not. But perhaps our guests will devour every crumb of whatever is not donated to the villagers and we will escape without the usual attacks of indigestion."

"Well, now, these are lady guests, Lord Henry. They eat like little birds, when they are not twittering about the house making happy mischief. But it will be nice to have company again. The house feels empty-like, with just you and me and herself as what we mentioned."

He noticed that the cook unthinkingly counted herself among the family, leaving out the other servants, but he did not correct her. The kettle came to a boil and Mrs. Hannigan poured the steaming water into the teapot she had prepared, wrapping a dishtowel around it to keep it hot.

She took down two cups and two saucers from the shelf that held the servants' plain china, adding a scone left over from the morning for herself. The cat left his basket and jumped up upon the table, uttering a barely audible meow.

"Now, Sir Puss. No cats upon the table, if you please."

The cook pulled the cat into her capacious lap, and she and Lord Henry chatted most agreeably about Christmases past—and the Christmas to come.

Two

He had overslept. Damn and blast the sun, which was shining into his eyes. The bare trees could not soften the brilliant light of day, but the sight of an impossibly blue sky was welcome.

From the cozy depths of his goose-down comforter, Lord Henry contemplated his fate. The cousins would be arriving, en masse, very soon. His valet was nowhere about, probably having fallen asleep in a distant closet, as usual.

But Henry needed a bath. And he needed to shave. He could not dress until these hygienic obligations, as Aunt Venetia referred to them, were met.

The warmth of his bed was a compelling reason to do none of these things. He dismissed the frivolous idea of coming down unwashed, unshaven, and in his nightshirt. Mrs. Hannigan would never let him hear the end of it, and Venetia would be conspicuously shocked.

No, there was nothing to be done but rise and greet the—

Female in his room.

"Oh! Good afternoon—I am sorry to have disturbed you, but I thought this was *my* room. Who are you?"

"I am Lord Henry Whittaker. Who are you?"

"Your cousin."

If she was indeed his cousin, which he doubted, never

having seen her in his life, she was a very pretty one. She wore a fur-trimmed spencer over a gown of wool that belled out from the warm petticoats beneath it, and carried a muff that was nearly the color of her glossy, dark brown hair, half-hidden under a charming hat also trimmed with fur.

Her bright brown eyes were soft as a doe's and her lips were pink from the cold day. He realized he was gaping at her and shut his mouth.

"Seventeen times removed," she added.

"On which side?"

"Your mother's, I believe."

That dear lady was far away in Constantinople, with his father, on diplomatic assignment, so he could not confirm this interesting new cousin with her.

"What is your name, if I may ask?"

"Peach."

He waited. "Is there more? Or are you called by that name alone?"

"Susan Elizabeth Catherine Jane Peach, if you must know. My unmarried aunts insisted on being remembered if they were to have just one niece."

"Ah. Then you are an only child, Miss Peach?"

"Precisely."

The gamekeeper, who had been pressed into service to help carry the luggage of the twelve young ladies who had just arrived—Lord Henry seemed to remember that being the number, one for each of the twelve days of Christmas—stamped into the room very much out of breath and dropped several bags with a resounding thud.

"Lord 'Enry—beg your pardon—some mistake."

"I should say so. You cannot leave those bags here, Felix."

He nodded, looking a little desperate. "The footmen 'ave the others. There is a mountain of them, sir."

"But they are not all mine," Miss Peach said reassuringly.

"Whether they are yours or not, they do not belong in my room and they shall be removed at once. Kindly remove yourself as well."

She simply stared at him impertinently, and Lord Henry felt suddenly too warm underneath the goose-down comforter. But he could not very well fling it off if she continued to stand there.

At that moment, there was a distant rumble that shook the floor and the bed upon it, as if a herd of sheep were approaching. He listened carefully—the sheep seemed to be giggling. The herd proceeded down the hall and stopped at his door.

Susan Peach turned to greet the other cousins and their friends. They crowded into the doorway of his bedroom and just outside it, full of unladylike high spirits, craning their necks to see inside.

A short one in the back jumped to see over her companions' bonnets and Henry cringed under the comforter.

"Ooh!"

"Who is he?"

"Are we sharing rooms?" the short one asked.

Miss Peach answered in a stagey whisper. "Not with him. That is the great Lord Henry Whittaker, who is not pleased to see us."

"Oh dear."

"Oh my."

"A pleasure to meet you," hallooed the short one in the back.

Felix, who had stood forgotten during this interchange, gave a long-suffering sigh to remind everyone of his presence. He then picked up the bags as best he could, holding a small valise in his teeth by its leather straps and everything else in his huge hands.

Miss Peach's eyes widened. "I will take that, if you don't mind." She relieved him of the valise, which was evidently hers, and examined the strap for toothmarks but found none.

She opened it and took out a peppermint drop, which she put into her pretty mouth.

Lord Henry looked away from this faux pas and tried to collect his thoughts.

"My dear ladies," he said at last, "though I am honored to make your acquaintance, I am not dressed."

A wave of laughter swept through the crowd of girls in his doorway.

"Ah!"

"Our apologies!"

"I can't see!" the short one in the back, of course.

Lord Henry sighed. "Now, if you would be so good as to follow Felix, he will show you to your rooms, wherever they might be. My Aunt Venetia would be dreadfully upset to find you in my chambers, I assure you."

"Henry!" There was no mistaking Venetia's stentorian tone—or her dismay. "This is most improper!"

The crowd of girls quickly moved back into the hall, followed by Miss Peach, who waved her arms to gather her skitter-witted companions into a group and whispered that they should wait and not wander off.

Felix did not raise his eyes to her ladyship's stern countenance. "Beggin' your pardon, ma'am. I am not in the 'abit of misleading young ladies, but I am unfamiliar with the wings of the 'ouse, never having gone nowhere but the kitchen and then only to bring in a brace of ducks."

"I understand, Felix," she said imperiously. "Please proceed to the south wing. You are now in the north."

"Beggin' your pardon again," he said. "It is rather confusin', what with the portrait gallery and them marble busts of the old dukes. They seem to look at you, like."

She waved him out. "Turn left at the eleventh duke. The housekeeper will be waiting for you by the glass-fronted cabinet that holds my collection of stuffed birds. They are a most edifying tribute to the art of taxidermy, Felix."

Here the gamekeeper looked up, perhaps sharing Venetia's interest in ornithology, Lord Henry mused.

"Taxi-wha—? Oh, indeed, ma'am," he said respectfully, trying to tug his forelock but impeded by the bags. He hoisted them all once more and went his way. Henry could hear him murmuring the directions. "Duke eleven. Stuffed birds."

Some minutes later, Miss Susan Peach and her companions explored the suite of rooms in which they would stay for the next fortnight.

These apartments had once been occupied by ducal offspring and decorated long ago in white and gold, very much in the rococo taste, with plump cupids adorning the ceiling and dizzying swirls upon the wallpaper. There were three beds to a room, as there had been many daughters in the last fifty years. The arrival of male heirs—Lord Henry's father, and that worthy young man himself—had been occasions for great celebration.

Each bed had an impressive canopy and curtains that could be drawn around it, and each had a white marble night table beside it, supported by the clawed feet of some mythical beast. Upon these tables, smaller beasts made of bronze held beeswax candles that smelled faintly and pleasantly of honey.

"La!" exclaimed Amelia, the short one who stood in the back at the door to Lord Henry's chamber. "It is all very grand." She disappeared through the connecting door.

Every effort had been made to air and prepare the rooms for their stay, Susan noticed with satisfaction. She would like being able to draw the curtains around her bed, as she preferred to sleep late when possible.

"Drafty, though," said Miss Fiona Givens, Susan's dearest friend, who was shivering, despite the hooded cloak she still wore. Her red hair had come down, as had the hood.

It was Fiona's mother who had been Venetia's closest cousin and bosom bow, and she was the reason they were all invited. "What do you think, Peachy? Shall we change or keep our warm things on?"

Susan set down her muff and took off her spencer. "Let us ask the housekeeper if we may have tea brought up. She is in the next room, I believe. That will help."

"An excellent idea." Fiona popped through the doorway to make this request and then perched upon the edge of the bed she had claimed. "I thought Lord Henry was looking well."

"What could be seen of him. He was rather starchy about our innocent mistake. 'Kindly remove yourself,' indeed." Susan imitated his haughty tone to perfection, and Fiona laughed.

"Do you know, he was once quite shy and funny, and not at all starchy—"

The rest of this interesting statement was cut off by Amelia's squeal of happiness. The two young women left off to see what she was making so much noise about and found her in the next room, rolling about in the luxurious bed.

"Ooh! It is very comfortable. And I do not have to share it with my sister, who could not come."

"We would have been thirteen if she had," a thoughtful miss pointed out. "So it is just as well."

The others nodded agreement with this ancient superstition and set about unpacking the most important things, like hairbrushes and ribbons, and hanging their gowns in the clothes presses, with the assistance of the upstairs maids.

There were only four maids to twelve guests—they had elected not to bring their own, as that would have required another two carriages—and some did without, quite cheerfully.

Susan was one of these, happy for the distraction of returning to her chamber to occupy herself with her things, as she could not help thinking of Lord Henry and how very handsome he had looked in his bed.

He seemed to be quite tall, even lying down, and broad in the shoulder. His nightshirt had not been fastened at the collar and she had caught a glimpse of his solid chest just before he slid mostly out of sight beneath the comforter.

His tousled dark hair had given him a raffish look that was most appealing. And oh, what soft and sleepy eyes he had. But he seemed rather staid, all the same. Not the sort of person who loved fun as she did.

Susan supposed such thoughts were unworthy, but they were only thoughts and there was no harm in thinking them.

His Aunt Venetia seemed a formidable sort—she had shown them her bird collection along the way and named all the previous dukes for their edification and enjoyment.

Seeming to assume that her young guests were too poor and too humble to set their caps at *her* nephew, she also pointed out that Lord Henry would eventually inherit the title, marry an heiress, and in due time join the row of marble men in the corridor.

Miss Peach thought Venetia ought not to be so sure of his future. Lord Henry seemed to be as haughty as his aunt and perhaps was not such a catch as all that. However, she was willing to be wrong. He was certainly a very attractive man and she was looking forward to seeing him fully dressed.

Three

An excellent midday meal quite restored the young ladies' strength after their long and fatiguing journey. Mrs. Hannigan had prepared a wondrous array of delicacies. These they devoured with enthusiasm, since there were no male guests present to make it necessary to pretend that they sustained themselves only on moonbeams and not food.

Afterwards, they gathered in the Green Drawing Room, as requested by Venetia, who seemed to speak in capital letters, as if determined to underscore the importance of everything. It was indeed very green: acres of emerald silk swathed the windows and covered the matching furniture.

The girls wandered about, admiring the decor, and Amelia peered into one of the massive Chinese vases that stood in the corners. It was nearly as tall as she was.

"Whatever are you doing, Amelia?" Fiona asked.

"I thought I heard a cat inside. But the vase is empty."

Susan smiled. "The cat is under the sofa, Amelia. If you sit down, he might make your acquaintance, but perhaps he is frightened to see so many of us."

Amelia sat, and soon enough Sir Puss came out to investigate her ankles. Two other cousins joined her on the sofa, and the cat jumped up to be petted by each in turn, looking well content.

The others found ways to amuse themselves for the next hour: several clustered around the pianoforte to sing while

Fiona played, and four picked up the cards that had been left upon a small square table and began a game. Susan looked through an uninteresting novel for a little while, then put it down, feeling restless. She rose and walked to a tall window that overlooked a garden.

It was formal in design, with boxwood borders along its brick walks, and bleak stone walls that dripped with ice where snow had melted and then frozen again. Her imagination filled it with brilliant flowers, though nothing bloomed there now . . . and perhaps a reflecting pool . . . and a dancing nymph . . . and a bench where one might while away an afternoon with some fond lover . . .

The sun suddenly disappeared behind a cloud, and with it, her daydream. The Berkshire sky lost its blue brilliance as heavy, dark clouds covered it, sweeping in over the Downs. A snap in the air hinted at more snow to come—Susan, who had grown up in the country, could almost smell it.

"Tra-la! Tra-la! How I do enjoy the old songs!" Venetia swept into the room, and the music-makers stopped in the middle of "Good King Wenceslas." They had lost their place several bars ago anyway and were making up new verses as they went along.

Susan noticed that Venetia held a box against her stately bosom. No doubt it contained something of great value, judging by the grip she had on it.

"My dear girls, how good of you to wait for me. I see that you have found—oh, that cat!" Venetia looked disapprovingly at Sir Puss.

"He is exceedingly friendly, Lady Venetia," chirped Amelia.

"He belongs in the kitchen. I wondered why I did not see him there. Mrs. Hannigan let him out, I suppose." She held up the box in her hands as if presenting some sacred object. "Can anyone guess what this might be?"

The young women in the room looked at her with wide eyes. The box itself revealed no clue as to its contents.

She opened the lid dramatically and a strong smell of whisky filled the room. Susan could just see the dark lump inside.

"It is a fruitcake! One of many. It was baked some months ago and has been soaked in spirits to preserve its goodness. But it is not for our enjoyment. No, these I give humbly to the poor and the proud, the shepherd and the squire alike. They are most grateful for my benevolence."

Susan, who disliked fruitcake, wondered about that— and wondered what Venetia was getting at.

"But they must be delivered ere the snow falls and keeps us inside. The village is just two miles distant and this task can be accomplished in an hour's time. If two of you would be so good as to accompany me upon this charitable errand, I would be much obliged."

Lord Henry chose that moment to stride into the room and nod affably enough at one and all. "Good afternoon."

All the cousins and friends of cousins sat up straighter when he appeared, Susan noticed with amusement. She was pleased to see that his eyes lighted first upon her and that he smiled slightly.

Certainly that was because she was the only one standing, she thought, not wishing to entertain romantic fancies. Her accidental foray into his bedroom had not been the ideal introduction, and perhaps he did not like her. His smile widened and she returned it demurely.

Perhaps he did.

He was indeed tall, as she had surmised, and well if soberly dressed in buckskins, boots, waistcoat, immaculate linen and a frock coat of superfine. "I would be happy to assist you, Aunt."

Venetia stared at him, astonished. "You? But you detest Christmas!"

"No. I detest fruitcake. I wish to get them out of the house as soon as possible." He held a greatcoat over one arm, and looked ready enough to brave the wintry chill.

"I will help," Susan said quickly. She looked at Fiona, still sitting at the pianoforte, who nodded and rose gracefully.

"Oh. Then come along. We shall not be long, my dears," Venetia said to the others, clutching the box to her stately bosom once more. "Do resume your entertainments. Tea will be served in a trice."

The old lady dispatched a maid to fetch Susan and Fiona's warm things, and her own, but the young women insisted upon going back to their rooms for a few minutes—girlish vanity, she supposed. They returned hastily, and soon enough all four of them were inside the carriage, rolling over the bumpy road to the village.

There was very little room, as the boxed, beribboned fruitcakes were stacked next to Venetia on one side. Lord Henry sat on the other, with Susan squeezed between him and Fiona, Lord Henry looking very pleased with the arrangement, and with himself.

Venetia, however, was not at all pleased by how pleased he looked. She had expected him to squeeze in next to her, but Lord Henry did not seem to care a fig for her expectations. She would have to have a word with his mother when Lady Alice returned from Constantinople.

As this would not be for another twelvemonth, Venetia could only bear and forbear, something she prided herself on.

The small windows of the carriage were frosted with crystals of ice, but the younger members of the party were warm enough, given their proximity to one another.

Lord Henry bestowed a slight smile, first upon Miss Givens and then upon Miss Peach. They were both charming, but it was Miss Peach who captured his interest in the greatest degree.

After she and her companions had quitted his room, he had gone back to sleep and awoken refreshed from a dream of a garden filled with a horticultural impossibility: peach trees that blossomed and bore fruit simultaneously.

He had wandered through this wondrous place hand in hand with Miss Peach herself, of course, and there had been no beady-eyed chaperon following them about. She had worn the lightest of summer dresses in this dream, and her figure had been most agreeably—but decorously—revealed.

His verdant dreamland seemed quite at odds with the sere winter landscape through which the carriage passed, but Miss Peach, sitting primly to his left and endeavoring to keep her position upon the cushions, was even prettier than in his vision.

He had decided to flirt with her. He would observe all the proprieties, of course, and nothing of consequence would happen. His heart would not be at risk, and she would leave in a fortnight. It seemed only logical to make the most of the time. Perhaps Christmas would not be so dreadfully annoying this year. He had begun to look forward to it.

Their first stop was at a cottage by the road, where the footman jumped down to announce their arrival. A buxom woman looked out at the carriage, and, noticing the coronet and crest upon the black-lacquered door, dropped a curtsy. Three small children clung to her skirts, which made the curtsy rather difficult, Susan thought sympathetically.

Venetia looked over the nearest stack of boxes and thrust a fruitcake into Susan's hands. "Here. Wish them a happy Christmas, but be quick about it." She watched with pursed lips as Susan clambered over Fiona, carrying a reticule that bulged in an odd way.

"Pray excuse me, Fiona—"

"Quite all right—"

Lord Henry got out on his side and went round the carriage to help Susan.

"There is no need for unnecessary gallantry, Henry. The footman can do that."

He bestowed his most boyish smile upon his frowning aunt. "It is my pleasure to be of assistance to you, dear Aunt Venetia. And to Miss Peach and Miss Givens as well. Christmas is the season of goodwill, is it not?"

The old lady gave him a suspicious look. "I have never known you to say so. Are you feeling ill, Henry? I will have Mrs. Hannigan send up a bowl of unsalted gruel before you retire tonight."

"There is no need. I am entirely well."

In fact, the warmth of Miss Peach's slender hand inside its kidskin glove was making him feel quite splendid. He would not mind handing her down from the carriage for the next thirty-two fruitcakes, in fact.

The footman, who had returned to the carriage, stood to one side and did not interfere, and Miss Givens gave Henry a conspiratorial smile.

Lord Henry and Miss Peach did the honors, and the fruitcake was handed over at the cottage door. The little ones left off clinging long enough to peek inside the box, but they wrinkled their small noses at the smell and seemed disappointed.

Susan reached into her bulging reticule, which she and Fiona had stuffed with candy drops and peppermints from her valise. To their joy, she gave the children each a few. She was saving the rest for other houses, and other children, and hoped there would be many of the latter.

When they had returned to the carriage and sincerest

thanks were called and pardon begged by the children's mother for not coming out in the snow to pay her respects more properly, Venetia gave the nod to the footman.

He wrapped his thick woolen scarf about his neck, jammed his tricorne hat down firmly over his ears, and called to the coachman. They rattled and rocked for another mile, coming to the village.

The houses of Bramblyside seemed to cling to the gentle hills upon which the town was situated, being made of the same stone that lined the twisting streets. Here and there, a house had been neatly plastered, standing out bright and white among its rougher companions.

Fiona rubbed a gloved hand over the window, trying to see out.

"Look, Susan—there is the church."

A lonely steeple soared into the darkening sky.

"Oh, we must stop by the vicarage," Venetia said anxiously. "The Reverend Lewes says Christmas is not Christmas without one of these 'cannonballs,' as he calls them. He is much given to levity, though it is inappropriate in a man of the cloth. Do you not agree, Henry?"

He merely raised an eyebrow. "I have no opinion on the matter, Aunt." The carriage drew up in front of a Jacobean house that seemed to lean in a friendly way upon the old church. "Please pass me a cannonball—a fruitcake, I mean."

"No, no," said Venetia somewhat peevishly. "I shall deliver it myself. I must speak to Reverend Lewes about the Sunday sermon."

Lord Henry went over the days of the week in his head. "Sunday is Christmas Day, is it not?"

"So you know when it is," his aunt said tartly. "Very good."

He gave her a quizzical look. Why was she in such an ill temper all of a sudden? Had the carriage ride rattled her—

or did seeing him ensconced between two lovely young women pique her prudery? Well and good.

His dear mama had explained, before her departure, that Venetia might attempt to introduce him to a Miss Letitia Curdle, the daughter of a bluestocking friend. Miss Curdle was reportedly very plain and some years older than he— and also heiress to a vast fortune. But Henry had no intention of submitting to Venetia's designs in the matter of marriage.

She fussed with one of the boxes and adjusted its ribbon. "I wish Lewes to exhort the congregants not to make merry. The consumption of spirits rises in direct proportion to the dropping of the temperature. Most of the villagers were quite drunk at the Christmas feast."

"A good time was had by all, Aunt. Surely there is no harm in that."

"What *has* got into you, Henry?" She did not wait for a reply but made ready to exit the carriage, and Lord Henry got out before her, extending a hand to assist her. They went up the walk to the vicarage, and Fiona and Susan settled back for a chat.

"Well, what do you think?" said Fiona, wrapping her cloak closely about her. Opening the door had let out most of the warmth of the carriage's interior.

"He is a handsome fellow," Susan replied casually. "And rather proud, like his aunt."

"All future dukes are handsome," Fiona said with a laugh. "But he is more fond of fun than you might think and not proud at all."

"Is he engaged?"

"No. He is but twenty-nine, Peachy. He seems determined to be friendly."

Susan shot her a look. "And what man would not be when presented, thanks to you, with a houseful of temptations. He might find it difficult to choose among twelve."

"I think he has chosen already," Fiona said slyly. "He seems quite taken with you."

"Piffle. He is only being polite."

"No. I have known Henry for some years. He does like you, Susan."

"How well do you know him?"

"Well enough."

"Have you not been here once before at Christmas?"

Fiona toyed with a lock of her red hair. "Venetia invited me and Mama to stay when I had just turned eight. Henry was nineteen, with excessively large feet that seemed to be always in his way. Gangly. Dreadfully shy. Afflicted with spots."

This picture did not fit the present-day Henry in the slightest. Susan was glad to know that he had not always been the embodiment of masculine perfection and impeccable manners.

"But he was kind, though very awkward. He is an only child, and treated me like a younger sister for the time that I was here."

"And what did you do?"

"Oh, we collected birds' nests for Venetia when the weather permitted us to be outside. And played at blindman's buff and ninepins in the halls when it did not. It snowed wonderfully one day, just before Christmas, and we cut out paper shapes and stuck them to the windows with our breath, it was so cold."

This playfulness also did not fit Henry's patrician demeanor, but Susan was very glad to hear of it.

"He has grown even taller since then, though he seemed very tall to me then. And he has acquired social graces and a passable education over the years."

Susan laughed. "He was a perfect bear when we entered his den this morning. But I own we surprised him, and it is not fair to judge his character from that."

Four

Fiona put a finger to her lips. "They are returning." She swung the door open before Venetia and Lord Henry reached the carriage, leaning back against the squabs as they entered. The footman shut the door.

"The vicar was not at home, but his wife accepted our gift most graciously," Venetia said with a sigh. "They have far too many children, I think. I counted seven."

"Perhaps they did not all belong to the vicar," Susan said sensibly.

Lord Henry nodded. "I recognized the offspring of the Stubbses and the Micklethwaites among them. But children grow so fast, it is sometimes hard to tell when one does not see them often."

"Stubbs and Micklethwaite—poor laborers, no doubt. Perhaps I have wasted a cake. Frumenty would be more to their liking."

The thought of this milky slop made Henry frown. "We could not carry a pot of frumenty in a carriage, Aunt. I am sure they will enjoy your gift."

Susan slid into Fiona as the carriage rounded a turn—and Lord Henry slid into Susan. They laughed merrily as they slid in the opposite direction at the next turn, which came up very quickly. Venetia stared out the window as if she did not want to see, stretching out an arm to keep the fruitcakes from falling.

The carriage stopped rather abruptly at a tavern with a sign that said "The Tankard & Tuppence." Loud roars of laughter came from the low building, its small mullioned windows aglow with firelight.

Lord Henry raised an eyebrow. "Have we come to spread good cheer at the inn? From the sound of it, they are much too cheerful already."

"Half the village is here," Venetia said firmly. "It will save us time. If you stand outside the carriage, I shall hand out the boxes to you and the footman, and then do the giving. The girls can wait here as before. A matron of my years is in no danger, but they should not mingle with low company."

Susan wondered why the old lady had asked them to come along in the first place if all they were to do was wait. It was clear that Venetia had not expected Lord Henry to accompany them—and that she was put out by his attentions to them.

Their exit took rather longer this time, as so many fruitcakes were involved, and they ended up pressing the coachman into service as well. The flagstone path to the rough-hewn door was icy, and Lord Henry took his aunt's arm, balancing three boxes on his other one.

They entered to find half the village, as Venetia had predicted—men, women, and even young children, who buried their faces in their mothers' skirts, looking sleepy. Though only ale was served, the villagers had drunk well and deeply of it, and many of the men were quite obviously intoxicated.

A brawny fellow spied the coachman and rose, swaying, to his feet, a belligerent look in his bleary eyes.

"Hoi! If it ain't owld Fred!"

The coachman muttered something and tried to hide behind the stack of fruitcakes he held. Lord Henry suspected that the two men had had some quarrel that had never been settled—and that it was about to be settled now. He put the boxes he carried onto a trencher table and put himself between the coachman and his aunt.

"Whatever are you doing, Henry? I cannot see—"

She also could not see the faces of Susan and Fiona, who had dared each other to leave the carriage and peep through the windows of the inn and see what went on there. They watched open-mouthed as the brawny fellow crossed the crowded room with some difficulty, shoving the other revelers out of his way.

"Will ye not look me in the eye? Ye have trifled with my Betsy and I shall know the reason why!"

The coachman set down his cakes and put up his hands. "She asked me to. She is a right lusty wench, Sam, and no mistake!"

"Damn you!" The brawny man swung a hamlike fist— and missed his target by a mile. He hit Lord Henry instead, who went down like a falling tree, revealing Venetia standing behind him.

The old lady picked up a stool and brandished it at Sam. "Back! Back, I say!"

Shocked into sobriety by what he had inadvertently done, Sam bolted for the door, almost tearing it off its hinges as he ran out. A brunette head looked around, followed by a red one—and Susan and Fiona entered the inn.

They rushed to Lord Henry's side. He moaned and opened one eye. The other had begun to swell and there was a trickle of blood from his elegant nose.

"So this is how my kindness is repaid!" Venetia shrieked. "My nephew is at death's door and my young guests are witness to scenes of utmost depravity!"

The villagers stood looking on, speechless, until the innkeeper's daughter collected her wits and rushed into the kitchen for a bit of beefsteak for Lord Henry's black eye. She came out, followed by her father.

"Take this, miss," said she. " 'Twill draw the humor and heal it right quick."

"The swelling is not too bad," Susan murmured. She took the beefsteak from the stout girl and applied it gently to Henry's eye until he reached up to hold it himself. Then she wiped away the blood from his nose with her hand-kerchief. "But we must get him home. Fred, can you and the footman carry him between you?"

The dumbstruck coachman nodded, just before Venetia, who still held the stool, struck him a smart blow with it. "This is all your fault! Trifle with Betsy, did you?"

"She asked me to," he repeated numbly, and fell on top of Lord Henry.

"That will do!" cried Susan, taking the stool away from Venetia. "Now how shall we get them home?"

Henry pushed the insensible man off his chest. "I can walk to the carriage, thank you—but not with Fred on top of me." He sat up, shaking his head to clear it.

"Oh, Henry! Oh, I am sorry!" Venetia collapsed into a chair and bawled like a baby. "So dreadfully sorry!"

"There, there. You did not punch me, Aunt. I have had worse, I suppose, as a boy. What shall we do with Fred?"

"Leave 'im 'ere," said the innkeeper placidly. The coachman, his face pressed into the sawdust strewn upon the floor, muttered something that sounded like a yes.

The footman and Henry exchanged a glance and nod-ded. "We shall have to leave the fruitcakes, Aunt."

"Bother the filthy fruitcakes! I am giving up good works forever!"

Certainly his distraught aunt needed to return home im-mediately. The young ladies seemed none the worse for witnessing the ridiculous brawl, Henry thought rather dazedly.

He himself had enjoyed looking up into Miss Peach's lovely, worried face as she had ministered so tenderly to her fallen hero—though he supposed he was not her hero, strictly speaking, but Venetia's—and he had merely been in the way of a blow meant for another man. Still, he hoped Miss Peach would think him heroic.

They proceeded by fits and starts back to the carriage, where the horses stood champing at their bits.

"I can drive, m'lud," the footman said worriedly. "Fred has taught me summat about it."

"Summat" would have to do, Lord Henry thought. This time the young ladies helped him in and he stretched out upon one of the seats, pressing the beefsteak to his eye and wishing his head would stop throbbing.

Venetia squeezed in next, still muttering fiercely, and threw the remaining fruitcakes out the door to make room for herself and the two girls. They sat in silence all the way home, but Susan reached out now and then to stroke Lord Henry's forehead, not minding what his aunt might think.

He rather enjoyed the attention, despite the pain. And Miss Peach insisted that he keep her handkerchief, in which she had wrapped a bit of ice to stop his nose from bleeding.

The snow that had threatened to fall by late afternoon now began to come down in earnest. The road ahead was soon covered, for which Henry was grateful, because the carriage did not rattle so much as it had.

When they had turned down the road that led to Hampstead Hall, the great house itself had entirely vanished into the swirling snow. But the footman drove on, marking his course by the black trunks of the trees that stood in noble ranks along the avenue. It was not long before they pulled into the circular drive.

The butler ran out just in time to see the very embarrassed Lord Henry step down, ably assisted by Miss Peach and Miss Givens. He noted his lordship's black eye without comment.

Mrs. Hannigan would have the whole story within minutes, of that the butler had no doubt. Perhaps he might ask her to grill that bit of beefsteak for him when his lordship was done with it. It would go well with the bottle of Madeira he had pinched from the cellar yesterday.

The butler peered inside the carriage. There sat Venetia, her countenance more stormy than the dreadful weather.

"Ma'am? You ought to come inside. The snow is falling fast."

"I can see that for myself." She gathered herself and turned to him. "What is the world coming to, Hinton? Answer me that!"

The story of the fight and the fruitcake was told in full detail, and spread through the house immediately. Within minutes, the lowest scullery maid knew that Fred, the coachman, had dallied with Betsy, the hussy, and Lord Henry, the hero, had bravely defended the ladies of his party against the brutish wrath of Sam, the spurned lover.

The wounded gallant had been made comfortable upon the longest sofa in the Green Drawing Room and seemed happy enough to be fussed over by the ladies who had not gone into town. Susan and Fiona had gone upstairs to change.

He would have preferred Susan's delicate touch, of course, but ten cooing females would do in the meantime.

Mrs. Hannigan bustled in with a bowl of steaming water and clean rags. "Now then, Lord Henry. I have not seen an eye like that on you since you and young Master Philip traded blows over the plums you stole."

The young women clustered around him waited eagerly to hear more.

"Philip missed the first time, you know," Henry said.

"Aye, and hit the tree with his right fist, poor lamb. But he got you with his left in the end."

"Do not remind me. But I suppose my steps were turned from a life of crime. I never stole plums again."

She dipped a rag in the bowl and squeezed it out, washing his face and wiping his bloody nose as if he were a boy of ten again.

"Ow!"

"Hush. You are a great baby, you are." She opened the swollen eye very carefully and looked at its bloodshot white. "It will mend in time. Now give me that bit o' beefsteak and put your head back upon the pillow so the bleeding does not start once more. Do you think you can remember to keep still, or do I have to knock you on the head myself?"

Lord Henry did as he was told, closing his eyes. Was there anything sweeter than feminine compassion?

Venetia came into the room and looked at him silently for a moment. "You seem to be in good hands, Henry. I suppose there is nothing I can do."

"Beggin' your pardon, ma'am, but you should be in bed." Mrs. Hannigan looked at her mistress with alarm. "You have been out in the snow and might catch your death o' cold. I will send the maid up with broth and ask the housekeeper to prepare a bedwarmer so that you are not chilled."

"Thank you, Mrs. Hannigan," Venetia said rather wearily.

"Girls, go with her. Lord Henry will be right as rain soon enough."

He opened his good eye to give her an imploring look but kept his head still. "I like my ministering angels. Do not send them away."

"Fiona and I shall see to him, Mrs. Hannigan."

He knew that charming voice by now. Henry heard the

light footsteps of Miss Peach and Miss Givens and sighed with satisfaction. "Ah. Perhaps Miss Givens might play some soothing melody to distract me."

"I should be happy to," Fiona replied.

"And what shall I do, Lord Henry?" Susan asked.

He waited until all the women but these two had left the drawing room. "Sit by me, and talk to me . . . until I fall asleep."

Five

The starch seemed to have gone out of him—she rather liked him this way. She nodded. Talking to him was easy enough, and she too needed to recuperate from the excitement of the evening.

"Is it still snowing, Miss Peach?"

"I believe so." She was quiet for a moment, listening to the gentle melody that Fiona had begun to play.

"Tell me about yourself. I did not know I had a cousin seventeen times removed."

"My aunts explained it once. It is complicated, but we are distant cousins."

She settled into her chair, looking at his peaceful though battered face. The odd sight made her feel—almost—oh, she could not quite name the emotion she was feeling. How was it possible for him to look so handsome after such a blow?

"Tell me more. Who are your parents?"

"My mother died when I was very young. I was raised by the aunts."

"Susan. Elizabeth. Catherine. Jane."

"You remembered." She gave him a surprised look that he seemed to sense though his eyes were closed.

He smiled weakly. "Yes, I remembered. I am not likely to ever forget our first meeting."

"I see." Perhaps she had made more of an impression on him than she had thought.

"And your father?" he inquired.

"What—oh. He is a scholar."

"We might introduce him to Venetia. Ornithology was once a passion of hers."

"My father is devoted to the study of ancient Sumerian and Chaldean texts. I do not think he has seen the light of day in months, let alone a bird. He is always deep in his books."

"Ah. Then they have nothing in common." He paused for a moment, as if trying to remember something. "Venetia came to live here years ago after some disappointment in love. She has never married."

They were silent for several minutes. Fiona had encountered a tricky arpeggio and was repeating it diligently.

"If she plays that one more time, I shall scream," Lord Henry whispered.

"You shall do no such thing," Susan whispered back.

She turned to gaze at her friend, whose red hair was swept up loosely, showing her profile to advantage in the soft candlelight. Bent over the keyboard, absorbed in her music, Fiona looked like a painting, remote and lovely.

"She told me that she came here as a girl—and that you were kind to her."

"Did she say that?" Henry opened his good eye. "Mrs. Hannigan instructed me not to tease her at the time—and I didn't. Yes, she was here one Christmas when it snowed a great deal. We amused ourselves well enough."

"We shall have to do the same. Some of the girls were thinking of putting on a Christmas pantomime."

He grinned—and winced. His head was beginning to hurt more and more.

"On what theme?"

"The twelve days of Christmas, as in the old song."

He thought about it before replying. "There is an entire barnyard in it. Six geese a-laying and seven swans a-swimming. Eight cows a-something."

"You have forgotten the four calling birds, three French hens, two turtledoves, and the partridge."

"You have forgotten the pear tree, Miss Peach. But I suppose you have enough maidens and ladies to manage. You are short several lords."

"I know. We could ask Felix, and the butler, and the footmen. And you."

"The lords are *a-leaping,* as I remember. I do not *a-leap.*"

Susan giggled. "You could *a-learn.*"

"No."

She looked at him askance. "May I ask why not?"

"It is not dignified."

"Fiona said that you were happy to indulge in all sorts of fun."

"Never." He tried his best to seem dignified, which was not easy with a black eye and no boots on—Mrs. Hannigan had insisted that he remove his boots for medical reasons, but he knew she was thinking about the sofa.

"You are teasing me, Lord Henry."

He nodded. "Do you mind very much?"

"No. I rather like it. But I think you must rest now."

He reached out a hand and found hers. "I cannot rest. Miss Peach—oh, Miss Peach!" he said, sotto voce. "You have given me a reason to live."

"Do not be so silly." Yet she did not pull her hand away. Fiona did not look up and Susan thought she might enjoy the moment as long as she dared.

His hand was warm and strong, with a few scratches on it from the scuffle in the tavern. She touched one with her fingertip.

"Ah—sweet agony! But it is only a scratch, as brave heroes say."

She snorted. "You are really very silly, Lord Henry. It *is* only a scratch, you know."

"Well, I am grateful for it, as it has caught your attention and kept you by my side. You did not finish telling me about yourself. Where are you from?"

"Hertfordshire. I grew up just outside the village of Braughey."

"Ye-es. The Hertfordshire branch of the family," he said slowly. "I seem to remember that we had some relations there."

"It is not much of a place. The church is the tallest building for miles around and there are more cows than people."

He nodded eagerly, as if he found the subject of cows fascinating. Susan realized that he was enjoying their odd tête-à-tête as much as she was. What had happened to the conservative prig of the morning?

"I myself have had many philosophical conversations with cows. They think before they speak, unlike men."

"And women?"

"Many women do not seem to think at all. You are a most interesting exception."

She gave him a wry smile. "I am not sure that is a compliment, my lord. I seem to be in the same category as a prize guernsey."

Henry rubbed his forehead. "No, no—not at all. I am having trouble finding the right words to say what I mean and I am feeling somewhat dizzy. Could I trouble you to fetch a headache powder from my aunt?"

"I am not sure where she is. This house goes on and on—there is no end to it."

He turned to one side, resting the unswollen half of his face on the pillow. "Well, never mind. Perhaps I needed to look at you and not at the ceiling or walls. This room is exceedingly green."

"There is a yellow drawing room across the hall very like this one. I peeped into it as I came down."

Lord Henry grimaced. "Yes. The tenth duke was fond of both colors. But I am not." He shifted, making himself more comfortable. "And how do you like your rooms, Miss Peach? Are you and the other young ladies comfortable in the Rococo Suite?"

"We are." She smiled and looked to Fiona for confirmation. But her friend was riffling through the music that had been left on the pianoforte, frowning slightly. She found another piece and began to play again.

"I hope that you will stay as long as possible. It would be a pity to lose such a peach to the wild woods of Hertfordshire."

"Why, it is not wild in the least," she said indignantly. "Nothing like here. People do not swing stools and fling fruitcakes in Hertfordshire."

Lord Henry sighed, remembering the fight and his aunt's distress. "I feel very sorry about Venetia's fruitcakes. But I daresay those who enjoy such sticky horrors will venture forth in the dead of night and retrieve them from the snow."

"We thought we might make other cakes, if Mrs. Hannigan allows anyone in her kitchen. Some cooks do not. If the snow keeps us indoors, we cannot play at cards all day and it seems that your library is lacking in romances."

"Mrs. Hannigan would be glad of your company, I assure you," Lord Henry said. He turned this way and that, and sat up at last.

"Are you sure you should?" Susan asked anxiously.

He touched his nose, which had stopped bleeding. He tried to open his eye. The swollen lid did not budge. He turned his face to gaze at her with the good one.

"Well, Miss Peach, how do I look?"

How to answer honestly? She pondered this question and his countenance for a moment. "Handsome indeed on the right—but not on the left."

He laughed. "Well said!"

She stretched out a hand unthinkingly as he rose, which he needed, as it turned out. He almost stumbled but stood up straight.

Fiona looked up at last, and her fingers fumbled. "Are you feeling better, Lord Henry?"

"I am, Miss Givens, thanks to your delightful concert, and Miss Peach's scintillating conversation."

Susan rose also, wondering whether scintillation was good or bad. "Let me ring for Mrs. Hannigan. You should not go to bed alone—Ah, I did not mean to say that. Not in those words. I do not know what I meant to say, Lord Henry. Oh, do not look at me like that!"

"My valet is upstairs. He will take care of things in his usual lackluster fashion." He smiled rather wickedly and gave her a most flirtatious wink, which she hoped Fiona did not see.

The next morning, Susan was the last to rise, which meant she had the suite to herself. The room was very cold, despite the fire in the Rumford stove that occupied the hearth. She wrapped herself tightly in the comforter and went to the window.

The snow had changed the world overnight.

It lay in deep drifts of sparkling white, shadowed with blue. Here and there, bare trees and leafless shrubs stood out against it, their branches startlingly black. The smallest twigs dripped with ice.

Looking at it almost made her eyes hurt. Thinking of

that made her wonder how Lord Henry was feeling this morning.

Susan dressed hurriedly, without summoning a maid, and pinned up her hair as best she could. She was tempted to swathe herself in the comforter once more, like the royal robes of a very eccentric queen, but decided it would undoubtedly be much warmer downstairs.

She turned right at the eleventh duke and made her way down the stairs to the breakfast room. The remains of what had been a considerable meal were still upon the table, though there was one unused place setting.

Picking up her plate, she went to the sideboard to forage through what was left. There were eggs—stone cold. And sausages—congealed in grease. And tangerines—most unexpected and delightful. Mrs. Hannigan must have been saving those in some hidden place for Christmas Day.

Susan decided to make do with the eggs, which she would eat quickly, and two tangerines, which she would savor. By great good fortune, some invisible being had just brought in a fresh pot of excellent tea and a plate of scones. She poured herself a steaming cup and sat down to her breakfast. She split the scone and buttered it liberally, as she was quite hungry.

She ate contentedly, hearing voices within the house but at some distance, perhaps in the Green Drawing Room or its evil twin, the Yellow. The voices seemed to argue at times and not at others, but Susan could not make out the words.

The door swung open and Mrs. Hannigan entered. "Good morning, Miss Peach. I thought you might be down shortly and I brought in fresh tea."

"Thank you, Mrs. Hannigan. It is very good. And so are the scones."

The plump cook smiled. "I am glad to see you enjoy them, miss. So did the others."

"Where are they?" She took another scone from the plate and buttered it a little less but added jam.

"In the library. They are practicing for a pantomime. It is like old times, when Lord Henry were young and brought his schoolfellows home at Christmas, which is to say, noisy. And nice."

Susan drank her tea and pointed with her butter knife. "Is the library that way?"

"Yes, Miss Peach."

"Thank you very much, Mrs. Hannigan."

The good woman left by the door she had entered through, and Susan positively gobbled the rest of her breakfast, hastily peeling and eating the tangerines and not savoring them at all. But they were delicious all the same.

Six

She left the breakfast room and headed down the hall to the library, a room she had glimpsed only in passing. She paused outside the heavy door and heard the familiar voices of her cousins and friends, raised in song—then raised in argument.

"It is five French hens and four calling birds, I am sure of it," Amelia said decisively.

"No, it is five golden rings, four calling birds, and three French hens," another girl answered.

"You are right," said Fiona's gentle voice. "Amelia, you are almost right. But I need you to stand still or you will be stuck with pins. I cannot turn you into a swan if you are going to behave like a goose."

Susan pushed open the door.

"Good morning!" the group chimed in unison.

"Good morning—I slept very late. Do forgive me. I see that you are all hard at work."

Amelia, who was swathed in layers of filmy white silk over her day gown, pirouetted. "I shall be a swan a-swimming!"

"You look lovely, Amelia," Susan said warmly. "Where did all this come from?"

"Venetia gave us permission to raid the trunks in the attic. There is no end of wonderful stuff inside—and we have not even opened them all."

Susan looked about at the rich materials tossed hig-gledy-piggledy about the room, and fingered a fine silk. "How is Venetia today?"

"She has caught a cold, and wishes not to be bothered. But she sends kind regards to us all," Fiona said. "I believe she is quite sincere. The fruitcake fiasco seems to have done her good. She said something about never becom-ing a prisoner in the kitchen again. Most odd."

"And how is Lord Henry?"

A gaggle of cousins spoke at once. "We have made him a most dashing eye patch—he looks like a pirate—he is in the study next to the library, Susan—he says he is think-ing—imagine that!"

"Men do think, you know, from time to time." She could imagine that he wanted to escape the feminine hubbub as politely as possible, and wondered if she should interrupt his privacy for the second time in as many days.

"He wanted to see you, Susan," Amelia chirped. "He said to send you in as soon as you came into the library."

Susan ignored the giggles of the women within earshot, and followed the direction of Amelia's pointing finger to a closed set of double doors. She knocked softly.

"Lord Henry? May I enter?"

She heard two bounding steps from within and the door was flung open. There he stood, looking very piratical in-deed in the black eye patch. He had not shaved, and his shirt was not done up properly at the neck, which added to the effect.

"Good morning, Miss Peach! Do come in!"

She entered the study, smiling. "You have excellent manners for a pirate, Lord Henry."

"Shiver me timbers, or whatever it is they say. Would you like some coffee?" He indicated a tray on the ma-hogany desk and the silver coffee service upon it.

"Thank you, but I have had two cups of tea." She looked

at him curiously. "Is this to be part of the show? There are no pirates in the song."

"No pirates prancing? Oh, well. The bright sunshine today hurt my eye, so Miss Lander and Miss Crandall made me a patch."

"They said you looked very dashing in it—and they were not wrong."

He bowed and clicked his heels together.

"Thank you, Miss Peach. Shall we join the others? We must practice for the pantomime, though the performers may have to double as the audience."

"What do you mean?"

He waved a hand at the snowy landscape outside. "The carriage cannot get through and no one can get to us."

Fiona entered. "It is like that winter of long ago—but there is more snow, I believe. Susan, can you come with me? We have a problem with the partridge."

They returned to the library, where Georgia was examining a moth-eaten stuffed owl from Venetia's collection, turning it this way and that.

"There is no partridge but we may use the owl. I thought we could make it a little costume."

"Why not?" Susan asked with a smile. "Have we feathers?"

"Yes, from an old pillow. Venetia saves everything."

"Have we paste?"

Lord Henry went back to the study and returned with a jar of paste.

"Then we have a partridge. Or will have, in an hour or two."

Amelia looked doubtfully at the stuffed owl, which was missing a glass eye. "But it is very large. I believe partridges are much smaller."

"This is a pantomime, Amelia, not a museum of natural history. We may permit ourselves some liberties," Susan said, laughing.

Georgia and Amelia sat down with the stuffed owl between them on a table and began to apply feathers to its bald spots.

"What next?" Lord Henry asked.

"Two turtledoves."

"Felix keeps pigeons."

Susan thought a moment. "Three French hens."

"Will plain speckled English ones do?"

"They will do splendidly."

He looked at her expectantly. "And then?"

"Four calling birds."

Henry pondered this one. "Venetia used to collect mechanical birds. She still has several, though some have lost their winding keys."

"You could whistle."

"I could indeed," he said cheerfully. "Please continue."

"Five golden rings."

"There are nearly twenty women in the house. That is easy."

"Six geese a-laying," she went on.

"I draw the line at live poultry in the house, Miss Peach. The hens and pigeons may be put in birdcages, but there is no birdcage big enough to hold six geese. And they have exceedingly bad tempers."

"We shall paint the croquet balls white for eggs to stand in for the geese."

"Most ingenious. If the croquet set can be found."

Susan counted upon her fingers. "Where were we? Oh, yes. Seven swans a-swimming."

"You have Amelia, but there is only one Amelia."

"Fortunately." She thought it over. "Amelia can run on stage seven times, trailing yards of tulle and flapping her arms."

"I look forward to that spectacle."

"Do you look forward to a cow, Lord Henry? Eight maids a-milking."

"We have the maids. Let us leave the cow to the last."

"Nine ladies dancing."

"Obvious." He gestured broadly at the women in the room.

"Ten lords a-leaping."

Lord Henry conceded the point. "I will leap if the others will."

"Eleven pipers piping." She sighed. "I had hoped to use the village children, but that seems impossible."

"We shall think of something."

"What about twelve drummers drumming?"

"Likewise."

Susan smiled brightly up at him. "Our pantomime shall be a success, even if no one sees it but ourselves."

Lord Henry pulled out a large repeater from his waistcoat and looked solemnly at its face.

"That explains it," she said impishly. "I knew one of us was ticking, but it was not I."

"We do not have much time, Miss Peach. You and your cohorts have gathered some materials, but we must begin to scour the house for the remaining items that we need." He extended an arm to her. "I believe there is a trunk full of pennywhistles and toy drums in my old room. Mrs. Hannigan has kept it faithfully, just as it was. And should the snow melt and the village urchins join the pantomime, they can make a glorious noise."

"Your old room? I should like to see that." she said. "Where is it?"

"I shall show you," he said. "And as you shared some of your family history with me last night, I shall return the favor."

She took his arm with one hand and waved good-bye to

her companions with the other as Lord Henry led her from the library to the long hall outside it.

"Before we begin—if you could remind me of the names of all of those young women, I would be very much obliged to you, Miss Peach."

"Has no one done so?" she asked, a little surprised.

"No, not formally. I thought I might figure it out for myself eventually, but I have not. I know Fiona, of course, and you—and our charming swan, Amelia FitzRoy. Miss Lander and Miss Crandall—Georgia and Jill, respectively—made my eye patch. That leaves seven."

They proceeded down the hall, observed only by a tweeny who was dusting some of the lesser statues.

"The remaining seven are Miss Penelope Dryfell, Miss Claire Ames, Miss Pamela Vereker, Miss Dorothea Small, Miss Anne Prinny, Miss Hermione Strong, and Miss Laura Inchbald. Can you remember all that?"

"Of course," he said breezily. "They are charming in their way. But none so charming as you."

Susan had thought that his stern demeanor would return—but it had not. Very good—she liked this Henry infinitely better.

Seven

They turned a corner into part of the house which Susan had not seen.

"Where are we now, Lord Henry?"

"Please pay attention." He cleared his throat. "Welcome to the stately home of my ancestors, the dear old dukes."

"You cannot welcome me to it, as I am already here and have been for some time."

"Then consider yourself welcomed twice over, Miss Peach. Now, where was I? Oh yes, the dear old dukes. They were fond of drawing rooms and there are many—too many. You have spent much of your time in the Green Drawing Room and looked into the Yellow, so we shall not bother with those."

She nodded.

"On your left, you may see a portrait in oils of the first duke. It is by Holbein, or someone very like him, perhaps the fellow who mixed his colors."

Susan stared up at the calm visage of someone who bore no resemblance whatsoever to Lord Henry.

"He advised a forgotten young princess on how she might keep her head from being severed from her neck, and was rewarded with a dukedom when she eventually became queen."

"She must have been deeply grateful. A head is a useful thing."

"Indeed it is."

"And how is yours feeling today, Lord Henry?"

"Somewhat better, thank you. But it still aches."

They moved on to other portraits of subsequent dukes, and their smug wives and numerous progeny. There was quite a lot to remember, and Susan sensibly decided not to.

"Might we sit there and catch our breath?" Susan asked, spotting a sunlit nook ahead. A velvet bench had been placed just under a mullioned window for the benefit of the weary traveler through history.

"Certainly."

They passed another maid, who rubbed a soft cloth over the occasional furniture in the hall while humming to herself, and they sat down upon the bench.

"However do they keep up with the dusting?" she whispered.

"They begin at one end of the house, and finish at the other a few weeks later. Then they begin at the beginning again."

"Your Aunt Venetia must be driven to distraction by so much responsibility. She supervises the house, does she not?"

Lord Henry nodded. "She takes it much too seriously. The housekeeper is a capable woman who could be entrusted with most of it, and Mrs. Hannigan is a treasure."

Susan remembered what Fiona had said. "I understand that Venetia has refused to be a prisoner in the kitchen after the fruitcake incident."

"That explains it!" He slapped his thigh and grinned. "I visited her this morning and she was still abed, reading Mary Wollstonecraft on the *Rights of Women,* or some such title— she was busily scribbling in the margins."

"Perhaps she has turned over a new leaf," said Susan.

"I hope so. Or taken up a new cause. She said—oh, what was it?—that 'women must be educated or the chains of ignorance will ne'er be broken.' There was a feverish gleam in her eye. I expect a school for girls will be founded in the near future."

"That is certainly more important than kitchen drudgery, I should think."

She stretched a bit, enjoying the warmth of the sun on her back and Lord Henry's company. His conduct this morning was quite different from yesterday—he seemed unfailingly cheerful, even kind. Had the knock on his head actually done him good?

Susan could not help but think so, though such a remedy was hardly recommended. Perhaps it was the excellent breakfast provided by Mrs. Hannigan—or the long sleep he'd had.

She did not dare to imagine that his sunny mood had anything to do with her.

"Are you quite rested, Miss Peach?"

"Yes—quite." She jumped up.

"Then we shall continue."

They walked on to another portrait gallery, a century or more forward in time. "These are not in order—but allow me to introduce the seventh duke."

This one sported a stiff peruke and a pinched expression.

"He devised much of the plumbing of Hampstead Hall."

She raised an eyebrow. "It does not seem like a noble occupation."

"Yet it is a necessary one. And he enjoyed laying pipe."

Susan had to laugh. "Well, good for him."

He moved along to three small portraits of three identical men with mournful faces, dressed in brocade coats and frothing lace collars.

"These were the triplets. They died of the sniffles within days of each other and the title descended to a first cousin."

"No one dies of the sniffles, Lord Henry." She looked again at the portraits, noting the red-rimmed eyes.

"Well, perhaps it was something else," he said amiably.

"I believe you invented the Sniffling Dukes to make a long story short. Or to hide a scandal. Perhaps they were smugglers—or spies."

A splendid picture of a woman playing a lute caught her eye.

"Ah—that was a scandalous aunt. She was the daughter of an Italian count and his highborn English mistress, and a musical prodigy. But she dared to perform in public and her family disowned her."

"Then why is she here upon the wall?"

Lord Henry shrugged. "Succeeding generations rather liked the painting. She is a beautiful woman, is she not?"

Susan studied it. The scandalous aunt was very beautiful. She could see some resemblance to her in Lord Henry's features, and his dark eyes and hair.

"That was her pianoforte that Miss Givens played so well last night."

Susan had noticed its old-fashioned design and intricate marquetry, but thought it an interesting antique and nothing more. She would have to tell Fiona of its history.

"These are the uncles who went to the American colonies and were never heard from again."

"I understand there are bears."

"One does not want to think of one's uncles being devoured by bears. Perhaps they are still growing pumpkins in Maryland and stealing good farmland from the Indian chiefs."

She took his arm again, as if it were the most natural thing in the world to do so. Lord Henry knew he would be unhappy when this tour ended. He would have to find another way to keep her close to him.

The housekeeper bustled by with her arms full of linens, clinking. He noted the ring of keys attached to her waist—keys that had formerly been worn only by his Aunt Venetia.

"Good morning, my lord. And miss."

"Good morning, Perkins. I see that you are now our chatelaine."

The woman smiled at him over the stack of linen. "Yes. Madame gave me the keys not five minutes ago. Said she had more important things to do than count raisins and annoy the servants."

"Congratulations. You will be sorry."

"How you do go on, sir!" Perkins bustled away, laughing.

Lord Henry patted Miss Peach's hand. "Speaking of the more important things on Aunt Venetia's mind, I sensed yesterday in the carriage that she thought you had designs on me. She has hoped to introduce me to an unpleasant heiress who might be able to afford the upkeep on Hampstead Hall, you know."

"I thought she did not like me," Susan said cautiously. "But I knew nothing of this heiress. What is her name?"

"Miss Curdle. Miss Letitia Curdle. Do not worry—"

Susan started. Had he read her mind? "I was not worried, Lord Henry. You have a perfect right to pursue any woman who takes your fancy." *But let it be me,* she added silently.

"My dear Miss Peach, if Venetia is busy with something new, as she seems to be, she will not interfere with us."

Susan did not reply. *Is he interested in anything more than a fortnight's flirtation?* She could not tell—and she could not allow him to trifle with her. Her fond feelings for him were perilously strong after only twenty-four hours in his company.

She supposed it was due to seeing him in such a vulnerable state last night. Let a man put on a bandage, even as a result of his own clumsiness or lack of caution, and women fluttered round, begging to be of aid.

Resolving inwardly to avoid such sentimental foolishness, she made the mistake of looking up into his dark eyes. And then he kissed her.

Eight

"Come back! Forgive me, Miss Peach!" He watched her positively gallop down the carpeted hall. Had he kissed that badly? She had seemed to like it, very much, as had he.

She yielded to his embrace in the most melting way, closing her beautiful doe eyes, fitting her body to his as if they were made for each other—as he believed they were.

Henry's dreams had been all of her, and all of love. He took that as a sign. He had waited with eagerness to see her in the morning, rising earlier than was his wont, and lingering at the breakfast table until it was clear that she would be late coming down.

When Miss Lander and Miss Crandall had suggested that they make a patch for his eye, he had agreed simply because it gave him a reason to stay with her friends and await her eventual appearance. He now took it off and threw it on the floor.

And he had been delighted to be included in the planning for the "Twelve Days" pantomime for the same reason. He would procure the necessary fauna for this entertainment by any means possible.

Why had she run away?

He had made his move too decisively—and too soon. That was it. Perhaps he ought to ask Fiona for advice on what to do.

No. She might tell the others and all would be lost. He would have to proceed as if nothing had happened, as if his lips had never touched hers, as if he had never held her in his arms—he would have to be Lord Henry Whittaker, the staid and stuffy, once more.

Fiona opened the library door to see Lord Henry standing there, his arms folded across his chest. Gone was the smile he had worn all morning, replaced by a stern compression of his lips.

She waved the fan she held at him, hoping to tickle the smile back.

"I shall be a lady dancing. We have decided to flutter our fans as we step, *one-two-three, one-two-three.* What do you think?"

"A charming idea, I suppose," he said indifferently. "Is Miss Peach dancing with you?"

"No, she will come on earlier with Amelia, as Amelia is nervous about doing seven swans by herself."

"But they are still only two."

"Susan has borrowed a very large mirror."

"Then they will be but four."

Fiona fluttered the fan under his nose. "Do not be so literal, Lord Henry. We do not have enough of anything. But we shall amuse ourselves all the same."

He sneezed.

"Are you catching Venetia's cold?"

"No. That confounded fan of yours is most annoying, Fiona—I mean, Miss Givens."

"Dear me. I see you have traveled back in time to yesterday. You seem as starched as your shirt. Have you quarreled with Miss Peach?"

He stared at her as haughtily as he was able. The knowing twinkle in her green eyes made him want to laugh, if only for the sake of their childhood friendship. "Is she here?"

"You have not answered my question. But no, she is not. She ran in, looking somewhat disheveled and quite pink in the face." *As if she had been thoroughly kissed and liked it very much,* Fiona did not add. "And she ran out again."

"I see," Henry said starchily. "Well, I will leave you gentle ladies to your labors. You may call upon me for any assistance you might require. I shall be in the Yellow Drawing Room, going over the household accounts."

He bowed and withdrew, and Fiona shut the door.

Perhaps Miss Peach was in the kitchen. Not all of the young women had been in the library, and she had mentioned that some of them might bake. If nothing else, Mrs. Hannigan might listen to his woes and prepare a treat for him: the delicious bacon that his aunt thought was not elegant enough to be served at breakfast.

It was now nearly noon and he was hungry again.

Yes. Bacon, bacon, bacon. Just the *thought* of it sizzling in a pan was enough to cheer him up. He could practically taste it now—and he took the stairs that led down to the kitchen two at a time.

Henry found Mrs. Hannigan alone in the kitchen, having a cup of tea at the deal table, Sir Puss purring in her aproned lap.

"Hello! Do not get up. I can see that you are comfortable." He slid into a chair across from her.

It seemed long ago that he had sat at this table with her into the wee hours of the morning, eating Stilton cheese and wheaten bread. In truth, little more than a day had passed. He had been hungry then—and he was hungrier now.

Ginny came into the kitchen, wiping reddened hands

upon the towel tied round her waist. "I have finished the dishes, ma'am. What should I do next?"

Mrs. Hannigan gave Lord Henry a wise look. "I suspect himself is hungry. Ask him what he wants, my girl."

She dropped a clumsy curtsy, but Henry saved her the trouble of asking. "Is there bacon?"

"Yes, sir." Ginny looked to the cook, not at him.

"Fry some, if you please," Mrs. Hannigan said. "Lord Henry has been fond of bacon since he took his first steps."

The girl went into the pantry to find it, followed by Sir Puss, and left them alone for a minute or two.

"And how is your poor head today?"

He slouched a little and draped an arm over the back of the chair, quite at his ease. "Much improved. And my eye is not as swollen. But I seem to be . . . thinking differently."

"I am surprised you can think at all after a punch from Sam. He is a blacksmith, you know."

Lord Henry shook his head. "I didn't. I suppose he makes shoes for our horses."

Mrs. Hannigan nodded. "He does at that."

"Well, see that he continues to do so. I bear him no ill will."

"You are most kind, Lord Henry."

"Do you think so? Not too . . . starchy? Or literal?"

"I am not sure of the meaning of the second word, sir. And starch is for gentlemen's collars. I have never heard it used to describe people. But I know that you are kind."

Ginny returned, holding a frying pan filled with slices cut from a raw slab of meaty bacon. " 'Twill be but a minute, sir."

He nodded and sat up straight again. "Do I seem different to you in any way, Mrs. Hannigan?"

She sipped her tea and regarded him thoughtfully. "No,

Lord Henry. You look exactly the same, except for that eye. And that will fade away without a trace soon enough."

"But ever since—" He stopped just in time. He had wanted to say, *ever since Miss Peach came into this house,* and go on from there, but not in front of Ginny.

"Ever since what?" Mrs. Hannigan inquired.

"I have felt different ever since the approach of Christmas. Something is in the air."

"That would be the snow, sir." Ginny looked up at the high window that illuminated the basement kitchen. "It is coming down again." She took the bacon from the pan and set it on a plate to cool in the middle of the table.

"Thank you, Ginny," said Mrs. Hannigan. "You may go."

The girl nodded and left, followed by Sir Puss, ever in pursuit of a warm lap and a patient female.

"Oh, dear. We shall have no audience for the pantomime and no Christmas dinner for the villagers. For all that Venetia complains about it, the traditional feast is something she likes to do, very much."

The plump cook looked at him curiously. "You never used to care about such things."

"Well, no—and I still do not. But I know that Venetia does. And that is what I mean when I say I feel different."

Mrs. Hannigan smiled. "I suspect that you are in love. I felt like that when I met my Wincent."

"You must miss him dreadfully—Christmas is nearly here."

"I do, sir." Her eyes filled with tears and Lord Henry swore inwardly. He had not intended to upset her but had done exactly that.

"Oh, but that can't be helped. I am happy that your heart belongs to—which one of the girls is it, Henry?" She dabbed away a tear with the corner of her apron, determined to distract herself.

"Ah—*hum.*" Should he tell her? Would she tell Venetia? Did he care? The answers were *yes, no,* and *no.* "Miss Peach."

Her smile returned, with only a few tears around the edges. "That is wonderful news, sir. She is the pick of the litter, if you don't mind a colorful turn of phrase."

"Not at all, Mrs. Hannigan. I am pleased that she meets with your approval."

"Why, she was here just before you came in, and I never knew she was your sweetheart."

He raised an eyebrow. "Ah, I am not sure she knows it yet, Mrs. Hannigan. Or even if she will have me. She ran away when I kissed her."

"A well-bred young lady is taught to be skittish, Lord Henry. You must be patient. She will come round in time."

"Did she stay here long?" He realized he had forgotten all about the bacon and picked up a piece, examining the proportion of fat to lean. It was perfect. He took a bite, and then another.

"Some of the other girls decided to make bread and it had risen too high. She came in to help punch it down. And a right strong punch she gave it, too."

He thought about that and was glad that she had not punched him instead. "They said they would come back when it was 'a-baking.' "

The lyrics of that damned song floated into his head as he ate. Was there any "a-baking" in it? There was not, he decided.

"They were quite covered in flour when they left. Perhaps they went upstairs to change."

Lord Henry decided to look there.

Nine

What with one thing and another, he did not find Miss Peach until the evening. She was sitting in the Green Drawing Room with Fiona, who shot Henry another knowing, decidedly mischievous look.

No doubt Susan had told her all about the unchaperoned tour of Hampstead Hall, and how strangely he had acted. Perhaps she had even mentioned that impetuous kiss.

The object of his affections stared down at the sewing in her lap when he entered. He reminded himself to be strong. Sincere. Anything to keep her from bolting.

Her hands trembled within the gauzy tulle—a swan in the making, certainly.

Henry gazed imploringly at Fiona, willing his old friend to read his mind. *If you would play once more upon the pianoforte—that I might speak softly to Miss Peach—if you would be so kind—dear, thoughtful Miss Givens—*

She got up. "Why, here is Lord Henry. Mayhap I shall play while you two converse."

"Fiona, sit down," Miss Peach said through her teeth.

She sat down—at the pianoforte.

Lord Henry listened as she ran her fingers through a few chords, trilling some nonsense to go with them.

"*Tara-deedle-tara-dumdiddy-dum*— How does that old song go? *Fiddle-faddle-feedle*-something. I cannot remember it."

Miss Peach bit off a thread rather savagely. "Obviously."

He edged over to the sofa where she sat, and lifted the tulle from the most distant cushion to sit down. She eyed him as nervously as if he were a tiger. Fiona played on.

"Please forgive my rash conduct of the morning," he whispered. "I kissed you well, but perhaps not wisely." *There—that sounded suitably restrained.*

She stabbed a needle in and out of the tulle. "Is a wise kiss worth having?" she whispered back.

"What?" He paused as Fiona flipped over a sheet of music. She began to play again—something Germanic, that crashed.

"What do you mean, Miss Peach?"

She heaved a huge sigh as the crashing reached a crescendo.

"I mean that I like to be kissed well, not wisely. And you did just that, as you said. But I hardly know you. Yesterday you seemed reserved to the point of rudeness, and today you are amorous and full of high spirits. Who are you, Lord Henry?"

That was a question that puzzled him most severely. But perhaps Mrs. Hannigan had known the answer.

"Why, I am a man in love. With you." He sighed himself, thoroughly frustrated.

"Prove it."

"Give me time, Miss Peach."

"Would you come to Hertfordshire if there were no other way to see me? I cannot leave my father alone in his old age."

"We will introduce him to Mrs. Hannigan."

"You are avoiding my question. Would you come to Hertfordshire?"

"Yes!"

"Would you keep all your promises?"

"Yes, within reason. The moon and the stars will remain

in the sky no matter how much I would like to give them to you."

"Would you—"

"Miss Peach, I would climb the highest mountain to pick a rose atop it—just for you. I would fight a rhinoceros—just for you. I would do anything for you." He stopped, suddenly realizing that Fiona had stopped too and was laughing hysterically.

"May I set that pretty poem to music, Lord Henry? *The Rose and the Rhinoceros*. How romantic."

"You are devilish, Fiona Givens! How dare you mock my feelings for Miss Peach!"

He looked at Susan. She too was laughing helplessly. "Oh, if you could have seen your face—those sweet words and that black eye. I do believe I love you, Lord Henry."

"This is outrageous—you cannot—*what?*"

Miss Peach endeavored to calm herself. "I said that I love you. And Fiona already knows that I do. She explained many things to me over the course of this very odd day."

He edged slightly nearer to her, avoiding the pincushion and the scissors. "What did she say?"

"That true love sometimes happens very suddenly. But it does not fade away. I hoped for more time, that I might understand you better—and know my own feelings for a certainty. But I cannot keep you at a distance, when you are so dear and so funny and so handsome and kiss so well."

"Thank you," he said, somewhat mollified. He looked at her and then at Fiona. "You will not tell Miss Givens everything I say and do when we are married, will you?"

"Certainly not."

He took Susan in his arms—still laughing—tulle, pins, needle, scissors, and all. Fiona hurriedly left the room, closing the door and standing guard outside. Then Henry kissed her again . . . very thoroughly indeed.

Ten

Venetia took the news of their engagement with an air of resignation. "What shall I tell Miss Curdle, Henry? She will be most disappointed."

"As I have never met that frighteningly rich young lady, she cannot say I broke her heart. You may tell her anything you like."

"I am founding a girls' school. Perhaps she will provide an endowment in perpetuity if I name it after her."

Henry thought about that for a moment. *"The Curdling Academy for the Crème de la Crème.* London mamas will enroll their darling daughters by the score."

The old lady sniffed. "You are being very silly. You have changed since you fell in love with Miss Peach, Henry."

He patted her affectionately. "And all for the better."

"Promise me you will postpone the marriage until your mother and father come back from Constantinople."

"Ah, that is a year away. And I have already obtained the license from the Reverend Lewes."

"Did he like his fruitcake?"

"He did not say."

"Ah, well. I shall never make another. Your mother will like Miss Peach, you know," she added absently.

"I hope so, dear Aunt Venetia. For we are to be married on Christmas Day in the village church."

* * *

The morning of Christmas Eve dawned gray and cold. The snow had melted somewhat but the sky threatened more by nightfall. Would they even be able to get to the little church tomorrow?

For the briefest of moments, Susan longed to be back in her father's cottage in Braughey, as quiet as it was, listening to Dr. Peach turn the pages of his books, lost in contemplation of vanished civilizations.

But the only man she would ever love had asked for her hand—and she had said yes with all her heart. She would leave this house on the morrow in bridal finery borrowed from one of Venetia's trunks, and return to it as Lord Henry's wife.

She moved away from the window and slipped on a robe over her nightgown and a mobcap over her brown hair, not bothering to comb it. For once she had awakened before her friends. There was no sound in the room other than Fiona's gentle breathing in the next bed and Georgia's dreamy murmurs within the curtains of the third.

The door to the suite opened without a creak, for which she was grateful. Susan looked down the hall. If Mrs. Hannigan had set out breakfast, she might slip down and avail herself of the comforting food that good woman provided in such abundance.

She padded down the carpet in thickly felted wool slippers, making no more noise than old Sir Puss. Once inside the breakfast room, she found that she was not alone—the plump cook was bringing out a chafing dish of something that smelled wonderful. A little kitchen maid followed directly behind her with a basket of muffins.

"Ah! Good morning to you, Miss Peach! Ginny, here is the blushing bride in all her splendor!"

Susan really did blush at this wildly inaccurate but pleasing description. "Slippers and mobcap, rather! But good morning to you, Mrs. Hannigan—and Ginny."

"Set the basket on the sideboard, my girl, and give Miss Peach a muffin. Then run along. You are up early, miss," she said kindly. "Nerves, I suppose."

Susan took a seat. "I am calmer than I thought I might be—for a few minutes now and then. Mostly, yes, I am nervous," she said, wrapping her robe tightly about her, though the coziness of the room shut out the dreary landscape outside.

"That is to be expected," said Mrs. Hannigan. "Do you know—oh, perhaps I should not tell you on an empty stomach. Have your tea. Have a muffin."

Susan reached for the teapot and took off the linen cloth that swaddled it to pour herself a cup. She added a drop of milk and took a sip. She nibbled a bit of her muffin. "There. I am properly fortified and ready for anything."

"Well, then. Felix took the cart into the village last night and stopped at the tavern. Them as what we know were in there hoisting pints, as cheerful as you please. He had a pint himself and told one and all that we had no audience and needed extras for the pantomime. They decided they would come, snow or no snow, in case there was a dinner. And they wanted to make amends for Lord Henry's black eye and Venetia's lost fruitcakes."

"None of that was their fault, Mrs. Hannigan. Two bumpkins got into a fight and he was simply in the way."

The cook put her hands on her generous hips. "But no one stopped them."

"There was not time."

"Well, be that as it may, miss. They are coming. Felix instructed the mothers to teach the children that there song—I cannot get it out of my head—and you will have pipers and drummers by the score."

Something outside the window caught Mrs. Hannigan's eye. She walked quickly over to look out and beckoned Susan to do likewise.

"They are here! And that is the hay wain they are riding in! What a sight!"

Susan stood behind her, looking over Mrs. Hannigan's shoulder. She could just see an immense wagon with wooden sides cresting the hill, pulled by a straining team of draft horses.

They stopped at the top. A few small heads popped up over the sides and she heard a faint "Huzzah!"

"Yes. We must awaken the others—and Venetia—and Lord Henry."

"So Venetia will have to give them the traditional dinner after all. But they usually come after Christmas and not before."

"Breakfast first, then rehearsal, then dinner, and then the pantomime with a full cast!"

"Oh, we shall be busy, miss. But I would not miss it for the world!"

She departed to find the other servants and Susan raced back upstairs.

Eleven

Felix ushered the crowd of villagers into the Great Hall at the front of the house, a place some of the younger children had never seen.

They stood in a huddle, looking up at the chandelier and down at the inlaid marble floor. One of the little imps played at hopscotch upon the alternating squares of tile until he was told in a ferocious whisper to stop.

The men took their wool caps off when the cold had left them, turning the brims round and round in their hands. An old woman tugged on the gamekeeper's sleeve. "And where is the breakfast you promised us, hey?"

A door that led into the Great Hall from the kitchen, which had been added to provide a shortcut to the dining room, opened slowly, and stayed open thanks to a large shoe holding it so.

The rest of the unseen being to whom the shoe and the foot inside it belonged stepped through the door. Alfred Pomfret, the biggest footman, was partly concealed by an enormous tray. Upon this was the promised breakfast.

The assembled crowd watched him walk by without saying a word to them—"Haughty as you please," muttered one bystander—though Alfred had been born in the village just as they had.

There was nothing like a double row of brass buttons to give a lowly man a sense of his own worth, thought

Susan. She found the scene, which she was watching from behind a column, most amusing.

A strong arm slipped around her waist and held her tight, and someone nuzzled the nape of her neck.

She would know those lips anywhere, she thought shamelessly. "Henry—not here."

"Why not here? We have as much privacy as we are likely to find all day."

"You must join Venetia at the table, and give healths, and huzzahs three times three, mustn't you?"

"Huzzah, huzzah, huzzah," he whispered very softly against her neck. She clapped a hand over her mouth to stifle a giggle.

"It tickles."

"Do you want me to stop?"

"Not just yet."

The old woman in the shawl brought up the rear of the breakfast parade.

"Well, I suppose I must take my leave of you, dearest." He kissed her hand and jumped down from their hiding place.

The huge footman looked round the Great Hall as he began to close the door, not seeing him at first.

"Ah, there you are, Lord Henry. We didn't want to start without you."

"Thank you, Pomfret."

They went inside together and Lord Henry bowed to the assembled company, who took up both sides of a long, long table. He shielded his eyes against the light coming from the far window—yes, that was his aunt, seemingly a mile off, presiding over the bacon she usually would not allow upon the table.

"Speech, sir! Speech!"

He bowed again.

"A happy Christmas to you all—" he began.

"That were an excellent speech!" There were more comments of this kind as platters were immediately passed and mugs filled by the fast-moving maids and manservants.

"Enjoy your meal, everyone. Mrs. Hannigan has outdone herself, and on rather short notice, too." If truth be told, Susan and her friends and cousins had not only gone without their own breakfasts, they had prepared much of this one.

The hearty fare vanished in an instant, as did gallons of hot tea and small beer for those who wanted it. Replete, the guests leaned back to digest. The old woman, who had seated herself next to Venetia, leaned forward with her elbows on the table and spoke without being spoken to. Actually, she asked a question.

Since it was almost Christmas, Venetia decided to answer it. She picked up a brass bell that had been placed by her glass and rang it vigorously.

"Silence, if you please! Mrs. Rawdon has asked if there will be a pantomime. The answer is yes," she said loudly.

Old Mrs. Rawdon leaned forward once more.

"She has also asked if there will be a dinner. Yes."

Lord Henry was not surprised that a third question was asked, though by this time the guests were not paying attention. Venetia rang the bell again.

"Despite the unfortunate and unavoidable loss of the fruitcakes, which Mrs. Rawdon says were eaten by a wandering donkey who did not live long enough to regret his greed—is that wild tale true, Mrs. Rawdon?"

The old woman nodded sadly. "It were my donkey, is how I know. The whisky killed him stone cold dead."

"I shall buy you a new donkey. How much are they?"

"Oh—a guinea." This bargain having been agreed to, his aunt rang the bell for the final time.

"Despite the loss of the fruitcakes, there will be a Christmas pudding! And brandy sauce!"

Appreciative murmurs ran round the table. "Very good, that!"

Before these honored but no longer expected guests had arrived, Venetia had run to the kitchen and thrown together the last of the currants, raisins, flour, spices, eggs, and sugar, adding an equal measure of minced suet—all with her own hands, as Mrs. Hannigan was simply too busy to do everything.

The result had been rolled up in cheesecloth and was even now steaming in a large kettle, where it would remain for several hours. It was the cannonball to end all cannonballs.

Lord Henry walked about the table, pausing now and then to chat affably with one guest or another. The snow was a popular topic, as was the incident at the tavern. The women clucked over the fading bruise and swelling around his eye, but the men admired it, as if it were a privilege to have your head half knocked off by Sam.

The blacksmith was conspicuous by his absence, Henry noticed.

He made one final conversational round and then borrowed his aunt's bell to get their attention.

"As you know, there is to be a pantomime this afternoon—"

"A pantomime!"

"Yes. If the men who are able could help with the sets and moving the cow—"

"A cow! A real cow!"

Venetia looked at him nervously. "Surely you are joking, Henry. You know what will happen."

"It is a papier-mâché cow, Aunt, for the 'maids a-milking' part. But it is not quite dry and must be carefully moved from where it was made."

"And where was it made, if I may ask?"

"My bedroom."

"I see."

He turned back to the villagers and explained the rest, enlisting the women who could sew to help with the costumes. The children were sent to the Green Drawing Room with their mothers to practice their caroling once more.

Several hours later, the candles were lit in the second-best ballroom and the audience trooped in. Half a Yule log was blazing merrily in the fireplace to warm the room, as a whole one had not fit.

It was a lively crowd: villagers and servants alike had been well fed over the course of the afternoon and drunk their fill of the rest of the small beer.

Susan peeked through a gap in the stage curtain, which very much resembled the draperies that had once adorned the Green Drawing Room. They looked quite handsome decorated with sprigs of red-berried holly and had only incurred a few holes.

The stage itself had been left behind long ago by a dance orchestra, as forfeit payment for the riot that had ensued on the night they played. It had been dragged hence from a distant storeroom by the butler and "every man jack on this damn ship," as he liked to say.

The rows of folding chairs were nearly full and the amateur performers milled about restlessly backstage. It was time to begin.

Swathed in tulle that in no way resembled a swan, Miss Peach stepped out to a burst of applause.

"Welcome to Hampstead Hall, ladies and gentlemen! And now, the premiere performance of—*The Twelve Days of Christmas!*"

The children walked shyly onto the stage and lined up in order of size. The smallest was pushed out by his mother.

"Sing!" she whispered.

"On the first day . . . day of . . . What is it the night of, Mama?"

"Christmas!"

After that, he sang every word perfectly, aided by the other boys and girls, who sang loudly if not well.

The partridge in a pear tree was a great success, bristling with feathers from every hen they had. No one knew it had once been a stuffed owl, least of all Venetia.

"Two turtledoves, three French hens . . ." sang the little boy.

Felix brought out two of his prized pigeons in one bird-cage and three beady-eyed hens in another, clucking madly. The four calling birds were wound up immediately before their stage debut, and all of them worked, opening their beaks with tiny peeps, to the great delight of the audience.

Five golden rings—that was easy, as Henry had said. The smallest girl held up one hand to show them and stepped back into the choir.

The six geese were represented by the croquet balls painted white. The audience fell silent, until a farm lad whispered loudly, "Them is heggs. Six geese a-laying. Heggs."

The little boy sang the seven swans a-swimming onto the stage. Seven young women clad in acres of white tulle flung themselves about to wild applause. Amelia's stellar performance as the Second Swan was particularly noted by a distinguished critic somewhere in the back.

Eight milkmaids with bright pink spots of rouge on their cheeks, wearing pink-checked aprons and billowing skirts, appeared next. The cow did not.

"Eight maids a-milking . . . " sang the boy. *"Eight maids a-milking . . . "*

Half the cow appeared—the back half. Lord Henry stepped on stage. "Ladies and gentlemen, owing to an unfortunate accident, we are not able to present an entire cow."

"But that there is the working end!" shouted a man. "Get on with it!"

The maids got on with it, and ran off, laughing,

"Nine ladies dancing . . ." sang the boy. There was more wild applause as the ladies, formerly swans, appeared without the tulle in their own dresses. They stepped, *one-two-three,* fluttered their fans, *one-two-three,* and scampered off.

"Ten lords a-leaping . . ."

Lord Henry appeared again. "Ladies and gentlemen, owing to a mutiny, we have only one lord. But I shall leap ten times." And he did.

"Eleven pipers piping . . ."

Here the village children came into their own, producing pennywhistles and threatening everyone's sanity.

"Twelve drummers drumming . . ."

The children made even more noise with the toy drums.

Thunderous applause greeted the reprise and the chorus, and there was a standing ovation for the finale. The little boy waved the partridge over his head and its hastily glued feathers began to fall off.

"Isn't that my owl?" Venetia asked Mrs. Rawdon.

"I wouldn't know, ma'am. But it is like no partridge I ever saw."

Lord Henry stepped out and announced a brief intermission. After the audience had refreshed itself with cold tea and peppermints from Susan's cache, they settled down to hear a poem or two recited. Then the children sang "The Holly and the Ivy," very capably indeed, and the little boy read the story of the wonderful night in Bethlehem from a worn Bible. Everyone cried.

* * *

Darkness had fallen by the time the pudding was brought in to the dining room, where everyone had gathered once more. It blazed a strange and brilliant blue that flickered over its round sides and the platter it rested upon. Mrs. Hannigan set it in the middle of the table.

There were rousing cheers, and healths given, and toasts both merry and sincere. Mrs. Hannigan toasted her Wincent in heaven, and was comforted by Lord Henry. Venetia wondered where Lord Henry had been keeping the sherry, which flowed freely.

The pudding was cut into small slices, dosed with brandy sauce from an enormous silver spoon, and dished out on the servants' china. It was quickly gobbled up, though most of the children did not like it, so their parents finished theirs for them. Susan consoled them with the last—the very last—of the lemon drops and peppermints.

By a miracle, the snow had held off. Coats and hats were gathered and put on, and handshakes and stiff hugs exchanged. And there were huzzahs at the very end of it all—three times three.

Just after midnight, the snow began to fall in earnest. Susan and Henry walked out into it, warmly dressed and not minding the cold. He brought her into his arms and let her nestle against his shoulder.

"Shall we always be this happy, Henry?"

"Yes, my love," he whispered, stroking her hair. "And tomorrow is our wedding day."

"We ought to be in bed."

"We shall share one tomorrow night." He held her closer still.

Twelve

The bells rang out on Christmas Day, their peals carrying far across the snowy fields and hedgerows in the clear air.

"We shall be late," Lord Henry growled. "The other carriages are already out of sight."

Venetia waved a gloved hand inside the carriage. "Reverend Lewes will wait."

Susan had stepped out to relieve the carriage of a little weight and watch the men dig out the wheel. She let her bonnet fall back from her head, enjoying the refreshing winter breeze that ruffled her hair, and looked inside the small valise she carried to make sure she had not forgotten her silk shoes and a few other things. She could not imagine being married in boots.

"Is there anything I can do?" she asked.

"Certainly, my darling. If you would but put your slender hand under the carriage and lift it back onto the road, we shall be on our way once more."

"There is no need for sarcasm, Henry. My question was sincere."

"My back shall be sincerely broken at this rate." He and Fred put their shoulders to the body of the carriage and gave a mighty shove.

The wheel moved up an inch and settled back down into the snow.

"Damn and blast!"

"Should I ask Venetia to step down as well?"

Lord Henry wiped the sweat from his brow. "No. Then she will offer idiotic advice and I shall really be angry."

He brushed the snow off a stump and sat down to catch his breath. Fred shielded his eyes against the bright sunlight, looking at an approaching cart and the powerful horse that pulled it so easily through the snow.

"It is the blacksmith."

"Sam?"

"Yes, sir."

"He shall take us to the church."

"But he is going in the opposite direction."

Lord Henry smiled diabolically. "Not anymore."

"I should not want to argue with Sam, sir," Fred said. There was fear in his eyes.

"You will not have to. Give me your bonnet, Susan."

She untied the loose ribbons and handed it to him.

Lord Henry put it on Fred's head and tied the ribbons in a fetching bow. "Get in the carriage and explain to Venetia. And don't look up."

Fred had no other choice but to do as he was told, as Sam was only a few minutes away and would see him instantly if he ran for it across the open fields.

Lord Henry put his hands in the pockets of his greatcoat and whistled nonchalantly as the blacksmith pulled up. The brawny man grew pale when he recognized the carriage—and Lord Henry.

"It is you! I am right sorry about that punch, my lord. I never meant to 'urt you—only Fred, the tosser."

The bonneted head in the carriage dipped low.

"Of course, Sam. I understand. But I was wondering—"

"'Ad a spot o' trouble with the carriage? Here, let me 'elp." Sam jumped down and put his shoulder to the carriage. It rose two inches this time—and sank two inches deeper.

"Oh, dear. Sam, old fellow, as I was saying—I was wondering if you could take us to the church. The carriage is a lost cause. We are to be married today. It will not take long with a horse like yours and we can return for the other members of our party in less than an hour."

Sam hesitated. "Why—you could say I owe you a favor, sir."

"You do indeed, my good man."

"Then I will do it. You and the lady may ride next to me on the box, as the cart is filled with horseshoes and farrier's tools."

"An excellent idea."

And so it was that Miss Susan Peach and Lord Henry Whittaker became husband and wife, with a blacksmith as their witness, and the entire village and most of their friends in attendance. Miss Fiona Givens took detailed mental notes on behalf of Venetia.

The bride wore a veil of tulle that no one saw her take from her valise, and all agreed she looked as lovely as a swan.

ONCE UPON A
CHRISTMAS

Melynda Beth Skinner

For Lammer,
who handed down
her love of words
and elephants
and Christmases,
and
for the family,
who loved her.

One

Stendmore Park, Buxley-on-Isis, England
December 18, 1818

David Stendmore, the Viscount Lord Winter, skidded to a stop in the narrow doorway of the nursery at Stendmore Park. He glared in the direction of the wide, blue-cushioned window seat, where his two daughters sat blinking innocently up at him, their rag dolls poised demurely on their laps.

David wasn't fooled.

"What was that thumping I heard *all the way down in the kitchen?"*

"Nothing, Papa," the girls chimed in unison.

"Humph!" David looked about the large, light-filled room for evidence of mischief. Finding none, he glared down at Rose and Rain and tried to remind himself that his daughters' intent was never malicious. No, they were simply drawn to exploration, as he had been at their age.

Irresistibly drawn.

Incessantly drawn.

Disastrously drawn—and *where was Miss Bull?* It wasn't like her to leave the Hellions alone.

If the viscount's daughters had inherited his taste for adventure, then it was fortunate they'd also inherited his old governess. Miss Bull was the Admiral Nelson of the nursery set. David had put her through her sea trials himself. Poor Miss Bull!

Raking his fingers through his tangled curls, he regarded his daughters with suspicion. They were being attentive and obedient—which meant they were up to mischief. Not that that was unusual. Rose and Rain were *always* knee-deep in mischief. Just like he'd been. As a lad, David had always been at the center of every spot of trouble. Hell, he'd been the cause of it, more often than not.

And no one had any reason to think he'd changed.

Not yet.

"Where *is* our Miss Bull?" he asked evenly.

A look slid between them. "We don't know, Papa," Rose said, looking and sounding much more adult than her nine years should have allowed.

"She was reading a letter—" little Rain began.

"From this morning's post," Rose clarified.

"—an' she gave a cry like this." Rain screeched dramatically, bit her wrist, rolled her eyes into the back of their sockets, and slumped.

"Then she ran out," Rose said.

"Yes, Papa, she ran out. Just like that." Rain, just six, tried to snap her fingers, without success.

"Like that." Rose snapped her own fingers, winning a glare from her little sister. "She probably went to the necessary, Papa. All this excitement, you know," she said in sage tones, leaning close. "And speaking of excitement, should you not be below stairs? Preparing to receive our guests?"

"No," David said, waggling a finger. "I should be below stairs preparing to receive *my* guests. Mine—not *ours*. You two are not to leave this nursery during the house party unless flanked by a regiment of dragoons armed with sharp—"

"Papa!" the sisters chimed in perfect, indignant unison,

though a sudden display of dimples spoiled the intended effect.

"All right!" He held up his palms in mock acquiescence. "I'll garrison the regiment, but for the duration of the war that is my house party, you'll still not to cross this threshold without an adult. There will be no more loud thumping and bumping up here, understand? You two will sit there and wait quietly for Miss Bull's return."

Rose and Rain nodded their solemn acceptance of his edict with too much alacrity.

With their wide-eyed, innocent expressions, their shining brown hair, and their delicate little hands, they looked like charming angels, but the earl knew better. Charming hellions was what they were—though David loved them just the same, God help him. Love them? He shook his head in resignation. He didn't just love them. He adored them.

And he'd been a damned fool to stay away from them so long. A damned fool.

They were his life—which was why this deuced, devilish house party was so important, *and where was Miss-blasted-Bull?*

There was so much to do before his guests arrived tomorrow. He hadn't a moment to spare. He was especially needed in the kitchen, where his undisciplined, untrained staff was sailing along without benefit of rudder, ballast, or keel. If he didn't get down there, he'd have to serve his guests naught but bread and cheese and ale!

David looked about the well-ordered nursery. He didn't see much that could go wrong if he left to attend to the thousand-and-one things that needed his input. Miss Bull, who ran a tight ship, wouldn't be gone long, and the nursery, as always, was battened down for rough weather. The hearth stood cold and empty, with the tinderbox safely locked away in the cabinet—along with the poker, the ink bottles, and anything sharper than a spoon. The Hellions ought to be fine left alone for a few minutes.

And he had to get downstairs. Though he could hardly hide Stendmore Park's strained circumstances from his guests, none but David realized the real danger. If a peer of the realm could not support his title and estate in such a manner that it brought honor to the Crown, the Crown could reabsorb them. It didn't happen often, but it was not unknown—and David was at low tide and on somewhat less than friendly terms with Prinny. He had to secure a hasty loan or two, which was why he'd called the house party.

He had to convince the surrounding gentry that he'd changed.

His children's futures depended upon it.

"You are still glaring, Papa." Rain's expression was full of genuine concern. She was a surprisingly compassionate child, considering her mischievous nature. "What's wrong?"

"My cravat is too tight, that is all." There was no need to worry them. Offering a smile of truce, he tousled Rose's curls, pinched Rain's cheeks, and then he made to leave—but as he turned his back, he thought he saw a look pass between them.

A conspiratorial look, a mischievous look, a look that foretold doom.

David crossed his arms and scowled some more, and their eyes widened, but as he opened his mouth to interrogate them, a flash of blue against the dull blacks and browns of winter outside caught his eye. Someone was crossing the lawn far below—*Miss Bull, perhaps?* Craning his neck, he moved to the window. Sure enough, there she was, heading toward the back of the house. No sense in tempting fate. He'd wait right here in the nursery for her to—

He stilled as he got a better look at the woman. It wasn't Miss Bull. This was a much younger woman, dressed in a stylish gown. She was short, dark, and slender. As she moved closer, he discerned that her gown was dirty and torn, and she carried a small portmanteau and—

And what if she were one of his guests come early?

Shock coursed through him. Her current heading was going to take her sailing right in through a back door that led to the chaos that was his kitchen!

"Bloody hell!" he cried, forgetting where he was.

"I thought hell was supposed to be fiery," Rose said, "not bloody."

Rain wrinkled her nose in disgust, but then a keen look came into her eyes. "Where'd the blood come from, Papa?"

His gaze didn't leave the window as he shook his head violently and held up one hand. "No, no. I did not mean—"

"It comes from fallen angels, I wager," Rose interrupted him. "It's a long way from Heaven to—*down there*," she finished in a whisper-that-was-not-a-whisper. "They must bang themselves up when they fall."

Rain's eye widened. "Do they get scraped knees?"

Rose nodded. "And bloody noses, and bulging eyeballs, and—"

"Enough!" David's head was pounding. "You will wait here for Miss Bull, and you will not cross that threshold."

Rose's eyes narrowed. "What if there is a raging fire, Papa?"

"Or if we cut ourselves?" Rain added.

The woman below still hadn't tacked away from her course.

"Fire and blood are the only exceptions. You see those, and you are free young ladies."

Rose's eyes flicked toward her sister and lit up. "Blood?"

"Yes," David said. "Yours. At least enough to fill a thimble."

"Oh," came the dejected reply.

David again raked his fingers through his hair, tangling them in his unbrushed curls, and sighed. He had a valet who preferred a liquid breakfast, a butler and housekeeper who'd run away to Gretna Green, and now his governess had gone a-roving. Perfect. What was next?

What was next was that the young woman set down her portmanteau and reached for the kitchen door.

"Pray, let her not be one of the guests!" He pivoted and ran, but not before the shy Rain squealed and hid under her bed, while her much more gregarious sister Rose squealed and pressed her nose against the glass.

"Oh! Truly, Papa? Already? I did not fancy any had yet arrived!"

"Away from that window!" he called over his shoulder. "And do not cross this threshold!" He charged through the door and down the hallway.

Two

When David walked into the kitchen affecting a calm he did not feel, she was already seated at the wide, oaken table, attacking a mug of milk and an enormous bowl of porridge.

Cook hastened over to him. "I hope you don't mind, my lord. I know we don't have much to spare, but look at her, the poor mite! She's half starved."

She was a beggar, not a guest! David nearly collapsed in relief.

Though the young woman didn't look especially emaciated to David, she did look hungry. She hadn't even looked up as he'd entered. "I have no objection, of course," he said quietly. "Pray do not disturb her, and keep her bowl and mug filled for as long as she can empty them."

"That I will, and gladly." Cook lowered her voice. "She looks like a lady, if you ask me," she said. "That ain't no calico her gown's made of, my lord, and I—" She gave a shriek. "My sauce!" She rushed to the stove, where a pot had boiled over with white stuff. An unpleasant odor permeated the room. "It's burnt! I'll never get this right!" she cried.

David was inclined to agree. Though he didn't know how to cook fine food, he knew it when he tasted it, and precious little of Cook's food qualified. It could not be helped. There was no time to hire another cook now, and there was no money for it anyway.

Cook wrapped a piece of leather around the pot's handle and shoved it aside in disgust. "Ruined," she said.

"Flour and butter we have plenty of," David said. "Try again."

"Yes, my lord. But before I do, will you take a look at these?" She wiped her hand on her apron and retrieved a sheaf of papers, which she thrust into his hands. "The menus for the party," she said.

"Show them to Miss Channing," David said with a dismissive wave.

"I did, sir. She said I was to show them to you, begging your pardon."

David sighed and took the papers to the window to catch the morning light. Miss Channing, his housekeeper, had been but a downstairs maid barely month ago, an astonishing leap in responsibility. But it could not be helped. Out of necessity half of the now senior members of his staff had been promoted in the same manner.

He'd come home from the sea to find Stendmore Park in chaos. A fever had swept over the countryside, taking many good people.

Including his brother.

David sighed heavily and flipped to the back of the page he was examining. Half of his staff had simply drifted away, not that he blamed them. Wages had gone unpaid and the house unprovisioned for weeks before David had returned. His homecoming meal had been the best the servants of Stendmore Park could offer: dry bread and cheese, washed down with the stable master's good ale. And things weren't much better now, six months later. Everything still balanced on the knife-edge of ruin. Everything.

A movement at the table pulled David's tired eyes from

the menus. A kitchen maid was serving the beggar another measure of porridge. The woman sat with her back straight, her hands folded politely on top of the napkin on her lap, as the maid finished ladling the plump oats into her bowl. Then the beggar inclined her head and murmured her thanks.

David knew instantly from her manner that the young woman was accustomed to being waited upon. *Who are you?* She was perhaps two or three years younger than David himself—call her five-and-twenty? And he did not know of a lady of her years living near Buxley.

Though the conundrum was intriguing and his sympathies aroused, David simply had no time to bother with her.

And yet, as he watched her slender fingers curl around the mug and lift it to her soft, bow-shaped mouth, he found himself setting the menus down upon the wide windowsill and approaching her. Her delicate, white hands looked more accustomed to playing the pianoforte than working or begging. There wasn't a callus on them.

She looked up as he approached, and David bowed. "I am David Stendmore, the Viscount Winter. Welcome to Stendmore Park."

She inclined her head gracefully. "Thank you, my lord."

He expected her to introduce herself, but the seconds ticked by, and she said nothing. "Where are you headed?" he asked.

"I come from the North," she averred. "I have no definite plans."

No definite plans. "Who are you?" he asked, deliberately blunt.

"I am no one." Her words carried no trace of impertinence. It was a fact, clearly stated.

"You used to be someone," he says, "and recently, I reckon. Have you no family?"

Her eyes became hard. "My name is Emily Jones, my

lord, and my past . . . is my own. Do you wish me to leave now?"

He felt an urge to smile at her defiance, but he beat it down. "Your bowl is still full of porridge, Miss Emily Jones. I would not want you to waste it. Pray stay as long as you wish."

She threw him a mischievous smile. "That you cannot mean." There was no shame in her expression, and her eyes were intelligent.

"I daresay Stendmore Park can spare a few bowls of porridge, Miss Jones. You may stay in the barn a day or two if you wish."

She nodded her thanks and smiled. It was a pretty smile, a ladylike smile, and David winced at the thought of a gently brought up young woman sleeping in a barn—his barn!—but he couldn't very well invite a gently brought up young woman to stay under his roof unchaperoned, now, could he? Not without taking the risk of having something go horribly wrong that necessitated marrying the chit!

"My lord?" the cook prompted. "I still need to walk into Buxley Village to place orders."

"Of course," David said, retrieving the menus. "But I am afraid the menus will need some modification before you strike out for the village."

"I knew it," Cook said, dejected. "The menu ain't good enough. I'll never make it as cook."

David shook his head. "You will, because you must. I'll have no more talk of failure. See here . . . is this wine the best we have?"

"Why, yes, my lord. It is the very best we have, of course!"

"Do not serve it, then. Serve something of lesser quality. We do not want our guests to fancy I am extravagant." He tapped the menu. "And the food is adequate, but it is too plain. Plenty of mutton and game, but no beef. Ample cream—but where are the spices and the sweets? We must have a Christmas pudding at the very least. And aren't there other dishes our guests will expect to be served? Special Christmas dishes?"

"Oh, indeed there are, sir. Wassail and frumenty and Christmas pies."

"Sugar plums!" a maid offered.

"Gingered nuts and shortbread," said another, and the rest of the kitchen staff chimed in: "Trifle."

"Twelfth Night Cake!"

"Syllabub!"

"Ooh," breathed Cook. "Heavens, yes! Syllabub. I love syllabub! She clapped her corpulent hands together in delight before dropping them to her sides and knitting her brows. "Though I don't know how to make it." She heaved a sigh. "And that ain't the only trouble." Moving to turn her back to the others, Cook bent closer to David. "None of it can be made without us laying in more sugar and spices, and there ain't enough money for more spices and sugar, my lord. Nor beef."

As soon as she'd bent toward him, all movement in the kitchen had stopped, and though she'd taken care to whisper, Cook's voice had carried to every straining ear. They were awaiting his response.

"Sell some more silver."

Cook flicked a glance at Miss Jones and David flinched. He'd forgotten she was there. He felt an inexplicable jolt of shame as he glanced over at her.

She was staring at him with an expression of sympathy.

A burst of movement rescued him from framing some sort of response as Miss Bull burst into the room. She wasn't in truth old—not even fifty yet—but David had been right and tight she was older than God when he was a lad.

"Oh, Master David!" she cried, waving a letter, her eyes full of panic and tears.

David took her hand. "Why, Miss Bull! What is the matter?"

"It is my mother." She waved the letter some more. "She is frightfully ill." Her eyes implored him.

"You must go to her at once, of course." Turning to a footman, he ordered, "Have the coach brought round. Make haste!"

Miss Bull's expression registered relief. "You always were a good boy," she said. "No matter what they said. I am sorry to leave you at a time like this, my boy, and I shall return as soon as may be."

"Do not trouble yourself, my dear Miss Bull. Take all the time you and your mother need. I pray she will recover fully."

"Poor thing," Cook remarked after Miss Bull was gone. "There ain't no good time to be sick, but Christmastime is the worst."

As murmurs of general assent filled the kitchen, David's eyes met the beggar's. *They?* The question hung in her eyes like a Christmas star, bright and clear, and David hesitated the barest fraction of a second before he allowed his face to break into an easy grin. It was a social ploy, a deflection, a tool he'd used so many times in the past that it came to him now without thinking about it. But it didn't work this time. Miss Jones averted her eyes, yet not before David could discern a deepening of the lines on her forehead.

But he had no time to ponder the significance of her expression, for a tumult erupted suddenly somewhere in the front of the house, and the hallways echoed with the sounds of arrival.

It was a barking, whining, nail-on-marble-and-wood

sound that could only mean one thing: Sir Basil and Lady Griselda!

Their arrival was confirmed a moment later by Mr. Crabbe, his new butler, who'd been but a footman a month ago.

"They ain't supposed to arrive until tomorrow, my lord!" he protested. "I have a copy of the invitation right here in my pocket. I wrote them out myself. It says clearly, 'Saturday, the eighteenth of December.' And that's tomorrow."

A strangled sound escaped David. "Today is *Friday* the eighteenth."

"Oh, dear! I wrote the wrong date, didn't I?"

David nodded.

"And at least some of the guests will be arriving today by mistake!" Poor Mr. Crabbe looked as if he wanted to melt into the flagstone floor, while Cook bounced off of it as she fainted. "Nice try," Crabbe muttered.

The scullery maids dashed for the hartshorn and collided, Sir Basil's seven mongrel dogs came charging into the kitchen—with their master not far behind, judging by the voice booming down the hall—and, outside, a flash of white heralded the fall of a bedsheet rope from the nursery window. The Hellions were attempting to escape!

In one smooth motion, David launched himself into action, snatching a plate of stale buns from a cupboard and rolling the lot down the hall. The dogs dashed after the things, snarling and shoving, effectively blocking Sir Basil's progress. "Dash around front and divert Sir Basil and Lady Griselda's attention!" he ordered Mr. Crabbe, and the young man rushed off to comply.

David ran out the back door. *"What* are you doing?" he shouted up at the nursery window.

"We're coming outside to play," came a small voice.

"And what did I tell you about leaving the nursery?"

"You told us not to cross the threshold."

"Stay right there!" Raking his hand through his errant hair, David dashed back into the kitchen. "Where is Rachel?" he demanded of the staff, referring to a kitchen maid. *She* could watch the children. She was particularly large and disconcertingly burly.

Cook grinned. "She's helpin' Young Tom cut the Yule log, sir."

"The Yule log!" David rolled his eyes. It was bad enough that he had to press undergardeners into service as footmen. Now he had serving maids out cutting timber. "Remind me to pay her an extra week's wage—when I can afford it," he added under his breath.

"Papa?" Rain called faintly from the window.

"What!"

"Are you sure we cannot climb down just once? We'll climb right back up again."

"You are not to come through that window! Or any other window," he added. "Or the chimney. Disassemble that rope and make up your beds immediately!" He turned to the staff with a feeling of mounting desperation. "Can any of you tie knots?"

"Aye," said one of the scullery maids. "I can." She wasn't a timid young waif. She looked strong and even a little mean.

"Then you'll do."

"For what, my lord?"

"You are promoted to nursemaid until Miss Bull returns. All you have to do is watch my daughters and see they do not find trouble."

A happy smile blossomed over the maid's face, but Cook blustered.

"No, no! Begging your pardon, my lord, but you can't take Betsy! I've only got two scullery maids as it is. If you take her, there'll be no one to wash up. What about the china and the crystal and the pots and the silver?"

A loud thump emanated from the open nursery window. David asked Cook, "Is there no other help available?"

"None, my lord. Mr. Crabbe, Miss Channing, and I have all scoured the countryside three miles 'round. There are none who will take a position here with no wages forthcoming and—er . . . and all."

David sighed. *And all,* indeed!

Stendmore Park barely had enough to feed its staff, and the fare was only barely edible, from time to time. Even the beggars had stopped coming to the back door. All except for the young lady thoughtfully chewing on her crust and watching him with unconcealed curiosity.

An even louder thump and a crashing sound rent the air. "Nothing broke!" chimed two little-girl voices.

The butler scurried into the kitchen, all seven dogs in his wake. "Sorry, my lord, but Sir Basil insists upon seeing you straightaway!"

"I say!" a booming voice echoed down the hall. It was Sir Basil! "Friends such as we do not stand on ceremony!"

David had known good Sir Basil since he was a boy. He and his lady wife lived in the next village, and David had been hard-pressed to avoid receiving them thus far. It had been rude of him, but it had also been unavoidable. He'd known the first night he'd come home what he'd have to do to resurrect Stendmore Park.

"Where is the viscount?" Sir Basil called. "Deuced fine of him to invite us to the house party. Deuced fine! Where is he? Want to thank him and congratulate him on his homecoming. First rate, first rate!"

The voice was growing louder.

David raked his hand through his hair—and then his eyes lit upon the beggar once more. She had most of her face hidden behind an ancient, tattered copy of *La Belle Something-or-Other.*

"You there, Miss Jones!"

Her eyes popped over the top of the magazine. "Me?"

"Yes. You have no place to stay." It was a statement, not a question. "Have you employment?"

"None."

"Good. I need a temporary governess. You are hired." He turned to Mr. Crabbe. "See that she's shown to the nursery," he said as a third loud thump reverberated through the house. "Quickly," he added, and out he charged. "Sir Basil!" his voice rang down the hall. "How good to see you!"

The kitchen staff quickly turned back to their work, and Emily, the new governess, was struck by the panic in their movements. What was going on here?

"Come on, then." The butler—Mr. Crabbe, was it?— motioned to Emily impatiently. "Let us find a maid."

What was she to do now? Become an impromptu governess? What choice did she have? *None,* came the answer. Well, then . . . she supposed she was a governess. *A governess!* Perhaps the duke wouldn't want her now that she'd been *employed!* Putting down the ladies' magazine, she smiled.

Everything was going to be fine. Not that she'd ever had any real doubt it wouldn't be—though this morning had stretched the boundaries of that faith. She'd been hungry and cold and tired. But she'd told herself the night was always darkest just before the dawn, and she had never given up hope. It just wasn't in her nature.

Retrieving her small portmanteau from outside the kitchen door, she scurried after the short butler and through the winding halls of Stendmore Park, being careful to avert her face from open doorways. Sir Basil and his lady were old, to be sure, but their eyesight was keen, and their minds were keener. They were a merry pair, a frequent addition to the ballrooms of London, and goodness knew Emily had been seen there often enough herself of late. It would not be at all the thing to be recognized, which they surely would, should the three of them come face-to-face—even as dirty and unkempt as Emily was. She would just have to stay out of sight, which shouldn't be too difficult, she reasoned, seeing as she was but a country governess. She would not be expected to dine with the family, not during a Christmas house party, at any rate.

She smiled. Everything would be fine. Everything was perfect.

Like a circus acrobat, she'd leapt into the air, and a net had appeared!

There was just one tiny problem—well, one rather largish problem, truth to tell, but that problem was stashed out in the barn, and the stable master had already offered to help her to keep it out of sight.

Three

It hadn't been hard to convince the stable master to help her, for the good man dearly loved animals, and the chance to care for a poor, mistreated baby elephant for a half-hour or so had proved too much for him to resist. Emily was a good judge of character, and she'd have bet her last guinea—if she hadn't already spent it—that he wouldn't balk too much about having to billet the elephant in the stable for a week or so, just until the real governess returned.

"Bantlings!" Gertie, a very young maid, called as they entered the nursery. "Miss Rose, Miss Rain, this is your new governess, Miss . . ." She turned to Emily. "Pardon me, miss. What did you say your name was?"

"Our new governess?" the taller girl asked, her eyes round.

"New governess!" the younger one echoed. "Bully is dismissed?"

Bully?! Emily shook her head. "It isn't like that," she began—but her sentence was drowned out by the cheering, whooping, squealing dance of two smiling, shouting little girls.

"They're heartbroken," Gertie remarked dryly.

"I am only here temporarily!" Emily cried, raising her voice to a pitch designed to carry. It worked. Both girls stilled. "I shall only be here until 'Miss Bully' returns."

Both girls giggled and covered their mouths, and then the eldest asked, "When will that be?"

"It is uncertain. Her mother is ill and she has traveled to be with her. I could be here a few days or a few weeks."

The girls looked at each other and grinned. "Weeks!" both shouted. Their eyes shone, and Emily wondered why. Miss Bull hadn't seemed the sort of dragon to inspire such disloyalty. In fact, downstairs in the kitchen, she'd seemed to possess an almost motherly tenderness for the girls' father. So why did his daughters despise her so much?

Emily looked about the room. It was a large, well-appointed space with tall, bright windows, thick carpets, and good, solid furnishings. Nothing amiss there. But, as she surveyed her surroundings, it suddenly occurred to her that it wasn't the sort of room one would expect housed children.

Where were the drawings? The birds' nests? The sea shells? Where were the toys? The storybooks? The dried-up old daisy chains?

Where was the mess?

"My," Emily said, "how tidy everything is!"

Rose and Rain slid each other a look. "Do you like things to be tidy?" Rose asked, her face wary.

"Well . . . yes, but this . . ." Emily began. Clasping her hands behind her back, she walked slowly along a row of bookcases, her back straight, trying to look like an officer surveying his troops. Down at the end of the bookcase, she ran one finger across its top and examined the dust she found there. "It is not as clean as I would wish . . ."

Behind her, she heard the girls groan.

"And," she said, "it is entirely too tidy."

"What?" exclaimed the maid.

"Yes." Emily turned. "I detest tidy nurseries. The neater they are, the less learning takes place." She turned to the girls. "It is clear your minds have been idle. I want you to get busy. Create a mess. At once!"

"In truth?"

"Do you mean it?"

"I mean what I say. Go forth and play. I want to see several toys scattered about, several storybooks out on the table, and several pictures drawn by the time I return."

Rain clapped her hands excitedly. "I like her!"

Rose wasn't listening. She'd made a dash for the bookshelf.

"Uh . . . where are you going?" the maid asked nervously.

"With you," Emily said, watching the girls with a satisfied smile on her face. "You are going to show me to my bedchamber."

The maid threw a baleful look in the girls' direction. "Do you fancy leaving them alone is wise?"

Emily smiled. "Not to worry, Gertie. Look at them."

The girls were already hard at work, both silent, with looks of intense concentration on their faces. It was obvious Miss Bull was a stern and unforgiving taskmaster. One look at the austere nursery had told Emily the sort of life these little girls led. Much too restrictive. "I expect they shall be too busy playing to make mischief. My chamber, if you please."

The maid lifted one eyebrow and shrugged, a gesture that clearly said, *So be it. It is on your head, not mine!* "Right through this connecting door, miss." She led the way into one of the unused rooms. "Afraid it's quite small."

"No matter," Emily said, following Gertie into the sparsely furnished chamber. "It is a vast improvement over what I have been used to."

It was true. For most of a month Emily had been sleeping at inns, farmhouses, crofters' cottages, and, after her money had run out a few days ago, barns or haystacks. To her, the well-appointed room looked heavenly. It held a sturdy bed with soft green hangings, a dressing table, a small sofa sandwiched between the window and the hearth, and a wardrobe—not that she had much to put into it. Emily placed her portmanteau on the counterpane and began to open it.

"Here, let me take that," Gertie said and began to unpack for her, clucking at the condition of Emily's two spare gowns and other things as she took them out of the portmanteau. Emily winced in embarrassment. Her clothes hadn't been properly laundered in a fortnight.

Before Gertie finished the job, a second maid came into the room with an enormous armload of clothing.

"The master had these sent up for you, miss. I took it upon myself to order you hot water brought up. You'll have it in a bit."

She left, and Gertie began to hang the gowns in the wardrobe. "I daresay," she remarked, looking Emily up and down, "these should fit just about right. All but *certain* places, but those can be taken in. Or plumped up a bit, sneaky-like, if you take my meaning."

It was an indelicate observation, to say the least, and Emily turned away to hide a smile. Lord Winter's staff was raw, indeed. This maid was young and untrained, but she was pleasant enough, and Emily decided she liked her.

"These gowns are lovely," Emily remarked. "But whose are they?"

A pained look appeared on the little maid's face. "I hope you won't take no offense, ma'am. They belonged to his lordship's wife. His dead wife," she clarified.

"Ah." Emily should have known. News of the infamous David *Spend*more had been all the talk in London six months earlier. But a rakehell viscount wasn't a proper subject for unmarried young ladies, apparently, so Emily didn't know much detail. She'd heard wild rumors, but all she knew for certain was that he was a widower who'd inherited his title upon his brother's death and returned from somewhere after a long absence—the army, was it?—and that he'd earned himself a reputation as a rakehell before that.

"Will Lord Winter not find the sight of the clothes disturbing?" she asked the maid.

"No . . . they say his lordship hardly ever saw his wife."

"Never?"

"Well, twice, at least." Gertie grinned. "Just long enough to get the girls, and then off he went, apparently."

"He served in the army, did he not?"

Gertie shook her head. "The navy. But not before he cut quite a swath through London, I hear tell." She looked around and lowered her voice, warming to the subject. "They say he was a very naughty lad there in London." She waggled her eyebrows.

"Oh." Emily said, suddenly wondering if perhaps she shouldn't have encouraged Gertie. But it was too late, and on Gertie went.

"Must have vexed his parents," the maid said. "Right cold fish."

"Mmm."

"Misers, they were. Went way beyond frugal. Didn't believe in boisterous carryings-on because that always led to spending money. No parties, no holiday feasts, no Boxing Day. And when their boys came along, they even stamped out music and dancing! The poor mites—they weren't allowed no high jinks at all. Why, I hear they didn't even burn a Yule log nor hang mistletoe at Christmas! And I believe it, for the kitchen don't even have a pudding pot!"

"Oh dear!" Emily said, forgetting she wasn't interested.

"Miss Bull was their governess, too, though she's a warmer sort than their parents must have been. She don't put up with anything nonsensical, though."

Emily nodded. She knew how that was. Her own governess was that way as well. And her parents. "When parents hold the reins too tight, the children pull at the bit," she said.

"Aye." Gertie nodded. "That's so."

"I suppose Lord Winter always was a wild one, then?"

"Oh, no, I don't fancy so, miss. It's said both lads tried hard to please their parents—though young Master David was always up to some mischief, Miss Bull says. He never did manage to curry favor as did Master Robert."

A pair of footmen came in bearing a small metal washtub and buckets of steaming water, which Gertie directed them to place on the hearth as she lit the fire. Closing the door after they left, she helped Emily undress and bathe.

"Not that being their favorite did Master Robert any good in the long run," she said out of the blue, as though their conversation had not been interrupted.

"What happened with him?" Emily asked, no longer even attempting to feign disinterest. She found she liked being a governess. A governess could ask questions and expect to get answers, it seemed.

"He rebelled," Gertie said. "Both of the lads did, though Robert was first. It was fast horses and even faster emptying of bottles for him. But Master David still tried to be a good boy—for a while."

"And then what?"

"Well, after a turn, he learned what was intended for him. He was the spare, not the heir, you see, and they expected to bundle him off to Northumberland or some such outlandish place where a cousin o' theirs had a living to bestow. I guess Master David was to take it and be a country parson. But he took the legacy left him by his gaffer and hied off to London instead. Threw over his traces spectacular-like. Squandered the lot, they say, on all manner of vices. Had himself a fine time! And when the money was gone, he up and joined the navy to displease his father and married beneath him to displease his mother. Stopped home only long enough to deposit his wife here before he went to sea."

"What was she like?"

"The missus?" The maid smiled. "Quiet. Shy. A timid little thing, but pleasant enough. No family whatsoever. He found her somewhere in London." She lowered her voice to a whisper. "In a bawdy house!"

Emily looked down at her hands and changed the subject. "Ah . . . wasn't she unhappy to be left alone here?"

"There are some who say she didn't mind," Gertie whispered. "Some say she and Master Robert fell in love." She clamped her lips together for emphasis before continuing. "But she died of childbed fever right after Miss Rain was born. There, now! You're all clean. How about choosing a dress? I dare say this one will do," Gertie said without waiting for a response from Emily. "You'll look fine in it." She held up a gown with a white, lace-trimmed bodice and bright blue skirts. "There's even a shawl to match, I think," she said, sorting through the other clothes. "Yes. Here it is."

Emily laid the shawl on the bed and began to dress. It felt strange wearing another woman's clothes, but they were fresh and clean, and, again, it was an enormous improvement over what she'd had.

Once more, things were working out just right.

"How long has Lord Winter been home?" she asked.

"Oh . . . six months, give or take. But you're making me get ahead of myself. There's more to the story. The influenza struck the countryside the summer after the girls' mama died. That was nigh on two years ago. I was but thirteen, which worried my own mama something fierce, thirteen being an unlucky number and all. Yet I was spared where a couple dozen others weren't, so I can't see as how it's all that unlucky, can you?"

Emily shook her head.

"Stendmore Park lost close on a dozen, including the old viscount and his lady. And the place never recovered, not with Master Robert quietly drinking himself to death." She clucked her tongue. "It was a sad state of affairs, and no mistake. I'm glad I wasn't old enough to be working up here, then. Wages unpaid and cellars bare. And none hereabouts knew what to think when the new Lord Winter come. We didn't know if we was in the frying pan or the fire, if you take my meaning. He was so Friday-faced."

She shuddered.

"They say he came back changed from the war. He's grim-like and cold most of the time. Like his parents, I reckon."

She worked on Emily's hair for a few moments, before saying, "They say the apple don't fall far from the tree, and I guess that's so. Still and all, he seems to care what goes on hereabouts. He's raised a good many of us up in our positions, when he might have called in more-experienced help, and everybody knows he's putting things to rights as much as he can. Still not paying wages, but we're all fed. Betwixt us, I fancy he'd have left the place to rot if it weren't for Wild and Willful."

"Who?"

"His little 'uns. Rose and Rain. Uncouth little things, ain't they? Not that it's their fault, mind you."

"Are they . . . are they unkind?"

"No, just high-spirited. Like him when he was a boy, I hear tell. Now, then, don't you look lovely?" She turned Emily around to peer in the looking glass.

Emily hardly recognized herself. She looked like a governess, for heaven's sake! Her mother and father would be mortified. *Good!*

"Well, if you won't be needing anything more from me, miss, I'd best be getting downstairs."

"Thank you, Gertie. I am certain I shall bump along just fine."

"It's the bumps I'm worried about, miss." The little maid nodded in the direction of the nursery, winked, and left.

As Emily put on her shawl and stockings and shoes, she thought about what she'd learned of the Viscount Winter. *When parents hold the reins too tight, the children pull at the bit.* She didn't doubt that's what had happened to Lord Winter. The more his parents had tightened their hold on him, the more he'd struggled. Eventually, he'd bucked and reared and wildly galloped off toward Ruination.

She thought about the austere nursery. Was he now doing the same thing to his own children?

A peek into the nursery told her they were still intently busy, one curled up with a book on the window seat, and another happily playing with her doll among a riot of wood blocks. Emily smiled. There was nothing to being a governess. It was easy. All one had to do was understand children, and Emily had four younger sisters.

Gathering her shawl about her, she stole past the children and out the nursery door on her way to the stables. It would take only a few moments to explain the situation to the stable master. She'd be gone no more than five minutes. All would be well.

Down at the stables, Mr. Sneed was pretending to be hard at work on a new harness, but Emily saw that he had moved his worktable to the far end of the barn, next to the stall where the baby elephant was hidden, and that he wasn't looking at the harness at all, but into the stall, a wide grin on his face.

"Hullo!" he called when he saw Emily approach. "You've been away a while. Must have had a grand meal!"

"Indeed," she replied with a smile, and she explained

about her new position as temporary governess. "And so," she concluded, "if it pleases you, I will accept formally the next time I see the viscount."

"You ain't already accepted the position?"

She looked cautiously about them.

"There ain't no one around to hear us," the old man said, guessing her concern. "I set the lot of 'em to other tasks."

She nodded. "I needed to speak with you first, for I cannot be the children's governess and the elephant's caretaker all at once. I shall have to ask you to care for her until Miss Bull returns and I leave here."

"Where will you go? What will you do with her?" He hooked a thumb toward the elephant.

She bit her lip. "I do not know," she admitted. "I thought I might find a way to send her back to India or Ceylon. Or perhaps I will discover another menagerie or circus that will take her."

"Aw . . . no, miss! Not another menagerie! What makes you fancy the next will treat that little baby any better than the last one did? You just can't!"

"She is an elephant, Mr. Sneed. I spent everything I had to acquire her, and now I cannot afford to feed her, much less to send her back to her probable birthplace. But if I cannot, then I will not have a choice. I can hardly keep her in—" She'd almost said London! "I can hardly keep her in your barn forever. Which brings me to another matter. If your master discovers her here without his permission—"

"Now, don't you worry none about that. He's not going to find out about it, busy as he is just now."

"Unless I tell him."

"Tell him?" A little-girl voice cried from behind her. "You mustn't tell him!"

"Rose!" Emily whirled around. "Go back to the nursery at once!"

"But we already know about the elephant."

"We were listening," Rain explained helpfully. "May we see the baby?"

"Please?" Rose pleaded.

"Yes, please?"

Emily put her hand to her suddenly pounding forehead. "Now I *must* tell him!"

"No, you don't," Mr. Sneed said. "If you're worried about Wild and Willful here spilling the beans, think no more on it. Little as they are, they know how to keep secrets."

"You mustn't tell him," Rose said. "Papa will be upset. Baby elephants are fun—at least I fancy they are, *since you haven't even let me see one, yet!*" She glared. "And Papa doesn't like fun."

"He'd be cross," Rain agreed.

"They're right," Mr. Sneed said. "If you tell him, he'll be vexed—especially now, during his house party. Why trouble him with it? I'll be up in the boughs happy to keep our little baby out here in the barn. And if his lordship discovers she's here . . . why, you can cross that bridge when you come to it. What can he do, dismiss you?"

"No, but he could dismiss *you*."

The old man smiled. "He could, but he won't. This ain't the first time I kept something hidden in my barn. The master ain't always been such a high stickler, an' I used to keep secrets for him when he was a lad. Brought me everything from baby ducks to hedgehogs. One time, he brought home a fox he'd rescued from his father's hunt!" His eyes twinkled. "No, he won't be dismissing old Mr. Sneed. Best not tell."

Emily considered a moment, while three sets of eyes silently implored her. She sighed. "You know him better than I. Very well. I shall not tell him."

All three gave a joyful whoop.

Mr. Sneed patted Emily's head as though she were a child. "Let's go in and see our baby."

Four

The next day dawned clear and fine, and Emily spent much of it outside with her charges, exploring—something they hadn't been allowed to do before. Emily let them choose where to go and simply followed, enjoying their delighted shrieks and giggles of discovery. They cavorted with Sir Basil's dogs and splashed their feet in the icy brook. With no flowers available, Emily showed them how to make daisy chains using ivy, and both children wore their green crowns throughout the day. They took them off only at luncheon, hiding them in the kitchen garden before going inside for the meal. They didn't want their papa to see them.

"Why not?" Emily asked. "They are quite lovely."

Rain's little face bunched up. "We never show Papa nonsensical things."

"Well, *I* do not think they are nonsensical," Emily declared, and outside she marched to retrieve the crowns. Back inside, she placed them on the girls' heads, so that everyone in the kitchen could admire them, and admire them they did—vocally, and with much enthusiasm.

They ended up eating the meal right there in the kitchen, a circumstance that delighted Emily. Meals in her parents' house were staid affairs, but the kitchen table at Stendmore Park was full of people laughing and chatting, and Emily had never attended such a lively and pleasant meal. It was good to be a governess!

Cook spoke to Emily when she went to refill her own teacup. "It was fine to see the little moppets outside on a fine day like today. Miss Bull keeps them inside most of the time, and they never get to run around making crowns and such." She smiled at the girls. "And they ain't misbehaving at all! You must have run all the steam out of them."

"No, no," Emily protested, "they just need somewhere to focus their energy."

"Well, good for you, I say. I was sure when his lordship hired you yesterday, you'd be eaten alive." She chuckled. "I'm that glad to see you're in one piece."

"Thank you," Emily smiled. "I shall endeavor to keep me that way."

Though she would have wished otherwise, luncheon did not last long. More guests had arrived and the kitchen was a hive of activity. Emily and the children helped by getting out of the way.

Three o'clock found them outside in the barren winter garden, skipping colored stones across the small blue reflecting pond there and listening to Emily tell stories.

She had discovered they were fascinated with anything having to do with Christmas, which, up until now, had been all but ignored at Stendmore Park.

When the staff had seen the crowns of green upon the girls' heads, they had remarked that Lord Winter had ordered the house to be filled with green stuff on Christmas Eve, six days away. Everyone was delighted at the prospect, and already pots and pots of fragrant fir, ivy, holly, bay, and rosemary stood at the ready.

"Why can we not bring the green stuff inside now?" Rose begged.

"It is considered unlucky to bring the greenery into the house before Christmas Eve," Emily answered.

"Do you fancy Papa will eat some of the Christmas pudding?" Rain asked dreamily.

"He did order it himself," Emily said, though she'd wondered at the same thing. If the apple didn't fall far from the tree, then why was Lord Winter making plans to celebrate Christmas so lavishly? She'd seen yesterday that he didn't even know what sort of dishes were traditionally served at Christmastime. What had changed his mind?

She supposed it was the house party.

"Papa has been awfully cross ever since he decided to have the house party," Rose said skeptically. "Maybe he won't let us have any pudding."

"Yes, maybe it's only for the guests," Rain speculated gloomily.

"Yes," Rose said, "Grandmama and Grandpapa didn't like Christmas at all. They called it 'fancy frippery' "—she lowered her voice and looked around—"and the servants say he's just like them."

"Nonsense," Emily said. "If he's just like them, then why is he holding the house party at all? Did your grandparents ever hold house parties?"

Both girls shook their heads.

"Well, then. Since this is the first Christmas you have spent with your father, perhaps you should not be so quick to foretell doom. Heavens, you shall probably have two portions of pudding, for the servants will be having their own down in the kitchen, and I am right and tight you shall be welcome to some of that. In fact, I know of a certain governess who will make sure of it. And you shall have other things as well: Christmas pie and—"

Rain's eyes grew big. "Christmas pie? What is that?"

Emily smiled. "It is delicious, that's what it is."

"What else will there be?" Rose asked, and Emily went through a catalog of all the traditional dishes. "And there will be a Yule log, and we shall hang greenery on Christmas Eve and play games and sing and—oh, girls, you shall have a wonderful time!"

They talked about it in minute detail for the next hour. The sisters were pitifully excited about a simple Yule log. They'd never had one. They were delighted when Emily told them that the Christmas pudding would have special favors inside. And the idea of mistletoe and stolen kisses had them giggling and rolling on the grass.

Emily let them be.

Though she had known them only for a day, she was certain she understood them. They were rebellious simply because they'd been under such strict control all their lives. No Yule log, no green stuff, not even so much as a plum pudding! These poor children had been deprived. If they were treated that way at Christmas, she shuddered to think how the rest of the year must have gone.

Well Christmas was only a week away, and Miss Bull was unlikely to return before then, so Emily had a chance to correct past injustices for the girls this Christmas.

And she'd decided something else, as well.

She'd thought that once this adventure was over, she would never find herself playing the part of governess again. But the past day had been so pleasant that an idea had crept into her mind: she could be a governess for as long as she wanted—or needed—to be. But first, she'd have to ask Lord Winter for a reference, and that meant that she had to do a good job. She was going to have to teach the girls something, yet she was certain that if she marched them up to the schoolroom, they would be vastly resistant to the idea.

Therefore, she would begin to teach them right here where they were, outside, and she'd let marching up to the schoolroom be their idea. It was a brilliant plan, and she smiled in anticipated triumph.

Being a governess was easy. Everything was going to be fine.

Gathering them close atop her large shawl, they basked in

the warm sunshine as Emily told them an old story she'd heard from her nurse, years and years before. It was a great favorite of hers, one she loved to tell her little sisters. And, like her sisters, Rose and Rain listened raptly.

"And so," Emily ended the story, "just at the stroke of midnight on Christmas Eve, if you listen closely, you can hear the animals talk."

"What do they say?" Rose asked in wonder.

"Oh," Emily answered, "anything that comes to mind."

"Have you ever heard them speak?"

Emily smiled, for she'd been waiting for that question. "Of course I have."

"What did they say to you?" Rain asked, her eyes full of curiosity.

"Yes, yes! What did they say?"

"I will tell you," Emily said, "after you tell me."

They threw her questioning looks. "What do you mean?" Rain asked.

"I mean that I have been telling you stories all day, and you have told me none in return. I wish to hear a story. I want you to tell me the story of *What the Animals Said to Miss Jones*. But you must write your stories down before sharing them. You will write them down in English, Rain— and Rose, you will write them down in French. And when you are finished, you will read them to the staff."

"In the kitchen?" Rain asked.

"Can I read mine to the servants myself?" Rose's eyes were shining.

"No!" The voice sliced through the air just behind them.

"Lord Winter!"

"Papa!" the girls exclaimed.

"I was just telling the story of the animals talking on—"

"Yes. I heard," he said with a frown. "What are you doing?" he asked Emily.

"Run along, children, and play down by the pond. Go practice skipping stones as I showed you earlier."

The governess turned to face David. He hadn't realized how short of stature she was. The top of her head barely reached his shoulder.

"I told you. I am teaching the children," she said evenly. "What does it look like I am doing?"

David almost smiled. She was bold and spirited, qualities he admired, but they would not help her in her capacity as a servant. Under other circumstances, those same qualities would have helped her cut a fine dash in the ballrooms of London. But in the vast majority of households they would get her dismissed. For her own sake, he needed to make her understand that before she left Stendmore Park.

"Teaching them? Why?"

"I am their governess," she answered.

"Only temporarily," he said. "I do not expect you to perform the duties of a true governess. I expect you to be more of a . . . a keeper."

"Ah . . ." She nodded. "I see . . . like the keeper of a lion, an ape, or—"

"Or any other wild animal you can name. Yes."

A smile burst forth upon her face, and David was struck by the sudden beauty of it. Her eyes seemed to shine with a merry light all their own, and he found himself smiling back in spite of his irritation a moment earlier.

"I know what your expectations are, but I hope you will not mind if I attempt to conduct myself as a proper governess would. If I perform my duties well, you may be willing to give me a reference for a similar position elsewhere."

"Are you always so bold?" he asked.

"I am. Does that displease you?"

He smiled again. "On the contrary. I prefer it." And he did. "Some people would call such plain speaking a virtue, Miss

Jones. If more people asked and answered questions truthfully, much strife would be avoided in this world."

She held his gaze as he thought about her request. He could see no harm in it. She was clearly an intelligent lady of good breeding—and he had to admit that he was pleased with her performance thus far. An entire day had gone by without disaster.

"Carry on," he said and turned to go. "Although," he paused, "a proper governess would focus the attention of her charges upon their lessons, not upon play. Upon reality, rather than upon fantasy. Especially these children. I know them well, and it takes little provocation for them to plunge into abandon."

"Abandon?" she asked, her expression bemused.

"My daughters are infamous for their rambunctious behavior."

"Do you mean that they are playful?"

"Call it what you will."

Suddenly, inexplicably, her face folded into an expression of irritation. "You seem to equate playfulness with evil, my lord. They are children. They need to play."

David flicked a glance over at the Hellions. They weren't playing as she'd directed them to but standing still, staring at them from a distance. They were probably trying to catch a word on the breeze or read lips. "It seems to me they have had quite enough play for one day."

"It seems to me they have had too little."

"They are my children," he countered, "and they need to learn responsibility. Miss Jones, are you aware that everyone within five miles of Stendmore Park calls my children Wild and Willful instead of Rose and Rain?"

It was true. David had discovered that fact a few days after he'd come home, and he'd been amused, even prideful—until he'd heard the whispers.

Wild and Willful—just like their father. No good will come of them.

He hadn't paid much mind to such talk at first, but the seeds were sown, and David had begun to think about them. While his parents were alive, Stendmore Park had prospered, but under his brother's care, it had withered and all but died. Six months of David's labor from sunup to sundown hadn't been able to bring it back to life. He hadn't the knowledge. And why? Because he'd hied off to London before he could learn any of it. Now he needed to hire a steward to help him and couldn't. And why? Because he didn't have enough money. And he didn't have enough money because he'd been undisciplined and irresponsible. He'd squandered his legacy and neglected the estate as his brother, who had drunk it all away.

It was his fault. All of it was his fault.

If he'd been home instead of in the gaming hells or his mistress's arms or on a blasted ship, his little girls would already be able to control the wild impulses they'd inherited from him. God knew they hadn't received any bad qualities from their poor, timid mother.

Though he hadn't loved her, he had admired her goodness, and he'd been sad when he'd heard she was gone.

He blinked once, twice, and, finding his attention had wandered, raked his hand through his hair.

"See here," he told Miss Jones. "My daughters need correction. They need control. You must not encourage their wildness. I've seen you roving about the countryside all day long. You ought to be giving them lessons," he said.

"I was until you interrupted us."

"You were telling them fairy stories. I heard you."

"I was telling them the story of the animals talking on Christmas Eve."

"It is fiction."

"You know that, and I know that, but they do not."

"Precisely. They believe you, which only proves my point. You should not be encouraging them to indulge in fantasy."

"People cannot do things unless they imagine them first, my lord. It seems to me that one of the responsibilities of a good governess is to develop her charges' imaginations. Your children need to exercise their imaginations more, not less."

"Do you realize how impertinent you are being?"

"Impertinent, my lord? Or merely possessing a different opinion?"

"Are you always this way? So incautious?"

"I do not understand."

"Miss Jones, you leap into the air when there is no net, trusting that it will appear."

Another dazzling smile blossomed on her face. "Yes. Exactly! You are right." She seemed proud of it. "Carpe diem. Seize the day!"

She just didn't understand. "Sometimes, Miss Jones, the net does not appear. Sooner or later, you will jump to your death."

"Better that than die of boredom," she countered.

The dratted errant curl that refused to stay in place fell over his brow, and David raked it back into place yet again. "Miss Jones, there are other ways to drill them in French without having them concoct some outrageous stories. I believe there are French books in the nursery."

"There are French books," she said. "Boring French books. And they are probably old enough to have bored you to tears, my lord. If a governess wants her charges to apply themselves, she must make the lessons interesting."

He sighed. He was getting nowhere, and he was beginning to doubt he ever would. She was a stubborn woman. Almost as stubborn as he was.

"I bow to your great experience and authority," he said, walking away. "I shall be pleased to extol the results of your pedagogy in your letter of reference." He meant his tone to be sarcastic, but somehow it came out sounding amused instead.

Emily watched him go, the sun glinting off his dazzlingly white cravat and his shiny brown hair. He was carefully dressed today, his bearing stiff and formal. But that hair! It would not be tamed. Tall and broad of shoulder, he was a strikingly handsome man with wide-set, intelligent eyes and a frank countenance. But as they'd spoken, she'd noticed something about him that didn't seem to fit. Deep lines in his face. Laugh lines. Dimples. He must smile often.

Yet she'd hardly seen him smile since she'd arrived.

Emily turned to the children and held out her hand. They came to her at once.

"Don't mind Papa," Rose told her, accurately guessing her father's state of mind. "He has been cross for a fortnight—ever since he decided to hold the house party."

"Well, if the mere thought of holding a house party makes him cross, I wonder why he decided to have one at all?" Emily mused aloud.

Rain gave her skirt a little tug. "Can we go visit the elephant? Please?"

Emily wasn't certain that was a good idea. What if Lord Winter should see them heading for the barn and decide to follow them? Yesterday, she'd merely thought he'd be annoyed. Today, she was absolutely certain he would explode like a firework.

"I fancy that is not a good idea," Emily said. "Not right now. What about your stories?"

"We can do them later," Rain offered.

"We could go to the barn later, too," Emily said.

"It will be dark later," Rose said, "and much colder. You wouldn't take us out in the cold, would you?"

"An' in the dark," Rain said, her face serious.

"Yes. Rain is afraid of the dark. She has nightmares . . ." Rose's voice trailed off, and Emily was suddenly alert, though she was uncertain why she should be. She did not have to wait long to find out, however, for Rose said after a moment, "I have nightmares, too."

"Oh?"

"Yes. And I talk in my sleep."

"I see."

"Sometimes I mention things I should not."

"Mmm."

"Like wanting to see elephants," she said, her face tilted up toward Emily and one eyebrow raised high on her forehead.

It was a threat. Rose was trying to blackmail her governess!

"Oh, dear!" Emily said carefully and walked on, considering what she should do. She was not surprised and even a little reassured to discover there was some truth behind their nicknames. She'd met strictly obedient children, and they always made her uneasy. It was as if something were missing in them somehow. But Rose and Rain were normal, happy little girls—or they would be if only they were allowed to play more.

"I believe I have changed my mind, ladies," she said after a moment. "I suppose it would do no harm to visit the elephant, as long as we are careful about how and when we approach the barn."

As Emily thought it would, Rose's face registered surprise. She hadn't expected her gambit to work. Like a bulldog who has chased a cat for years only to discover he does not know what to do with her when he finally catches her, Rose was unsure of herself. Her steps faltered and slowed as emotion marched across her face. Satisfaction, then worry, then guilt. Inside, Emily smiled and walked on, chattering with Rain about the possibility of Christmas snow.

"Miss Emily?" the voice from behind them came at last.

"Yes, Rose?"

"I didn't mean it."

"I know, dearling. But then, neither did I. We are still going to the schoolroom—after a short visit to the stables."

Beside her, Rose said nothing, but after a moment, she giggled and placed her hand in Emily's. Emily's fingers closed around the little girl's, Rain joined them on her other side, and off they went to the stable yard.

When at last the elephant saw the children, she ran around her stall excitedly throwing straw into the air. Emily laughed. "It looks like she is vastly enthusiastic this afternoon."

"Yes," said Mr. Sneed, "she's happy to see the girls again."

A sly look passed between the sisters, and again Emily was instantly alert again.

Heedless of the dynamic, Mr. Sneed chuckled. "I'll wager she wants more syllabub."

"More syllabub?" Emily asked.

The girls were suddenly terribly interested in their frocks, the manger, the door lock, their hair—anything to avoid Emily's gaze.

"She loves it so," said Mr. Sneed. "Fortunately, there's plenty to go around." He hooked his thumb toward a crock stationed just outside the stall door. "Cook can't get the recipe right. New to the job," he added. "But Baby don't mind."

"She likes it," Rain said, unable to keep still any longer. "She tossed it about just like the straw at first, but then she tasted it, and—"

"And it seemed a shame to let it go to waste," Rose said, discerning the secret obviously had been exposed.

"And I couldn't see much harm in it," the stable master said, "seeing as how it's cold out, and she loves it so."

"Obviously," Emily said, eyeing Baby's eagerly questing trunk and roving eyes. "And you named her 'Baby' last night, I presume? In the middle of the night, when everyone else was asleep?"

The girls lowered their eyes to the floor. "Yes, miss," they said in unison.

Mr. Sneed scowled. "I thought you'd given your permission, miss."

Emily sighed. "Ladies, you must not do that again. It is dangerous for little girls to be up wandering about at night, and I do not want you to be hurt. If I find you've done it again, I will have to punish you for it. Do you understand?"

"You are not going to punish us this time?" Rose asked, incredulous.

Emily shook her head. "I cannot punish you for a rule I have not set down, now can I?"

"Well, you could," Mr. Sneed said, "but I'd have wagered you wouldn't." He smiled broadly at her and patted her hand.

The visit with Baby went all too fast. It was delightful to see the girls scampering about the stall, playing chase with the elephant, who was so obviously enjoying the game, too. She was surprisingly agile and quick for her size. The top of her back reached Emily's shoulder. She was gentle. A little lady. But Emily reminded herself that the "little" lady would not remain so. "Baby" was an appropriate name for her now, but someday it would seem comical. Nevertheless Emily shrugged off the thought with her usual optimism. No need to worry about it. Everything would work out well in the end. It always did.

Five

As her charges worked on their stories, Emily went for a walk. She was the type of person who needed solitude each day in order to function properly. She didn't intend to go far, just down the corridor a short distance and back. She would avoid the public rooms entirely, keeping to this floor, which was reserved for the children and the servants' quarters. All the guests would be downstairs playing at cards, embroidering, playing billiards, or just plain gossiping.

And so it was that Emily was surprised to see the viscount coming toward her down the hall.

"Miss Jones," he said with a bow. "Where are the children?" He glanced behind her.

"They are working on their lessons," she said, neglecting to tell him that they were writing down their stories, or that they were alone in the nursery. Emily was certain there would be no trouble while she was away, for she had told the girls that if they behaved, she would allow them access to her wardrobe upon her return. They knew the gowns she was wearing had been their mother's. Neither of them had any memory of her, and they were eager to explore the gowns and fripperies. She'd even promised they could try them on. And so Emily was one hundred percent certain there would be no mischief from either of them while she strolled the halls.

But the viscount—a man!—would not understand that.

"Miss Jones. I . . . uh . . ." He shifted uncomfortably. "I find myself in the position of having to apologize. Your presence these past two days has been a godsend. I've not heard one thump or crash all day, no ropes have been lowered from upstairs windows, and the Hellions haven't once been seen below stairs. I commend you."

"The Hellions?"

"My pet name for them," he said. "A joke between us. Proof that I am not always such a curmudgeon."

She felt herself dimple. "I am indeed glad to hear it, my lord." And she meant it. It was good to know that he was sensible of his bad moods.

"I wish to make it up to you," he said, and tucked her arm into his.

So, Emily thought to herself, Lord Winter wasn't made of ice! No . . . on the contrary, his arm felt quite warm— and so did Emily's face!

"You look charming today," he said. "That gown suits you."

"Thank you for lending it to me," she said.

"You may keep it and all the rest. I have no use for them."

"Thank you!" she said. "But are you certain? You would look lovely swirling about the floor in them at Almack's."

He laughed aloud, a lovely, surprising sound, and they chatted amiably as they strolled the hallway. Emily was so absorbed in their conversation that they were halfway down the stairs before she realized they were on them.

"I—I must go back to the nursery," she stammered.

"Why? The children are fine with whomever you left in charge. My staff knows not to let them out of their sight." He smiled easily. "You must come with me."

"Why?"

He gave her a kind smile. "Many of my guests have younger sons," he said cryptically.

"I beg your pardon?"

"No," he said, "it is I who should be begging yours, for what I am about to say. Pray forgive me, Miss Jones, but I must speak freely."

"I give you leave," she said.

He bowed. "Miss Jones, it has not escaped my notice that you must have come down in the world, for you are clearly a well brought up young lady, and I find I cannot in all good conscience dine in company downstairs without inviting you to join us. Pray come downstairs with me. It is nearly dinnertime."

"Oh!" Emily panicked, knowing she could not do as he suggested without being recognized. "Oh. I . . ."

At that moment, she was saved from having to find a plausible excuse by the appearance of Sir Basil and Lady Griselda.

"Well, well!" Sir Basil smiled. "Who do we have here?"

Emily watched as recognition sparked to life in Lady Griselda's eyes and she opened her mouth to address Emily, but Emily quelled her with a look and a small, frantic shake of her head. Biting her lip, she nodded almost imperceptibly toward Lord Winter.

Lady Griselda's eyes widened, and she flicked a glance up at the viscount. "Who is this lovely creature?" she trilled. "Why have we not seen her before now? Where have you been hiding her? Sir Basil, have you ever seen such a lovely creature as this? Of course you haven't," she said, without waiting for him to respond. "Because there is no one like her, and *you have never seen her before*." She coughed delicately.

An expression of surprise flooded her husband's face, but he closed his mouth and said nothing.

Lord Winter made the necessary introduction—using her false surname, Jones, which made Emily hold her breath, but neither of the older people goggled at it, bless them. "Come," Lord Winter said. "Dinner is waiting."

Emily wilted in relief and implored God to remind the "Hellions" of their mother's gowns while Emily was away. Dinner might take a while.

She needn't have worried, however.

"Dinner" turned out to be little more than an elaborate tea, and the guests were eager to leave it in favor of a planned evening of dancing, cards, and more gossip. It was over within an hour.

As she'd known by stealing a look at the guest list that morning, Sir Basil and Lady Griselda were the only ones present who knew her, and during dinner Emily was able to relax, knowing they would not betray her. She'd always found the pair pleasant, but now she knew they were much more canny than they appeared—and that they were kind, as well.

In truth, she enjoyed herself, once she'd been introduced, deriving special pleasure from the disapproving glare of the harridan seated directly across from her. It was obvious the woman did not approve of the governess's presence. She looked as though she were tasting sour pickles every time their eyes met.

Emily was hard-pressed not to laugh out loud several times, for if the harridan knew who Emily really was, she would no doubt be groveling and fawning and declaring Emily an Original or some such claptrap.

It was the first time Emily had ever dined with the country set, and, apart from the harridan, she found the experience unexpectedly pleasant. The guest list included Dr. Brown, the village physician; several old landed squires, who between them apparently owned a considerable amount of property; and a few younger merchants and farmers, obviously prosperous, judging by the cut of their clothing. Most of the men—all but the doctor—were accompanied by their wives, and a few marriageable daughters and sons rounded out the company. It was a lively group, and she hated to leave them after dinner was finished.

As she made her way toward the dining room door, Lady Griselda touched her wrist. "A moment with you, my dear."

"Of course," Emily said, throwing a look toward Lord Winter, who was speaking with the doctor.

They moved to one side of the room, and Lady Griselda whispered, "Tell me, my dear. Quickly, quickly!"

Emily hesitated. "I am here for a very good reason."

Lady Griselda smiled. "Of course you are, my dear. Avoiding the Duke of Besshire is the best of reasons."

"You know?"

"Doesn't everyone?" She winked. "Not to worry. I will not betray you, and neither will Sir Basil. Our lips are sealed."

"Thank you!" Emily whispered.

"Oh, no. Thank *you,* my dear. For you have turned a vastly dull house party into a much more intriguing one. Lord Winter is not what we were expecting—or hoping for, I am afraid."

"How so?"

"We thought he might be more . . . well, more lively." She threw a warning look over Emily's shoulder. "Speak of the devil," she muttered and glided gracefully away.

Emily had to admit Lady Griselda was right. At dinner, the viscount had been completely respectable, which meant that he had also been completely boring. Stiff, inane, and formal. She saw nothing of the rambunctious boy that by all accounts he used to be.

And yet she refused to believe he had become like his parents, as some said. He was reviving some of the Christmas traditions they eschewed, after all, and his apology to Emily for his earlier set-down had been tender and sincere.

What he needed was someone to reintroduce him to spontaneity. And Emily was the person to help with that, for if she was not spontaneous, no one was!

Six

It snowed. The ground was covered in white, and the guests' moods had become quite festive over the past two days. David congratulated himself on his timing. Christmas was the season of goodwill. He'd hang some greenery, light a fire, stuff everyone full of sweets, and everything would proceed just as he'd planned it.

Late in the afternoon, as David was crossing the lawn on his way back from the ruins, where he'd been strolling with some of the younger set, he came upon a battlefield. Miss Jones and the Hellions were having a snowball fight.

At first, he frowned. They should have been in the schoolroom, not cavorting outside. But they hadn't seen him yet, and as he stood for a moment, watching, he realized Rose and Rain were laughing so hard that they couldn't even toss their snowballs! And Miss Jones wasn't in much better shape.

He smiled in spite of himself. He'd never seen his children laughing like that. They were usually solemn around adults, but Miss Jones was an adult, and she was laughing right along with them!

He wished he could do that. *Should I be?* Guilt and regret stabbed him, but, just as quickly, he beat the emotions down. No, such behavior as Miss Jones was displaying wasn't what his children needed from him. He needed to maintain high expectations of them to ensure they grew up to be responsible. He would not be as rigid as his parents had been. He would be different. He would have a Yule log next year. But he wouldn't let his daughters remain wild and willful.

Still, it was difficult not to wave his arms and shout, "Look at me!" To provoke them. To join in the fun. Unconsciously, he raised his hand and took a step closer to them before stilling.

He'd almost done it, by Jove!

But he'd stopped himself, just in time. He had to be an example for his children. He had to behave responsibly. And responsible adults did not become involved in snowball fights.

He turned to go, berating himself for the feeling of sadness that had suddenly come over him. It was not logical. It was not reasonable. It was not—

Thwack!

A snowball hit him right on his bottom!

David spun around. Behind him, Rose and Rain stood, uncertain, while Miss Jones stood grinning, her hand—the one that had previously held the enormous snowball—empty, her eyes sparkling with challenge.

He didn't think about what happened next. One moment he was fifty yards away from them, and the next, he was running, while simultaneously shaping an armload of scooped-up snow into the patriarch of all snowballs.

Three sets of eyes widened, three smiles appeared. And three girlish screams mixed with laughter erupted across the expanse of white.

They ran and David pursued, letting out a war whoop, an echo from his childhood. Freedom and pleasure and exhilaration rushed through him like a torrent, upwelling from his past, and David laughed.

He chased them until they ducked behind a snow wall, where they began lobbing bombs of cold and wet from the cache they'd hidden there. Taking cover behind a tree, he laughed some more. The war was on.

None of the snowballs hit their targets, but everyone enjoyed the battle. And when the ladies finally ran out of ammunition, they shrieked and ran, giggling and shouting. David grinned and chased after them, stopping long enough to load his arms with three huge snowballs, intending one for each of them. They had a good lead on him, but he was a fast runner. He overtook them just as he was rounding the corner of the icehouse and blindly threw the first snowball.

Which splattered—*thwack!*—right in the center of Mrs. Kellerman's forehead, before sliding down over her face and chins and falling with a *plop* into her enormous décolletage!

David froze.

"What is the meaning of this?" she thundered, wiping snow from her eyes. "Outrageous! Who threw that?"

David dropped the two snowballs he held and reflexively smoothed back his errant lock of hair.

"Lord Winter!" she blustered. "Did you throw that missile?

Miss Jones and the Hellions were nowhere to be seen. "I apologize, Mrs. Kellerman. I was playing with my children," he said.

"That I do not doubt," she said. "You always excelled at play, young man. I trust other aspects of your personality have *not* remained the same." She turned away, dismissing him haughtily.

David closed his eyes and, smoothing his hair yet again, sighed heavily and groaned. She was the biggest stickler in the neighborhood. And he'd just plastered her with a snowball.

About that time, Emily came skulking from around the

far corner of the icehouse, just in time to see the harridan walking away from Lord Winter. Neither looked happy.

Before Emily could stop them, Rose and Rain rushed at him with fresh snowballs. Holding up his palm, he quelled their enthusiasm with a baleful look. The joy in their little faces evaporated. It was easy to see that they were hurt.

"Run along, ladies, and gather ivy and holly for the kissing boughs," Emily said quietly.

"Are you going to argue with Papa again?" Rain asked.

"Nonsense. What is there to argue about? We are having a lovely time, are we not?"

That seemed to satisfy them both, and they scampered away on an eager search for greenery.

"What is wrong?" she asked Lord Winter as soon as the girls were out of earshot.

He scowled. "What is wrong is that you have turned the place upside down!"

She felt as though he had struck her, and her face must have reflected it, for he was instantly contrite.

"No, no! I am sorry. I did not mean that." He looked down at the ground and shook his head. "What happened is entirely my fault. I should not have lost control as I did."

"Lost control!" she cried, incredulous. "What do you mean 'lost control'? I'd say you embraced spontaneity."

"Exactly."

She shook her head. "And what, may I ask, is wrong with that?"

"Rash behavior leads inevitably to doom, Miss Jones."

She planted her hands on her hips. "What doom can possibly have befallen you because you were tossing a few little snowballs?"

"One of those 'little snowballs' hit Mrs. Kellerman."

Emily couldn't have kept her bark of laughter down if she'd tried—which she didn't.

"How dare you laugh!"

"Forgive me, my lord!" she said, chortling the while, "but I do find it funny, for Mrs. Kellerman is exactly the type of woman I wish to avoid. London was full of them, haughty, self-righteous, disdainful Town pugs, snapping and quarreling amongst themselves."

Quarreling over me.

She sobered and gave an involuntary shudder.

He rolled his eyes skyward. "Though I will concede that Mrs. Kellerman is not a great favorite of mine, she is still my guest—and as such you will treat her with respect, whether she is present or not."

"Of course, my lord," Emily said, knowing he was right. "I am too outspoken. It is one of my faults." She would have thought Lord Winter would be satisfied with her capitulation, but, inexplicably, he scowled.

"You hail from London?" he asked. "I thought you said you came from the North."

Emily's heart gave a flutter. "Oh, I . . . I did, but . . . that is to say, I . . . I am not originally from the North, my lord, but from London." Which was true enough. Emily was born in Grosvenor Square at the very height of the London Season, and she'd been an inconvenience to her parents ever since—one they fervently wished to be rid of.

"I see," said the viscount, and Emily felt a stab of guilt, for she knew he did not see clearly at all. No, she was obscuring his view at every turn, and it chafed at her. Secrecy was not in her nature. In fact, she was often accused of being too forthright. It was one of "the Emily crosses" her mother bore—vocally and with much relish.

"Come to think of it, I know precious little about you, Miss Jones. If I am to write a letter of reference, there are certain questions I should ask."

It was by sheer force of will that Emily held herself still and swallowed down the lump that formed instantly in her throat. "Go on," she said evenly, though her heart was trying to pound its way out of her chest.

For the next five minutes, Lord Winter asked her personal questions. She answered truthfully whenever she could, but most of what she said were half-truths and lies of omission. And when the viscount was finished asking questions and had disappeared into the house, Emily was left behind with a deep sense of shame and guilt.

He'd been kind enough to take her in and give her employment—when she was alone and starving, for all he knew. And here she was, lying to him, spoiling his children, and keeping an elephant in his barn.

She thought about him all the rest of that afternoon and evening. His frown, his scowl, his glare . . . his smile, his laugh, his shining eyes, his outrageous war whoop . . . More than once, her mind went a-begging, reliving the moment when her snowball had hit his well-shaped rump and he'd turned around and let fly that outrageous battle cry and then thrown his head back and laughed with complete, glorious abandon.

She wondered if he was even aware that he'd laughed at all.

It was late. David had been working in his study ever since his last guest went to bed. Thank goodness they did not keep Town hours! He set his spectacles down and rubbed the bridge of his nose. He couldn't concentrate. He kept thinking about having lost his temper with Miss Jones. Why had he been such an ass?

He'd scared himself, that was why. He'd scared himself with that savage cry he'd given and that willy-nilly snowball fight and the utter lack of restraint he'd shown.

He couldn't afford to go back to the way he'd been before the war.

But, blast if he hadn't enjoyed himself today!

David couldn't remember the last time he'd laughed like that. And his children had laughed right along with him. His children and Miss Jones . . .

He drifted into a memory of the snowball fight. How lovely his little girls had looked, their eyes sparkling with excitement . . . how lovely *she'd* looked, with her cheeks all pink and her dress flipped up over her ankles and her expression full of joyful defiance! She was so unlike any lady he remembered from the ton.

"I saw the light . . ."

As though he'd conjured her with the memory, there she was, her slender form silhouetted in the doorway. She was holding a tray with something hot on it. He could see steam rising.

"I guessed you would be down here working, probably with no fire," she said. "I . . . I thought you might be cold."

He was touched. "Thank you."

She set the tray down on his desk. "I do not know how to make coffee, but I do know how to make chocolate. Have you ever had it? I make it for myself in the middle of the night, sometimes," she confessed. "When it's available," she added. "Cook had a bit extra. I hope you do not mind my using it."

"Not at all."

She poured them both a cup of the thick, brown brew, and David tasted it. It was hot and bitter and surprisingly good.

"Why do you have to conserve so, my lord?" she asked suddenly. "No fire on your hearth, so little food."

"Why do you have to pry?" he countered, not truly offended. After all, she had warned him she was direct.

"Because that is the sort of person I am," she answered. "I ask because I have questions."

"Do you always do things without regard for the conse-
quences?"

" 'Leap and the net will appear,' " she quoted him with
a grin.

"I also said, 'Leap often enough, and someday the net
will *not* appear.' What would you have done if I'd taken offense at your impertinent question and dismissed you just
now? Where would you have gone? Where would you
have slept this cold night?"

"I do not know." She shrugged. "But things would have
settled themselves favorably, I am sure. They always do."

"That sort of attitude leads inevitably to disaster." He
tapped the newspaper on a side table. "The papers are always full of such stories."

"You exaggerate," she said, scooping up the paper and
opening it up.

To prove him wrong, he supposed. She obviously intended to read the wedding announcements or some dry
financial information or an advertisement for a hair tonic.
But, her eyes scanned the paper for only a moment before
they widened and she snapped the newspaper shut.

He choked down a laugh. "Oh, yes. Pray do read it. I
haven't the time for it."

And for the second time that day, Emily felt her heart
trying to beat its way out of her chest. She'd seen her name
in the paper. Her real name. "Ah . . . since you do not read
the paper, may I have it, please? Thank you!" she said,
not waiting for a reply and, tucking the paper under her
arm, she stood up—too quickly, for she accidentally
swiped the paper across the corner of his desk and
knocked to the floor several small objects there. "Oh! I am
so sorry!" she cried and bent to pick them up.

"No, no! Leave them. They are of no importance," he
said, looking vaguely uncomfortable.

"Nonsense," she said, replacing the things on his desk.

They were tiny silver figures. A hedgehog, a frog, a horse, a lamb, a bell, a sixpence, a pea, and a bean. Suddenly, Emily realized what they were, and laughed with delight. "These are favors for a Twelfth Night!"

"Cook asked me to keep them in my study. It is one place the Hellions never go," he explained. "She wants them to be surprised."

He looked embarrassed, and she wondered why. But for once, she did not pry. "I see," she said quietly, and they drank the rest of the chocolate in silence before Emily beat a hasty retreat, taking the tray and her incriminating newspaper with her.

After a stop in the kitchen to drop off the tray, she headed for the stairs. But her path took her right past the study, and she followed an impulse to peek in on the puzzling viscount. Creeping to the door and peering past it, her eyes goggled.

For there was Lord Winter—the rigid, responsible viscount—*playing* with the Twelfth Night favors, a gentle, little-boy smile on his face, and, instantly, Emily Jones, the improbable, imposter governess, realized she was in love.

Seven

It was late. For the second night in a row, she'd gone to her bed but couldn't sleep, and so she'd slipped outside, thinking the cold night air might help to clear her head of the emotions that swirled like snow, obscuring reason. But it was too cold, and she'd ended up in the warm glasshouse. The moon was just past its last quarter, but its weak light bounced off the snow, bathing everything in a luminous blue-white.

"Dear God," she whispered. "How could I have let this happen?"

How could she have fallen in love with someone so unsuitable?

She didn't even like him. At least, she didn't like the man he was trying to become. And he certainly did not like her. She sighed heavily.

And then, like a dream—or a nightmare, she wasn't sure which—he appeared in the doorway of the glasshouse. She saw him before he saw her.

"What are you doing here?" she demanded, her voice cracking. *Stupid question. Stupid, stupid.*

"I am working," he said.

"Of course you are," she said. "I should have known. Do men not always work in the small hours of the morning in their glasshouses in the middle of winter?"

"I was working in my study," he said, "and my eyes

started to cross. I needed to stretch my legs." He held up his hand, his fingers wrapped around a ball of twine. "I roll it off the roof outside and catch it. It helps me think. But I saw you inside, so here I am instead."

"I will wager you never come here during the day," she said.

"What do you mean?"

"Only that you pretend to be what you are not. You pretend to be all business, when in truth, you would like to play."

He scowled but issued no denials. "What are you doing here?"

"I could not sleep," she said.

"Is something troubling you?"

"Indeed, my lord, there is. But I do not wish to burden you with my bumble broth."

"Nonsense," he said with a disarming smile. "If you did not wish to burden me with it, you would not have mentioned it."

"You are right, of course," she said.

"Of course," he said, deliberately arrogant.

She laughed. "Be careful with those jests, my lord, or someone will learn your secrets."

"I have no secrets."

"No. Not at first glance. But you are more than you seem, and I find myself on uneven ground. Frankly, I do not know what to make of you. I wonder . . ." She regarded him thoughtfully. "Since you interrogated me about myself earlier, I wonder if you will answer some questions about yourself?"

"You may feel free to ask whatever you like," he said, "and I shall feel free to answer your questions as truthfully as you did."

She looked at him sharply, and one masculine brow climbed high upon his forehead. "You are very astute," she said. "You know I was not completely honest with you yesterday afternoon."

"Not completely honest?" he asked. "Miss Jones, I reckon very little of what you told me yesterday was unvarnished truth."

She could feel her cheeks stain themselves pink. "I am not accustomed to telling lies," she said.

"If I thought you were, I would have dismissed you and had one of my men escort you from my land."

She waited for him to demand she divulge her secrets, but the moment stretched into seconds, and he stood mute, regarding her with an expression of . . . of what? Respect? Is that what she saw there? Because she knew it was not admiration. No. He thought her impulsive and undisciplined, everything he despised.

"It is true that I am grateful for your kindness," she said.

He held up one hand. "Your secrets are your own. I believe all people of good character are entitled to them."

"You have decided I am good, then, my lord?"

"I have."

"And what led you to that conclusion?"

"Your reaction to Mrs. Kellerman."

"Mrs. Kellerman? The harridan? But I was impatient, vexed, and excessively strident."

"Some would call that honesty."

"And others would call it impertinence, as you pointed out to me. Did you in truth hit her with that snowball?"

"Right in the middle of her forehead. And the bulk of the snow slid into her gown." Unexpectedly, a chuckle escaped him. "I used to plot against her as a child—though the worst I ever did was steal apples from her orchard."

"Of course. For you are every bit as good a person as I am. Lord Winter's heart isn't quite as cold as he wishes everyone to believe."

"What do you mean by that?" he asked. "No!" He held

up his palm. "I do not wish to know." He looked like he wanted to say something else, but then, suddenly, he bowed and moved toward the door.

"Lord Winter," she called after him. "I wonder if I might take the children into the village tomorrow to buy some watercolors and some paper. The children want to illustrate their stories."

"Do not tell me you are still allowing them to indulge in fantasy!"

"I am afraid I am," she said, trying hard not to look contrite.

"Miss Jones, I thought I told you that we must set limits, and they must learn to accept them!"

Emily was tired of all his talk of rules and limits. *Balderdash!* She knew it was claptrap, and it was time someone pointed it out to him. "Must they also be rebuffed by their father as they were today? To have their creativity strangled out of them? To be bored to tears?"

"What rubbish!"

"Rubbish? That is exactly what happened when you dismissed their stories and again yesterday when you dismissed them! Did you see the hurt in their eyes? For heaven's sake, they are pitifully eager to please you. And if they manage it, God help them, they shall end up bored and boring. Just like you!"

"Good. Better that than lying one's way through the countryside. For the last time, Miss Jones, my children are not to be indulging in silly fairy stories. Do not tell them any, and do not encourage them to create them."

"I will tell them stories whenever I wish, and I do not care if you dismiss me."

"Good. I'll do that as soon as possible."

"Good. In the meantime, I will do whatever I think is right."

"I detest needing you." He sneered.

"I detest that you need me." She sneered right back.

"There's a kissing bough above our heads."

"Yes."

"I detest kissing boughs."

"Good."

"I am going to kiss you now."

"Fine!"

And then he kissed her.

He pulled her against him, enclosing her in the cocoon of his embrace, shutting out the world and all conscious thought. His arms were strong, his body solid, and the scent of him filled her nostrils. His mouth was unexpectedly soft as it quested against hers, and she melted against him like a late spring snow and kissed him back.

After what might have been a second or an hour—Emily couldn't have told—he grasped her shoulders and set her away from him.

Blinking once, twice, he gave his waistcoat a downward tug before taking a swipe at his errant curls.

"Yes," he said. "Well then."

"Well," she said. "Fine."

"Good," he murmured.

"Indeed."

And then they kissed again.

If Emily's emotions were swirling before, now they were a blizzard. *I cannot believe this is happening!* she thought. Afraid that if she opened her eyes, she'd find it was all just a dream, she risked a peek—only to discover that Baby was standing right behind the viscount!

Eight

She froze.

He noticed.

When someone is kissing someone and that someone stops, it is difficult not to notice! He had, and again he broke their kiss. Behind him, Baby waved a pilfered bouquet joyously about.

Emily had to distract the viscount! There was only one thing to do. Grasping the lapels of his coat, she pulled him to her and kissed him with what could be described more as zeal than passion.

And this time, her eyes were open.

Wide open.

He responded to her wanton kiss. La, did he respond!

As they kissed, Emily took one step backward. And another. And still another, hoping to draw him outside of the glasshouse, and it was working beautifully! The trouble was, her ploy was also working on Baby, who was matching them step for step.

She groaned with frustration.

He groaned with . . . something else.

At that moment, Baby lost interest in her tatty bouquet. And a normal, happy, active baby elephant just has to find *something* to do with her busy little trunk!

She found something. She found the viscount's hair!

Her questing little trunk, with its three fingerlike appendages, got busy exploring his bouncy, wayward curls.

The viscount kissed Emily harder.

Then, apparently tiring of his hair, Baby turned to his ear.

The viscount groaned and kissed her even more ardently. "Oh, Miss Jones!"

Baby's restless trunk moved on—only to caress his neck . . . his shoulder . . . and then down his back—

"Ah, Miss Jones . . . Emily!"

—until she was drawing careless circles on—

"Your bottom!" Emily thrust herself away from him.

"Yes," he drawled. "You expected to find someone else's back there, perhaps?"

"My Lord Winter!"

"Miss Jones?"

"My Lord Winter!"

"Miss Jones!" He chuckled.

"Oh, la! My lord! It was not me!"

"Oh?" He was laughing now.

"It was . . . it was—" She closed her eyes. "My lord . . . it was my elephant."

He wheeled around, which was definitely an imprudent thing to do, for now Baby's trunk was situated one hundred and eighty degrees opposite of what it had been, through no fault of her own. Lord Winter danced away, sputtering. "Wh-what is that? Your elephant? *Your elephant?* Yours? *Yours?* How can it be your deuced elephant?"

Emily took a deep breath. Now was not the time to panic. "She was being mistreated," she began. "And I rescued her." And out tumbled the entire story.

Lord Winter listened calmly, considering that an elephant was standing next to him, ripping apart and tasting plant matter the entire time Emily talked. If Baby liked whatever species it was, it was loudly and enthusiastically consumed, and if she did not like it, it was enthusiastically waved about before it was even more enthusiastically tossed aside. Oh, yes, Baby was having a grand time!

Emily was not.

The longer she talked, the angrier the viscount appeared.

"And they just let you take her?" he finally burst out.

"Well . . . no . . ."

"So you took her without asking them? Just like that? Are you mad? You cannot just go about the countryside pilfering pachyderms whenever the mood strikes!"

"It wasn't like that."

"Oh? I suppose you *planned* to take it, then? You awakened that morning and said to yourself, 'Emily, my girl, today is a lovely day to relieve someone of his elephant?'"

"It wasn't like that, either," she said stubbornly. "I had no other choice."

"No other choice? You could have left it right where it was! Instead, you followed one of your bacon-brained impulses and landed us both in high seas. What did you imagine you were going to do with her once you'd spirited her away? What will you do with her when you leave here? And how can I convince everyone I've changed with a stolen baby elephant *in my house?*"

Emily stilled, blinking. "Is that what this house party is about? You trying to convince the neighborhood you are no longer a rakehell?"

He shoved back the curl that always seemed to be astray. "There's more to it than that," he said. "Much more. I am destitute, and the Prince Regent would enjoy reabsorbing my title and estate."

"Ah yes, the infamous peacock feather and the duchess incident!"

"How do you know about that?" he demanded.

"One of the servants," she averred, neglecting to tell him

it had been one of *her* servants back in London who had told her.

"I should not be surprised you know. There isn't a person in the kingdom who doesn't know about that episode and a thousand others, real or imagined. I earned the reputation I have. But, devil it, my children did not! And this house party is my last hope for them."

"How so?"

"By proving I've changed, I hope to secure loans from my guests in order to bring the estate back from the brink. But no one will make me a loan if they find I've got a stolen elephant in my house!"

"She's not in your house, and I did not steal her. I bought her with a ring my grandmother gave me." Emily's eyes pricked with tears. The ring had been important to her, but not as important as saving Baby. "I just did not tell the owners that I was buying her, that is all."

"You did not even ask if they wanted to sell her!" He growled. "You are outside of enough! Leap and the net will appear! Seize the day, carpe diem! Just like my children! Just like—"

"Just like you." she interrupted. "The real you."

He waved one exasperated hand in the air. "You keep saying that over and over, but you cannot possibly know what I am like!" Once more, he pushed that endearing lock of hair off of his forehead.

"You are just like that hair of yours," she said. "You cannot be tamed. It's just not in your nature."

"My nature is to be responsible, cautious, and controlled."

"Oh? Then why did you kiss me just now?"

His face registered shock, but then he clamped his lips together and shook his head.

She grinned. "Oh, la! I just figured it out!"

"What?" he demanded.

"You are afraid of yourself! Of the part you've buried!"

"What buffleheaded nonsense are you spouting now?"

"But it surfaces unbidden," she went on, as though he hadn't spoken. "All of it. The spontaneity, the joy. The sarcasm, the irreverence. And the purely human desire to share those things with others. You are no different from anyone else—even though you fancy yourself an automaton!"

"You go too far," he said, his voice rigid with anger.

"No, my Lord Winter, I do not go far enough! And I'd best speak my mind before you have me banished." She pulled herself up to her full height. "You can suppress those human qualities in yourself if you wish, but you have no right to try to turn your little children into automatons as your own parents tried to do to you!"

"Pack your bags," he said. "You are leaving."

"I have no bags," she said and turned to go. "Come, Baby."

As though the elephant understood her, she wrapped her trunk around Emily's wrist and walked toward the door behind her. It was cold outside.

"Oh, God," Lord Winter groaned behind them. "Stop!"

She stopped, but did not turn around. "Yes, my lord?" In the reflection of the glass, she watched him rake his fingers through his hair.

"You cannot go."

"That is not a very good apology, my lord."

He sighed. "You are right. And I was wrong. Again. Miss Jones . . . Emily . . . you seem to bring out the worst in me. Please stay."

"Thank you, my lord. Well done. I will stay of course—since I have no other place to go."

"And yet you would have walked away from here."

"Indeed."

"What am I to do with you?"

"Well, since you shall have to wed an heiress if you cannot convince Mrs. Kellerman and her ilk that you are a paragon of respectability, I suppose kissing me again is out of the question?"

"Unfortunately," he said with a wry smile.

"Then I suppose you had better write that letter of recommendation forthwith. I will use the time until Miss Bull returns to secure a position elsewhere."

"And your elephant?"

"She is unskilled, I am afraid. And you cannot send her out into the cold. Not without a sweater, lunch, and pocket money."

He smiled a little and then sobered. "Be serious."

"Could she not stay here? Please?"

He sighed. "I suppose Mr. Sneed is aware of her presence?"

She hesitated.

"Speak. He will receive no punishment. Not even a setdown. He helped me hide many animals when I was a boy, and I knew even then it wasn't for my benefit, but for theirs. I revered him for it, and it would be hypocritical indeed for me to punish him now for the same offense."

She gave him a warm smile. "In that case, he is quite aware."

And you are too attractive, David thought. *Blast!* She wasn't at all the sort of female David needed or wanted. She was too forthright, too impulsive. The sooner she left Stendmore Park, the better.

"Good night," he said with a bow and beat a hasty retreat before he kissed her again.

Nine

". . . and so,"—he motioned toward the brown-skinned boy who stood uncertainly beside him— "I've brought him out here."

Early that morning—too early!—he'd been dragged from his bed to meet two visitors who were demanding their elephant back. David didn't listen to what they had to say, for the boy standing behind them, silent and eyes averted, told David all he needed to know.

David knew a servant from a slave. He'd seen both. He'd seen beloved, well-cared-for slaves and neglected servants. Neither especially aroused his sympathy. But this little boy flinched whenever the men moved too suddenly, and anger tightened David's chest.

"It's ours," the shorter of the two men said. "We can prove that. And you've got it. We seen it down there in your glasshouse."

David stood and leaned over his desk. "We deal harshly with trespassers in this part of the country, a thing you . . . *gentlemen* would be well advised to remember."

"We wants our elephant," said the other man, pale and gaunt.

"It is snowing outside. How will you keep her warm?" David asked, noting the little boy had nothing but a thin cloak to keep him warm.

"That's our concern," the skinny man said.

David clenched his jaws together and then demanded. "Show me the ring."

The men traded cold, calculating looks. "What ring?" said the first. "We don't have no ring."

"In that case," said David, "my elephant cannot possibly belong to you, for the ring was left as payment for her. Good day."

"All right . . . what if we did have a ring?" the other man said. "It wouldn't be near enough to compensate us for losing the elephant."

David smiled a smile that did not reach his eyes. "Gentlemen, I intend to keep *my* elephant. Let us settle on a fair price."

Five minutes later, the men left the house with the rest of David's remaining silver, and David left the house with a little boy and a receipt for one baby elephant.

"This is Rohan," he said to Emily, who stood beside him now in the glasshouse. "He is the elephant's mahout. Back in Ceylon, they were meant to stay together their whole lives. But they were sold into slavery a few months ago."

"Laleeta!" the boy cried, spotting the elephant. "Laleeta!"

Baby trumpeted in recognition and rushed up to him, her trunk extended. He wrapped his thin brown arms about her neck, and with her trunk, the elephant gave him what could only be described as a hug before she ran off in the opposite direction, clearly daring him to chase her. They dashed off toward the opposite side of the overgrown glasshouse.

"Thank you," Emily said, looking up at David with shining eyes. "It was a good and generous thing to do."

"It was an impulsive and stupid thing to do, and I am certain I shall regret it," he countered.

"Nonsense. Everything has been settled admirably."

"Nothing has been settled. What am I to do with an elephant?"

"You should have thought about that before you bought her," Miss Jones said with a mischievous grin.

He should have been irritated with her. Hell, he should have been livid. But she looked at him that way, and all he could think about was kissing her.

But he couldn't. Not again. He shouldn't have kissed her in the first place. He had no right.

"Miss Jones . . . last night, I—"

"La, it was only a kiss!" she said. "I hardly fancy we are the first pair to be gripped by a sudden momentary passion."

"Momentary?"

"Indeed. I am, as you pointed out, much too spontaneous. It is I who should apologize. I am the one who hung the kissing bough out here. The girls couldn't wait until Christmas Eve to hang some greenery, and I couldn't see the harm in it. It cannot in truth be bad luck out here."

"We kissed because of it," he said.

"Yes, we did," she agreed.

"And that was not a lucky thing," he said.

"No," she agreed. "It was unlucky, I'd say."

"Then we are in agreement?" he asked.

"I believe we are," she answered.

"It was just a momentary passion, then," he said.

"Yes."

"A passing ephemera."

"Indeed."

He couldn't help it. His gaze flicked down to her lips. "The kissing bough is still there."

"It is."

"And the boy is at the far end of the glasshouse cavorting with Baby."

"I hear them."

"Which means I could kiss you again, and no one would know."

"It does."

"And I want to."

"Good."

"Fine, then."

And, for the third time in twelve hours, David found himself kissing his children's blasted governess!

She broke the kiss first and stepped back from him, eyes wide. Pointing up to the kissing bough, she said, "I shall remove the thing forthwith."

"Please do. And pray do not hang any more."

"Heaven forbid!"

He turned on his heel and left, and Emily stood staring after him, feeling she might shatter into a thousand pieces and blow away. What was this madness? What was she doing kissing the viscount *again?* What if they were discovered? If the news got back to her father there would be no escaping the parson's mousetrap—and she'd be stuck with Lord Winter for all eternity. She was here trying to avoid marriage, not to be trapped into one! *Dear heaven!* She didn't want a man who sneered at play and scowled at levity. Lord Winter was entirely too deliberate, too controlled, too rigid.

And entirely much too tempting.

He was a man who rescued baby elephants and laughed at snowballs tossed down harridans' necklines!

But he was trying to convince everyone he had abandoned that sort of behavior. And he was trying to convince *himself* he'd changed even harder than he was trying to convince the neighborhood. What if he were successful? What if he managed to transform himself into the person he thought he should be?

The point was moot anyway, Emily told herself. For she wasn't what he'd want in a wife. And even if Lord Winter suddenly lost his ordered, plodding, calculating, unbending mind and decided he wanted a woman of Emily's temperament, Emily just couldn't risk it. She didn't want a husband like him—no matter how endearing his rare smiles or how hard her toes curled when he kissed her.

Behind her she heard rustling and turned to see Baby and her little mahout come forward through the thick, untended growth of the shrubbery.

"This is like the forest in my land," he said with a grin. "It will be very good for hiding."

"Hiding?"

"Sahib says it is my task to keep Laleeta hidden."

"Is that her name? Laleeta?"

"Yes. It means 'play' in my language."

Emily laughed. The name was certainly apt. "Your name is Rohan?" At his nod she asked, "Does it have a special meaning, too?"

"In Hindi, it means 'ascending,'" he said proudly. But then his little brown face wrinkled up in uncertain lines. "I am wondering, can ma'am sahib tell me if in coming here I have ascended or descended?"

She laughed. "I am afraid I do not know, Rohan, for I am still trying to answer that question for myself!"

"Hullo!" Mr. Sneed called from the door. Rose and Rain had been helping him modify a horse blanket for Baby. Emily made the proper introductions, and Mr. Sneed explained to her that he'd transferred Baby Laleeta into the glasshouse at around midnight because he'd worried that the stable was too cold. "It's cold enough in here, as it is."

"Sahib is wise," the little boy said and looked worried. "Elephant children sicken and die if they are not kept warm."

Cries of dismay rent the air.

"What if it snows again, Miss Jones?" Rain said.

"What if it gets too cold?" Rose moaned. "Oh, our Baby must be kept warm!"

"But how?" Mr. Sneed said. "We can't take a chance on her kicking over a brazier and burning the place down, and she ain't going to climb up the ladder into my place over the coach house."

"She could stay in the nursery," Rain said.

Rose snorted. "We cannot bring her into the house, silly. Papa would be cross."

"I can help her up stairs," Rohan said proudly.

"How else are we to keep her warm?" Rain asked.

"How indeed?" Emily murmured, chewing her lip. Peering up through the roof of the glasshouse, she could just make out the nursery windows. *How indeed?*

Ten

Christmas Eve dawned clear and cold. The temperature dropped steadily all day, until the wind began to howl and a steady, swirling snow covered everything in a tempest of white. But David barely noticed what was going on outside, for inside, Miss Jones was busy turning his household upside down.

She'd appeared with the children downstairs just after breakfast, declaring that the holiday was one time when it was right and proper for children to take part—indeed, without them there would be something lacking! David was horrified at first, but when the guests remarked upon his children's pretty manners and congratulated him on finding such an effective new governess, David relaxed—until he discovered that the guests were hanging kissing boughs all over the house!

Somehow, Miss Jones had taken charge of the decorating, and she'd been commanding the servants—and even the guests—like Nelson his fleet. They'd hung miles and miles of greenery and paper flowers about the ancient great hall. She'd enlisted the elders to cut foil stars and silk flowers, and the young people were balanced atop chairs and tables hanging the blasted things and laughing. Those not otherwise involved were singing or playing the pianoforte. The servants had already broken out bottles of Mr. Sneed's cottage ale, and, though their mistletoe was already devoid of berries, no one paid any attention and the continued stolen kisses were the source of much muted laughter coming from the direction of the kitchen. The world had gone mad.

It was unsettling. His only comfort was that the guests didn't seem to think anything was out of the ordinary. In fact, Mrs. Kellerman had declared David to be a paragon of good taste and refinement! The entire room was buzzing with it. And so, amidst the ritual Christmas chaos, he tried to be calm. Everything was proceeding as he'd planned, after all.

And, while the viscount and the governess stood at opposite ends of the room—as far away from the kissing boughs as they could—they were both trying to convince themselves of the same thing.

She ought to feel happy, Emily told herself. The day had been a complete success. Indeed, the entire journey—her journey—had been a complete success. She'd avoided being endlessly pushed toward the Duke of Besshire for an entire, blissful month. She'd become a governess, easily tarnishing her reputation enough to discourage all but the most ardent or avaricious of suitors. And she'd probably cause her parents enough humiliation that they would give up their campaign to force her to marry altogether and allow her to settle into a life of contented country rustication.

On top of that, she'd made new friends. Children, servants, country gentry, and an elephant! It had been an adventure. She'd leapt and the net had appeared. It had been glorious.

And it wasn't over. A letter had arrived that afternoon, an answer to an advertisement the viscount had helped her place in several newspapers. If her parents would not see reason and let her escape into the country, she could threaten them with the letter—or she could make good on that threat and in truth continue on as a governess!

Everything would have been perfect if she hadn't been faced with the fact that her next assignment would not include the Hellions or Baby Laleeta. And neither would it include her blasted employer, with whom she'd fallen in love like a silly mooncalf. Even now, the mixed-up man was trying his best to look like he wasn't interested in the festivities, whereas any fool could see he was about to burst with the desire to join in.

Shortly before nine o' clock, as she stood staring into the flames slowly consuming the enormous Yule log, he found her there.

"You will come to supper, will you not?" he asked quietly. "I have no doubt you are responsible, in part, for my impending success. I would like you to be there at the pivotal moment, when I finally ask and receive pledges for the loans I seek."

And she was.

She was there when he stood up and confessed his past sins. When he expressed his regret for his wild, misspent youth. When he asked them all to forgive him for bringing scorn upon the neighborhood. When he explained that he'd worked hard to reform and that he intended to continue working for the good of the neighborhood till the end of his days. And she was there when he finally asked for his loans.

She was there when Mrs. Kellerman, the harridan, declared publicly that she'd been watching Lord Winter for signs of being a wastrel but that she'd found none. "In fact," Mrs. Kellerman said, "I believe he has changed completely. I would not have believed it, but he is as stiff and sober as a gravestone. No adventures. No high jinks—except those instigated by others." She glared at Emily before continuing, "He has nothing to hide, and Mr.

Kellerman and I will be happy to pledge a loan in the amount of five thousand pounds. I am sure that if our neighbors will do the same—each to the extent of his own ability, of course," she said, knowing full well there wasn't one family who could pledge half so much and obviously enjoying the knowledge immensely, "I am certain Stendmore Park will prosper. With the proper management and supervision from the investors, of course."

And Emily was also there when Baby Laleeta, having escaped from the nursery and smelling the food and the wine, charged into the dining room trumpeting and swinging her trunk and reaching for the punch bowl, which was full of syllabub.

David gasped.

All hell broke loose.

Most of his guests screamed. Two fainted. He watched as the blasted elephant grabbed the punch bowl and tipped it, sending its contents cascading over Dr. Brown and from there onto the floor. Sir Basil's dogs rushed into the room to investigate the ruckus and began to bark and whine. The elephant ran around the table trying to avoid them. Half the guests scrambled to stand, sliding in the syllabub and colliding, and the other half cowered under the table.

Miss Jones was trying to herd Baby Laleeta out the door, but the elephant, apparently reassured by her presence, only made a mad grab for a cup of syllabub that sat on the table. This time, she was successful, and the syllabub made its splashing, dribbling way into her pink mouth. But it was a pitifully small amount for an elephant, and she quickly discarded the goblet with a crystalline shatter and reached for another.

Into the melee charged Rose and Rain, followed by the little mahout, who was shouting in Hindi.

The only person not standing or prone was Mrs. Kellerman, who, imperious, sat looking as though she smelled something bad—until Baby reached for her goblet of syllabub, and the old harpy tried to snatch it back. It slipped, flew into the air, and David watched as, seemingly in slow motion, the goblet tumbled against her expansive chest, the syllabub flowed between her bosoms, and Baby saved the situation by plunging her trunk into the lady's décolletage and loudly slurping the concoction.

Mrs. Kellerman let out a bloodcurdling scream, and into the shocked silence that followed, Emily Jones dealt the final, crushing, killing blow.

"Lord Winter did not know about my Baby! I swear it."

Eleven

"Your *baby?!*" The harridan screeched.

Everyone was suddenly staring at Emily, their mouths open, and Emily realized what she'd said. "No!" she cried. "Oh, no! That is not what I meant! It is not my baby. It is *his.*" She blanched. "No! That is not what I meant, either!"

Most of the company averted their gaze, and Emily looked to Lord Winter, whose expression registered dismay, defeat, and despair as the horrible scene coalesced and began its journey into local legend.

Elephants were not the only ones who never forgot.

It didn't matter what she said now. Nothing she could do could repair the damage she'd done. Her heart broke in half. Because of her, everything was ruined. But—oh, la!—she couldn't just sit there and not try! She had to do something. Say something. But she hadn't the first notion what.

With one last, impulsive leap into the unknown, Emily opened her mouth to speak.

"My name," she began, "isn't Emily Jones, and I am not in truth the governess. My name is Miss Emily Fairwell, and if you need proof, Sir Basil and Lady Griselda can confirm that."

The pair nodded solemnly as the harridan blustered. "Fairwell!"

"Do you mean to tell me, Lord Winter, that you have

been harboring a runaway heiress under your roof? Un-chaperoned?" So word of Emily's disappearance had echoed even here.

"An heiress? It would seem so," the viscount drawled. His beautiful eyes, once sparkling with anticipation and promise, were now dull and dark, and Emily's heart was crushed.

Mrs. Kellerman sniffed. "Our pledge is withdrawn."

"You have the wrong of it," Emily said, "There is a perfectly reasonable explanation for all of this."

Fervently wishing she knew what that explanation was, Emily let her mind whirl and click like a well-oiled machine, and, as usual, an idea came to her. It was outrageous. It was risky.

But it was all she had.

"I am not unchaperoned," Emily said. "Lady Griselda is my chaperon."

"And why have I not been informed of this?" the harridan asked.

"Perhaps," Emily responded in a deceptively civil tone, "because it was *none of your business.*"

As Mrs. Kellerman sputtered, Emily realized she would *have* to go home now. There would be no position waiting for her. She could not stay at Stendmore Park, and she had no money to run. Lord Winter was right: impulsive behavior was a wild, unpredictable beast. One time it could lead one to sweet baby elephants, charming little girls, and gentlemen who stole one's heart, while the very next, it led to ruination.

Across from her, the harridan had subsided, perhaps sensing, as everyone else scattered about the room clearly did, that Emily had more to say. Emily looked about the room and forced herself to smile.

"I was sent here by my father on a matter of utmost importance," she said. "He will be glad to hear you have withdrawn your investment, Mrs. Kellerman. He will be pleased to have a larger share."

"Share?" the harridan demanded. "Share of what?"

Emily reminded them that the neighborhood had long been known to the ton, but only as a sleepy village with a coaching inn on the road to Bath. The inn did a very brisk business, but none of the travelers lingered.

"Lord Winter proposes to change that. He has formulated a bold plan to transform the village, to bring economic prosperity and cultural refinement to your very doorsteps. You will no longer be forced to travel to Bath or to London to seek it. Indeed, those who live in either town will come to you—bringing their sons and daughters and their riches."

She spared a glance at the viscount. He was staring at her in shock, and Emily plunged on.

"He cleverly arranged to have the expensive elephant brought in as a token of his good faith, to prove to you that he meant to do as he said."

"Which is?" Doctor Brown asked.

"Lord Winter means to build a pleasure garden right here in Buxley-on-Isis, a garden to rival Raneleagh or Vauxhall, a garden full of music and light. There will be assembly rooms, a hall for presentations, a green that will host everything from balloon ascensions to fireworks to races, and a water garden. And the crowning centerpiece to these Winter Gardens will be a grand menagerie—with that adorable baby elephant as its first permanent exhibit."

Baby was busy waving an ostrich feather pilfered from Mrs. Kellerman's turban. Someone snickered.

Griselda began applauding gently, and, slowly, all the guests except the Kellermans joined in.

Emily beamed. "It will be a glorious success. A place for the weary traveler to rest his bones—and empty his pockets. Everyone travels that road. And everyone would like a place more hospitable to stop. Why not give them one?"

"Why not indeed!" Sir Basil chimed. "Splendid idea! Splendid!"

The applause grew louder.

Emily stood a little taller. She'd succeeded! But she thought she could do a little more . . . "The viscount has always believed pleasurable pursuits are important for a healthy mind and body, which is why he thinks it necessary to bring a pleasure garden here, seeing as how there are so many illustrious personages about and nothing fanciful for them to do."

"Humph!" Mrs. Kellerman said. "The viscount is a great expert on the pursuit of pleasure—as we all know."

Emily gave her a sweet, sympathetic smile that said she thought Mrs. Kellerman was possibly the most stupid woman in all England. "While some still believe the viscount was simply a rakehell," she said, "most in Town have heard he was in truth conducting scientific research. He is to be presenting a paper on the subject later this year." Emily's eldest brother was a junior member of the Royal Society, and Emily knew he could be persuaded to help her. Daniel was a good man.

But Mrs. Kellerman clearly didn't believe her story. "And what is your postulate, my lord?" she asked.

"He has concluded that pleasure and personal beauty are directly connected." Emily said. "You, for instance, must certainly indulge in pleasurable pursuits, as your noted beauty does not come from a cream pot." She paused. "Does it?"

Mrs. Kellerman opened her mouth, clapped it shut, and opened it again before answering. "I should say not! But why all this havey-cavey skulking about? Why all this false name business and pretending to be the governess?"

"Madam, in business dealings of this magnitude, timing

is everything. Were Lord Winter to reveal his intentions too soon," she said in a patronizing tone, "the deal—and the neighborhood's future—would have been spoilt. Is that what you would have wanted?"

"Why no, I—"

"And will you allow a little spilt syllabub to ruin this chance for the neighborhood to flourish?"

"Of course not, I—"

"Very well, then. I think all is settled. The misunderstanding is cleared up."

"Except for one small detail," Mrs. Kellerman said with an acid curl of the lip. *"What about your baby?"*

"Baby?" Emily said in confused tones, giving a convincing performance. "Oh! My baby!" She tittered dramatically behind the back of her hand. "That," she said, pointing to Baby, "is Baby Laleeta. We call her 'Baby' for short."

Uproarious laughter erupted. Even Mrs. Kellerman's wispy husband chuckled, and she had no choice but to chisel her hard features into the semblance of a smile and force a laugh—a brittle sound that told Emily beyond doubt that the lady's humiliation this day would keep her in check for years. The neighborhood would not allow her to live it down. The cat was belled.

The dining room erupted with a dozen excited conversations: *Isn't it grand? The Winter Gardens! What an appropriate name! What an insightful idea!*

One old squire declared he'd always known Master David would come home to roost and make the neighborhood proud.

"He's quite the gentleman," said a matron with a gleam in her eye. She had several unmarried daughters.

The pledges rolled in.

As Lady Griselda rose and led the rest of the ladies into the parlor, Emily's eyes found Lord Winter's.

He was seething.

She was stunned.

Their gazes locked and he strode around the table. "A word with you," he said, gripping her arm and drawing her into the library. He closed the door.

"A closed door my lord? Propriety demands—"

"It wasn't enough to come waltzing in here and turn my life upside down, was it? No! You had to turn the entire village upside down. You have committed me to building a vast pleasure garden. If I go through with it, life in Buxley will never be the same. And if I do not, I shall be reviled and Rose and Rain will suffer for your thoughtless impulses. So now I must not only resurrect this ruin of an estate, but I must also construct a pleasure garden. All on the charity of the neighborhood."

"Loans are not charity."

"And they're not enough to do the job, either. The sum is barely adequate to rescue Stendmore Park. It's not even a tenth of what I would need to construct your blasted pleasure garden! Once more, your thoughtless devotion to impulse has left ruin in your wake."

"You do not understand, my lord," she said quietly.

"I understand perfectly. With nowhere to go and no real plan of action, you skipped blithely away from your family in the middle of winter with nothing in your pocket. You stole an elephant and walked off into the country. You came to my kitchen door looking for a meal and accepted employment. And then you decided to become a governess for God only knows how much longer. You lied. You deceived. Did you think about how your family would feel to find you gone? Did you consider your employer's mortification when he discovered he'd hired some rich man's precious daughter? Did you consider your charges and how they might fare under the tutelage of an inexperienced and spoiled debutante? Did you even consider what would happen to the poor elephant if severe weather had caught you on the road with no place to stay? No. You considered none of that. You never do. And you have no remorse for any of it. Do you?"

"Everything worked out well," she said quietly.

"For you, perhaps, Miss Whatever. But I see no net under my daughters," he said in bitter tones, and, turning away, he leaned heavily against the mantel.

"You do not understand," she said again. "My father will pledge any amount to see me wed and be rid of me."

"What makes you fancy I wish to wed you?" he said, misunderstanding her intent. "As you said, it was only a silly kiss. A momentary passion, ephemeral and soon forgotten. We are complete opposites. You are a slave to impulse, and I the architect of my own destiny. I do not even like you. Just because you announce in my dining room that your father will give me money does not mean I am obligated to wed you. I will find someone else to wed. And you—"

"Will marry the Duke of Besshire."

He stilled. The moment stretched as the mantel clock ticked off the seconds. "The Duke of Besshire?" he asked.

"It is time I told you the truth," she said and then plunged on. "In Town I am not called Emily. I am known as Anomaly—a name I have earned, for I learned early that when one's family sees one as an embarrassment, one is left blissfully alone in the country.

"But I have younger sisters old enough to wed, and it is apparently not at all the thing for them to wed before me. So my parents have asked me, ordered me, threatened me, bribed me, blackmailed me, and begged me until we have all grown weary of it. But years and years ago I decided that I would never marry unless it was for love, and I have remained stubborn. And unwed.

"Then, a month ago, at some crush of a rout my parents attended, Father let it be known just how much he was willing to settle upon me. He forced me to come back to London, and every Town pug with an unwed son gathered nigh, and I suddenly had more beaux than I could count ardently professing their undying affection.

"Father is just as stubborn as I am, and he says that without a husband this is the way things will be for the rest of my life. Surrounded by insincerity and artifice, plied by greed and deception. To have any peace, I must wed."

"But why Besshire?" Lord Winter asked. "He is dull. He smiles all the time and never blinks. Blast it, Emily, the only two memorable things about him are his moist hands and extreme overbite. You can do better."

"You still do not understand," she said tiredly.

"I understand that once more you are leaping into the air."

"Indeed. I shall leap into marriage, and I am certain I shall be quite happy," she said, though she was certain she would be miserable instead. "After all, he is a duke. How could I not be happy?"

Twelve

David was still reeling. Everyone had become so excited about the Winter Gardens that before the evening was over, their pledges had doubled. Doubled! No one cared—or even seemed to remember—that he'd been an infamous rakehell. Mrs. Kellerman had retired to her chamber with a megrim. Merriment prevailed. And his girls had stared up at him all evening with rapturous expressions, until Miss Jones had taken them up to bed. It had felt good, damn good. And he'd made a decision.

He'd have enough blunt to save his title and his estate, and enough to at least start on the pleasure garden. And, even if he couldn't complete the project, the neighborhood would watch him try, by Jove. He'd dedicate the rest of his life to it. His daughters' reputations would not suffer. Their futures were assured. And David's life would have meaning.

He should have been happy, but he wasn't.

Sir Basil and his lady noticed. They flanked him and cornered him. "Out with it, my boy," Sir Basil said. "What is wrong?"

It was no use hiding his feelings. "She will be leaving soon. She is to marry the Duke of Besshire."

"*Besshire?*" Lady Griselda scoffed. "Pish-tosh! She'd sooner marry a hedgehog! That is nothing but a rumor."

David shook his head. "She told me so herself."

The older pair looked at each other with raised eyebrows, and then Sir Basil spoke. "It is a well-known fact that she has refused Besshire many times."

His wife nodded. "If she has decided to accept him now, something is quite amiss."

Sir Basil gave David a piercing stare. "She knows her father would do anything to be rid of her. Including giving a huge sum to help found the Winter Gardens." His bushy white eyebrows rose and Lady Griselda patted David's hand before they both moved off.

The snowstorm finally diminished, and David left the party soon after. He sat up for a while in his bedchamber, staring outside at the darkened nursery windows. Emily and the children were asleep, or he would have gone to question her. Why had she decided to marry Besshire? Was it because he was a duke and she longed for freedom? Or was it as Basil and Griselda suspected—that she was wedding Besshire only to gain her father's support for the Winter Gardens? Was it a convenience? Or an immense sacrifice?

He lay in bed for a time, unable to sleep. Either way, he'd behaved badly. In fact, he'd behaved badly several times. As a woman, she did not have the opportunities in life that he had. She did not have the freedom he enjoyed. Any deviations she made outside of the narrow vein of expected behavior would be seen as anomalous and impulsive and unacceptable. How could she not chafe at such confinement?

He needed to tell her he understood her at last. He needed to urge her to go forth and find the love match she desired. David knew what it was to be wed to someone without love, and he could not wish it for Emily. If she did not marry, her father would not invest in his pleasure garden, but David was determined that he would find another way to complete the project.

He wanted her to be happy. After all, he owed her so much! He needed to tell her that her wild spontaneity, at least this once, had been a good thing.

Abandoning his bed a little before midnight, he padded up the stairs toward the nursery. At first, he told himself that he was just checking on the Hellions, since they'd been up so late and had had so much excitement, but he threw that excuse overboard halfway there. What he really wanted was to gaze upon Miss Jones, to memorize the contours of her sleeping face. She'd distanced herself after supper, and though he knew it was irrational, he'd missed her presence at the party.

All he wanted was one look. One peek and he'd go back to—

The room was cold, and his daughters' beds were rumpled but empty.

Expecting to find them in her room, he looked there, but found only another empty yet still made bed. Where were they? Darting back into the nursery, he looked around, only then noticing that the window was open and that a bed sheet rope lay over the windowsill. Rushing to peer outside, he saw tracks in the snow leading off into the darkness.

He panicked.

Cursing himself for a fool, David ran outside and followed the tracks. *Blast it!* She'd run away, by the devil! She'd decided not to marry the Duke of Besshire after all. She was following another one of her buffleheaded impulses, and his poor children were following right along in her wake, with snow on the ground! Terror gripped his soul. *They could die out there!*

Damn it. Damn her! And damn himself for believing she was anything but a selfish, unthinking—

Suddenly he noticed a soft, faint glow of lamplight inside the stable. He ran.

He found her standing alone, bathed in lamplight and leaning against the rough doorway of the elephant's stall, still as the night. He was yet in shadow, and so she did not see him approach. A soft smile graced her features. At her feet lay three children and an elephant, jumbled together in a ball of arms and legs and trunk, all sleeping in the hay and covered with Emily's enormous shawl.

And there she stood, shivering in the cold.

All at once, he realized he'd been terribly unfair.

She hadn't been running away at all. No, it was obvious the children had sneaked out of the nursery to come see the elephant talk and had fallen asleep during the wait.

"Why did you not wake them up and take them back into the house?" he asked softly. "You are frozen," he said, taking off his bed robe and placing it over her shoulders.

She gave him a grateful smile. "I am waiting until after midnight to wake them. They will be disappointed if they are awake at midnight and Baby Laleeta does not speak."

David's heart swelled with tenderness. "Miss J—uh . . . Emily. You are too impulsive, but when it counts, you can be depended upon." She'd jumped into the air trusting the net to appear, but the net was already there, woven of her own intelligence, her own creativity, her own loyalty—and of her willingness to take a chance in the first place.

"But by admitting who you are and marrying Besshire, you are sacrificing your freedom for my children's happiness."

She looked down at her hands and said nothing.

"Tell me . . ." He swallowed hard. "Is it foolish to hope that you make this sacrifice for me as well?"

Did she care for him? Did she love him? David couldn't expect it. He hadn't proven that he was worthy of her—and until that very moment, he hadn't been. In his quest to become responsible, he'd been unbending and insensitive. He'd been so busy trying to control life, he'd forgotten how to enjoy it. But no more. She'd changed him.

How could he convince her of that?

For once, David followed an impulse, a wild impulse. An impulse that seemed right. Taking her hand, he knelt before her.

"May I tell you a story, dear lady?" he asked.

Her eyes registered surprise and then confusion. "What are you doing?"

"A story. I wish to tell you a story," he said.

Finally, after a long, searching moment, she gave a nod, tentative and wary.

He swallowed. "Once upon a Christmas," he began, "there lived a lonely gentleman and his two beautiful daughters . . ."

It was their story he told, the story of two unhappy people named David and Emily. He told of little girls and an elephant, of lies and confusion, of joy and awakening. "But my story has a happy ending," he said at last. "For, in the end, David asks Emily to marry him."

"And what does she answer?" she whispered.

David shook his head. "I do not know. You will have to finish the story yourself."

"Must I write it down?"

"No . . . but you may have to repeat it several times before I will believe you, whatever the ending is."

"I will finish it," she said, "on one condition."

"Anything."

"Promise me you shall tell stories every day."

"Every day of our lives?"

Emily nodded, her heart beating wildly.

"I promise," he said. "I swear it. And I shall enjoy it."

She smiled, content at last. "Then of course Emily says 'Yes!'"

In the distance, the church bells rang through the clear, cold night air, heralding the arrival of Christmas Day. As Emily and David kissed, three children slept at their feet.

And as the last, clear tone of the Christmas bells faded away, a lilting, girlish, and slightly nasal soprano, redolent of sandalwood and spices, whispered, "And they lived happily ever after!"

ABOUT THE AUTHOR

Melynda Beth Skinner lives with her husband and their own two charming hellions in Florida, where she leaps into the air, decorates like mad for Christmas, and visits with elephants whenever she's able.

She enjoys hearing from readers. You may write to her at:

7259 Aloma Avenue
Suite 2 Box 31
Winter Park, FL 32792

If you wish a reply kindly enclose an SASE. Or visit her at www.melyndabethskinner.com, where you can send her an e-mail, chat with her online, or view her Christmas gallery. She wished you a Merry Christmas and a New Year filled with love.

More Regency Romance
From Zebra